B. Milton Hyde is a native of Charlottesville, Virginia, and currently resides in southwest Virginia with his family. He is a proud alumnus of both, Grand Canyon University in Phoenix, Arizona and Liberty University in Lynchburg, Virginia. This is his debut novel.

In memory of James Irvin Baber and Travis Sexton. Gone too soon but never forgotten.

B. Milton Hyde

BEHOLD A PALE HORSE

THE LEGEND OF THE PALE RIDER PART I

AUSTIN MACAULEY PUBLISHERS™
LONDON * CAMBRIDGE * NEW YORK * SHARJAH

Ordering Information
Quantity sales: Special discounts are available on quantity purchases by corporations, associations, and others. For details, contact the publisher at the address below.

Publisher's Cataloging-in-Publication data
Hyde, B. Milton
Behold a Pale Horse

ISBN 9781647505226 (Paperback)
ISBN 9781647505219 (Hardback)
ISBN 9781647505233 (ePub e-book)

Library of Congress Control Number: 2021920876

www.austinmacauley.com/us

First Published 2021
Austin Macauley Publishers LLC
40 Wall Street, 33rd Floor, Suite 3302
New York, NY 10005
USA

mail-usa@austinmacauley.com
+1 (646) 5125767

While there are many people who deserve to be mentioned here, I will mention but a few:

I must first acknowledge, Greg Collier. It was his words of wisdom in the aftermath of an unexpected death in the family that first motivated me to stop talking about writing a book and actually start writing one.

Of course, I could not have persevered through the lengthy process without the love and support of my family.

I must also acknowledge the efforts of my first readers, those rare few individuals I could trust to give me their honest and unbiased feedback of the first draft. Their contributions to the finished product cannot be underestimated.

Many thanks to the editors at Austin Macauley Publishers who saw enough merit in the first draft of this manuscript to give an untried writer an opportunity.

Of course, none of this would be possible without the hard work of the dedicated team at Austin Macauley: the editorial staff, production, design, and marketing teams who turned that manuscript into the finished product you now hold in your hands.

Last, but most certainly not least, I must acknowledge my Lord and Savior, Jesus Christ, through whom all things are possible and to whom goes all credit and glory.

Chapter One

**North Bank of the Oostanaula (Near Resaca, Georgia) –
May 1864**

A heavy mist rose slowly from the river and rolled over the sea of tents picketed on its north bank. Close behind it came the roar of cannon fire and the rattle of musketry, all punctuated by the agonized screams of the wounded being treated in the medical tents. It was these screams and cries of anguish that weighed most heavily upon the young officer who strode quickly by on his way to the command tent.

Lt. Matthew Lloyd Garrison wore a grim expression upon his face as he made his way through the camp. Though only in his mid-twenties, four years of bitter combat had aged him beyond his years. His dark hair was cut short and he had chiseled features with a square jaw. There was something in his icy blue eyes that lent a hint of cruelty to an otherwise handsome face.

As Garrison neared the command tent, he was acutely aware of the mud that caked his uniform and the smell of gunpowder that clung to him like a shadow. He was fresh from the field, although the battle clearly still raged on. He was a member of General Kilpatrick's cavalry division, part of the Army of the Cumberland under the command of General Thomas. The unit had been ordered up from their position at Snake Gap Creek that morning to reconnoiter the area around Resaca. They were surprised by Confederate infantry forces and General Kilpatrick had been wounded and removed from the field of battle.

Led by Garrison's own brigade commander, Colonel Eli Murray, they rallied and dispersed the Confederates before moving aside to allow the infantry forces of General McPherson to move forward and continue the assault. The cavalry was subsequently ordered to picket the north bank of the river. With Colonel Murray assuming command of the division, leadership of the 3rd Brigade had fallen to Lt. Colonel Samuel Benjamin.

It was the tent of Lt. Col. Benjamin that Garrison now approached as a foreboding sense of dread descended upon him. He had never been summoned to the command tent before and had never met Lt. Col. Benjamin. He couldn't fathom why Benjamin wanted to see him, but his instincts told him it probably wasn't good. With a deep breath to gather his nerves, Lt. Garrison stepped through the flap and into the tent. What he could never have known was that doing so would change the course of his life forever.

Chapter Two

The interior of the tent was dark, lit only by a single oil lamp. As his eyes adjusted to the gloom, the first thing Garrison saw was the smiling face of his best friend, Major Jack Garnett. Garrison's anxiety immediately began to dissolve.

He and Garnett had grown up together, first in Virginia and later in Kentucky when both families relocated. They had gone to West Point together, graduating the same year. Both of their families had become wealthy raising thoroughbred horses, so it was only natural that both men would gravitate toward the cavalry and they had been fortunate to be assigned to the same unit. When war erupted, both men felt their loyalty belonged to the Union rather than to their birth state.

Although Garnett had risen in rank much more quickly than him, Garrison felt no jealousy. Garrison knew he belonged on the battlefield where his horsemanship and firearm skills made him deadly. His friend's strength, on the other hand, lay in the areas of administration and organization, making him ideally suited to serve on the command staff. Now that Garrison found himself standing before the acting brigade commander, Garrison was especially glad to have Garnett there with him.

Garrison's thoughts were interrupted by the sound of someone clearing their throat. His attention was drawn to the large man who sat behind the field desk that dominated the small space. As he took in the presence of Lt. Col. Benjamin, Garrison felt his anxiety begin to return. Benjamin appeared to be in his sixties with a nearly bald head surrounded by a ring of gray hair located just above his small ears. His jowly cheeks were covered with matching gray hair styled in muttonchops. His green eyes were now focused upon Garrison with an intensity that the younger man found more than a little uncomfortable.

Benjamin held Garrison in his icy stare for a moment longer before breaking into a welcoming smile. "At ease, Lieutenant," Benjamin said in a gravelly voice. He then sat back in his chair appraising Garrison's appearance another moment before continuing. "It seems that you have made some additions to the standard issue armament for cavalry soldiers. Tell me about that."

Garrison hesitated for a moment, wondering if he had been called to the command tent to be reprimanded for his custom gun rig. Cavalry officers typically carried a single revolver along with their sword. Garrison found a sword to be useless on the modern battlefield and no longer carried one. Instead of a single revolver, he carried five. An Army Colt .44 hung low from each hip. A .40 Le Mat taken from a dead Confederate cavalry officer was holstered on the front of his left hip for a right-handed cross over draw. Two more Army Colt .44s hung from a dual shoulder holster and were positioned for a dual cross over draw.

Gathering his courage, Garrison finally spoke. "It doesn't take long to empty your revolver when engaged with the enemy and there's seldom time to stop and reload. The additional pistols give me the edge over the enemy," he explained. "They were approved by Col. Murray," he quickly added. He knew for a fact that he was not the only one in the unit to supplement his weaponry.

"So, I've been told," Benjamin said, eyeing Major Garnett. "Something like that seems far more suited for a guerrilla soldier than a uniformed officer of the United States of America, if you ask me."

Garrison struggled to keep a neutral expression on his face as he felt his temper begin to rise. His armament had been approved by his commanding officer, and he would be damned if he was going to let this pompous ass of a man make him change it now. *How would he know what was needed in battle? Hell, his fat ass probably couldn't mount a horse if his life depended on it, much less actually ride into battle,* Garrison thought to himself.

"Relax, Lieutenant," Benjamin said as if reading Garrison's thoughts. "It's actually perfect for the assignment I have in mind for you, which brings me to the point of why I called you here in the first place."

"Are you familiar with the town of Bent Pines, Georgia?" Benjamin asked. Garrison shook his head silently and Benjamin continued, "Well, there's really no reason that you should be. It's a tiny little town located southwest of our present location and barely worth its dot on the map, if you ask me. Most importantly, it is absolutely and positively devoid of any strategic or tactical military value."

"This is what makes it such a great hiding place," Benjamin added with an almost childlike gleam in his eyes.

Before Garrison could process this last statement, Benjamin suddenly changed the topic. "You know this war is almost over, don't you?" he asked. He continued without giving Garrison a chance to respond, "And the South has lost. It's only a matter of time now. They just don't have the manpower or resources to continue the fight indefinitely. In the East, Grant is taking heavy causalities but he keeps moving forward, pushing that wily fox, Lee, ever closer to Richmond. We'll do the same here and Atlanta will eventually fall. It makes me wonder why they don't just end this now. What could they possibly hope to achieve by dragging this destructive conflict out longer than need be?"

That childlike gleam returned to Benjamin's eyes as he continued, "It just so happens that we intercepted a wounded Confederate courier with a dispatch that sheds a little light on the subject. Their one chance, the only chance really, is the intervention of a strong foreign power such as Great Britain or France. Now the Brits are out of the question because of their strong anti-slavery stance. The French, on the other hand, might be willing if the incentive was right."

"Of course, that begs the question: what on Earth could the Confederates have to offer that could possibly entice the French to get involved at this point in the war? How does twenty million dollars in gold sound? That might pique some interest. Don't you think?" This time, Benjamin actually paused to allow the young officer to answer.

"Permission to speak freely?" Garrison asked. When Benjamin nodded, Garrison continued, "With all due respect, sir, if they had that kind of resource, don't you think they would have used it long ago?"

"And what precisely do you think they could have done?" Benjamin asked with an air of condescension. And now Benjamin resumed his annoying habit of continuing without giving Garrison a chance to answer. "They lack the infrastructure needed to mass-produce war materials. The blockades have effectively cut off any chance of importing what they need. The only real question worth asking is why they waited so long to make this move. The answer to that is relatively simple. Until last July when Vicksburg fell and Lee was defeated at Gettysburg, they had every expectation of winning this conflict."

"Despite your doubts, the French are prepared to enter into this conflict on behalf of the Confederacy. In fact, according to our captured intel, there is a French fleet in route to the continent with the intent of breaking the blockade in New Orleans, landing troops there, and driving our forces out." Benjamin's voice had been slowly rising as he spoke, so that now he was nearly shouting.

"The only thing holding them back at this very moment is the fact that they are awaiting confirmation that the Confederates actually have the gold. Our captured courier was the one tasked with gaining that proof. That's why he was carrying camera equipment when he was captured. He was to get photographic proof that he would then hand off to a French spy somewhere between here and Louisiana. That spy would then send the signal that would launch the French assault on New Orleans."

"And you really think that this intel is reliable?" Garrison asked, forgetting to request permission first.

Benjamin gave him a hard glare. "In fact, I absolutely do," he spat. "And Lieutenant," Benjamin added, his tone dangerously menacing, "please consider your permission to speak freely revoked. It's time for you to shut up and listen to me very carefully."

Garrison visibly bristled at the harsh rebuke. Benjamin, his tone softening, resumed his briefing. "This all brings me back to that little town of Bent Pines, Georgia. That's where the Confederates have hidden their gold stockpile. According to the intelligence, the town has virtually no military presence. They knew that if they placed a garrison there, they risked the town becoming a tactical or strategic target of our campaign to subdue Georgia." Garrison couldn't help but notice how pleased with himself Benjamin sounded.

But Benjamin had still more to say, and Garrison had the sinking feeling that he wasn't going to like it one bit.

Chapter Three

Five Miles Northeast of Bent Pines, Georgia – One Week Later

As Matthew Garrison stared into the embers of the dying campfire, he knew that his thoughts should be on the details of the mission he was about to undertake. But try as he might, his mind refused to cooperate, his thoughts dwelling instead on the final minutes of his audience with Lt. Col. Benjamin.

Benjamin, adamant that his intelligence information was accurate, had devised a covert operation to steal the gold he was convinced the Confederates were hiding in the small town of Bent Pines. Garrison had listened in trepidation as the Lt. Col. had laid out his plan.

"We are convinced that a small force of five men should be able to discreetly enter the town, steal the gold that's being held in a custom-built vault room in the town's bank, and make their getaway before Confederate forces can offer any resistance," Benjamin had said.

Garrison still wasn't sure who Benjamin was referring to when he had said 'we,' but in the end it didn't really matter. Garrison was a good soldier and good soldiers followed the orders of their superiors, even when they didn't believe in the mission. And Garrison definitely didn't believe in this mission.

The idea that the South had been hoarding and hiding twenty million dollars in gold in this small Georgia town sounded absurd to him, and he had said as much to Lt. Col. Benjamin when he was given the opportunity. He well remembered Benjamin's response. "So, what? You think the Confederates shot their own man, loaded him on a horse, and sent him hurtling toward our picket lines, all just to feed us some false information about imaginary gold?" Benjamin had asked, his voice dripping with sarcasm. "To what end? What good could that possibly do for them?" he had added.

Garrison hadn't bothered to answer. By this point, he had come to accept that Benjamin had little interest in what he had to say. Again, it didn't really matter. He was a soldier and he had his orders. He would carry them out to the best of his ability. Now, here he was in enemy territory about to embark on a fool's errand. He didn't know what to expect, but he had little doubt that it wouldn't be the easy task Benjamin made it out to be.

Chapter Four

"Alright, we're all set, Lieuten…um, I mean Boss." Garrison, his reverie interrupted, looked up at the young man that had just addressed him. His gaze was met by a sheepish grin. "Sorry, once you get so used to addressing your superiors by rank, it's a hard habit to break," the young man said.

"It's alright, Johnny," Garrison replied, having to remind himself to address the young man by his first name. This was a covert mission. If any of them were killed or captured, there could be nothing tying the Union to the mission. That meant civilian clothes and not addressing each other by rank. Garrison gave him a smile and added, "Just do me a favor and don't do that once we get to town, okay?"

"No problem, Boss," the young man said with a big smile.

Garrison took a moment to consider his companion. His name was Johnny Watkins. He was the youngest of the five men Benjamin had assigned to this mission, having just recently turned eighteen. *Just a kid really,* thought Garrison. He had a baby face and an infectious smile that made his brown eyes sparkle.

In the few short days since they met, the young man had managed to endear himself to Garrison. As it turned out, his family, like Garrison's, was in the business of raising horses, and this provided the common ground over which the two could bond. All of this, combined with Watkin's young age, was probably the reason Garrison had decided to keep the young man close to him for the duration of the mission. They were the last two to leave camp and make their way to Bent Pines.

Garrison knew that five strange and heavily armed men arriving in town together would immediately raise the suspicions of whatever authorities resided there. He had therefore devised a plan that spread their arrivals out over three days with him and Watkins arriving last, just moments before beginning the operation. He had sent Robert Barnes in first. He was the reconnaissance man. He'd take a room in town and await the arrival of the others. If he detected a heavy Confederate presence or any signs of a trap, he was empowered to abort the mission by checking out of the hotel and returning to camp. That hadn't happened, so they would proceed as planned.

Bobby Sexton and Billy Jenkins went in next driving a buckboard wagon, appearing to be in town to load up on supplies from the general store located next to the bank. The amount of gold they expected to find would be too heavy to carry in their saddlebags, so they would use the wagon to get the gold out of town quickly. If all went according to plan, they would abandon the wagon once they reached a safe distance from the town, torch it, and carry the gold the rest of the way on pack mules.

Garrison took one last look around the campsite. His keen eyes swept every inch of the ground to ensure they left no trace of themselves behind. "Alright, kid. Let's get on with this," he said to Watkins as he swung himself into the saddle.

Watkins mounted his own horse, flashed Garrison his boyish smile, and said, "Right behind you, Boss."

Chapter Five

On the Outskirts of Bent Pines, Georgia – May 1864

They were on the outskirts of town when Johnny Watkins suddenly drew back on the reigns, bringing his horse to a stop. Garrison pulled up short and gave the younger man a quizzical look. Much to Garrison's surprise, the boyish smile he'd come to expect from Watkins had vanished. Taking its place was a grim expression unlike anything Garrison had seen from the youth since meeting him.

Watkins opened his mouth to speak but no sound came out. He closed his eyes, took a deep breath, and tried again. "Look, before we ride in there, there's something I gotta say. We ain't talked about it none, but I think we both know that there's something that's just not right about this whole thing." Watkins paused as he reached into his jacket pocket and pulled out two folded pieces of paper. He thrust them out toward Garrison as he continued on with what he had to say. "Before we go in there, I want you to take these, just in case something goes wrong. There's a map and a letter. I told you my folks had a horse ranch, but what I didn't tell you was that it's not too far from here. It's close enough to get to if we run into trouble but far enough away to make it a safe rendezvous spot. I'm pretty sure that's the only reason Benjamin put me on this team. The map will show you how to get there. The letter…well, that's for my folks. You know…um…just in case I don't make it there." A single tear escaped Watkins's eye as he said this. He quickly brushed it away with the back of his hand, clearly embarrassed at the show of emotion.

As Garrison looked at Watkins, he was overcome with a growing sense of affection toward the young man. He silently vowed to do everything in his power to make sure Watkins came through this in one piece, while simultaneously cursing himself for letting the kid get to him. Garrison reached out and took the papers from Watkins's shaking hand. He gave the kid what he hoped was a reassuring smile as he said, "Relax, kid. Everything is going to be just fine. Now let's get a move on. The others are waiting."

As they both gave a kick to get the horses moving again, another thought occurred to Garrison. "Hey Johnny, how is that you ended up on this side of things after growing up down here?" he asked.

Watkins gave a quick smile. "I grew up in Ohio. We moved down here to build the horse ranch a few years before the war started. Great timing, wasn't it?" he asked ruefully.

Garrison flashed him a quick smile and said, "Okay, that makes sense." By now they had reached the very edge of town. "Alright, enough idle chatter. It's time to get down to business," Garrison said, his tone now grim and serious.

Chapter Six

Bent Pines, Georgia – May 1864

Lt. Col. Benjamin had been right about one thing, Garrison mused as he and Watkins made their way slowly down the street. Bent Pines was definitely a tiny little town. It consisted of one main road through the town center. The street was lined with the few businesses the town needed. In addition to the bank, there was a general store, a butcher shop, a saloon, and a hotel. Spreading out behind the buildings on either side of the street were the modest homes of the town's inhabitants.

The bank was located on the right side of the street in the center of town. The hotel sat directly across the street from it. The general store was on the same side of the street as and directly next to the bank.

These were the three buildings of primary interest to Garrison. As he and Watkins approached the primary target, Garrison's eyes swept over the bank looking for any signs of trouble. He noted only one horse hitched directly outside the bank and took that as a good sign. After examining the bank, Garrison turned his eyes toward the hotel. He was relieved to see Barnes sitting upon a bench on the hotel's porch, seemingly absorbed in reading a newspaper.

Next, Garrison looked toward the general store. Again, relief washed over him as he saw the wagon that Sexton and Jenkins had driven to town, parked right in front of it. As Garrison watched, Sexton and Jenkins emerged from the general store with another man, whom he could only assume was the store's proprietor. They appeared to be giving the man some instructions. He nodded, turned around, and headed back in the store. He emerged a moment latter with a cart full of supplies that he began loading on the wagon. Sexton and Jenkins watched for a moment and then made their way to the bank.

Now Garrison knew that the mission could go forward. This was the final failsafe in his plan for robbing the bank. If any one of his men had not been in place as they were supposed to, the mission would be aborted, and he and Watkins would simply ride through the town without stopping. Any of the others who were able would then leave town as well.

With everyone in place, Garrison and Watkins came to a stop in front of the bank. As they hitched their horses, Barnes closed up his paper, walked across the street, and entered the bank. Watkins and Garrison would be the last to enter.

Chapter Seven

Garrison entered the bank with Watkins close on his heels. As he entered, he surveyed the scene before him. Sexton and Jenkins had the full attention of the bank manager under the guise of being there to open a large account. Barnes stood in line directly behind the one citizen in the bank who was conducting his business with the bank's lone teller. *Perfectly according to plan,* Garrison thought to himself as he made his way toward the teller.

As soon as the door closed behind him, Watkins spun around to flip the sign to 'closed' while simultaneously locking the door. He then moved quickly to pull all the shades down to keep any passerby from seeing what was going on in the bank. His actions caught the attention of the bank manager, but before the man could offer a word of protest, he was confronted by the sight of two very large guns pointed directly in his face. Sexton and Jenkins both smirked as they watched the color drain from the man's face.

For his part, Barnes had moved in close to the man in front of him, jabbing his pistol into the man's back. The citizen wisely threw his hands in the air in the universal sign for surrender. The teller began to reach under the counter before thinking better of it as he found himself staring down the barrel of the Colt revolver that seemed to materialize out of nowhere into Garrison's left hand.

"Don't," Garrison said as he gave the teller a cold stare. His voice was hard as steel as he continued, "No one has to die today. We're only interested in what you have in the vault. Once we have it, we'll be on our way."

Watkins quickly took his position, standing back-to-back with Garrison, a pistol in each hand as he watched the bank's entrance. Garrison looked over to Sexton and Jenkins, giving them a quick nod. The two proceeded to hustle the manager around the counter to the vault door.

The door was massive, spanning the width of the vault and reaching from floor to ceiling. Garrison watched closely while also trying to keep tabs on the teller out of the corner of his eye. The bank manager was clearly frightened as he fumbled to open the combination lock on the vault door without much success.

Sexton eased the hammer forward and holstered his revolver. "Just relax," he said to the manager. "You take your time and get it right on this next try." He gave the manager a toothy grin and added, "But do hurry it up…We ain't got a lotta time here."

The bank manager steadied his hands as he made another attempt to open the vault. He got it right this time and when he pulled the lever, the two deadbolts sealing the vault shut slid back. He then grabbed the metal handle and began to pull the heavy door open.

As he did, Garrison's sharp eyes saw something that chilled him to the bone. It had only been a second or two, but Garrison was sure that he had seen a wicked grin cross the man's face before he began tugging the door open. The hairs on the back of Garrison's neck stood on end as a sense of impending doom fell upon him.

Before he could utter a word, the vault had swung open completely. Almost immediately, a volley of gunfire erupted from inside the vault. Sexton and Jenkins, who had been standing directly in front of the vault, were hit multiple times. Both men were dead before their bodies hit the floor.

Barnes had turned his head toward the sound of the shots. The man he was covering immediately spun around, producing a large knife as he did so. He proceeded to bury it hilt deep in Barnes's gut. He gave the blade a vicious twist as he pulled it out and then plunged it back into Barnes's gut a second time.

The bank teller used the distraction as an opportunity to reach for the gun he had hidden under the counter. Garrison shot him between the eyes without a second's hesitation. He simultaneously drew the Colt from his right hip. He used it to gun down the man who was in the process of stabbing Barnes a third time.

To his credit, Watkins had reacted immediately to the sound of gunfire. He spun to his right, toward the open vault with his pistols cocked. Inside the vault were six Confederates working quickly to reload their muskets. He opened fire on the men. Garrison joined him and together they quickly dispatched all six.

With the fight concluded, silence fell upon them. It was then that they heard multiple gunshots from outside, accompanied by panicked screams. "Go take a look and see what's going on out there," Garrison said to Watkins. "I'm going to check on the others," he added.

Moving around the counter toward the vault, it only took a quick glance to realize that Sexton and Jenkins were beyond his help. Peering into the vault, he could see that it contained only the six dead Confederate soldiers.

Lastly, he cast his cold, hard gaze upon the bank manager. The man had thrown himself to the floor and now lay there shaking like a leaf with his hands over his ears and his eyes screwed shut. For a brief moment, Garrison considered killing the man for his role in setting the trap. In the end, he decided against it. He may be a killer, but a cold-blooded murderer he was not.

Garrison now moved back to the other side of the counter to check on Barnes, although he was pretty sure what he would find. To his surprise, the man was still alive but in agony. The bastard who had stabbed him had twisted his blade around multiple times to inflict maximum damage. Garrison held little doubt that Barnes's insides were completely ruined.

He looked the man in the eye as he kneeled by his side. They both knew that there was only one thing Garrison could do to help him. Garrison hesitated, hating what he was about to do. Barnes looked up at Garrison, imploring him with his eyes, and gave a little nod. Garrison stood, drew his revolver, aimed carefully, and ended Barnes's suffering with one well-placed shot.

Chapter Eight

"What's it look like out there?!" Garrison shouted over to Watkins.

"It ain't good. Johnny Reb is everywhere!" Watkins shouted back.

Noting a hint of panic in the kid's voice, Garrison stood and strode quickly toward him. The young man had acquitted himself well so far, but everyone had their breaking point. He couldn't let the kid lose it now if either of them wanted any chance of making it out of here alive.

Arriving at his side, Garrison placed a steadying hand on the young man's shoulder. "We're all in here. So what the hell are they shooting at?" Garrison asked.

"Anything that moves," Watkins said in a bewildered voice. "That's not all. The whole damn town is on fire," he added.

Garrison pulled one of the blinds aside to see for himself. He was just in time to see the Confederates forming a firing line right in front of the bank. "Get down!" he shouted, giving Watkins a hard shove before diving to the floor himself. No sooner had they hit the floor than they found themselves covered in glass as the bank's windows were shattered by the fusillade from the Confederates.

Still lying on the floor, Garrison felt a rush of heat pass over him. Rolling onto his back and looking back toward the bank's interior, he was just in time to see several flaming torches land on the floor. Just then, five more torches came sailing in over the two men. Almost everything in the bank was made of wood, so it didn't take long for the flames to spread until Garrison and Watkins found themselves confronted by a raging inferno. On the plus side, there no longer seemed to be anyone shooting into the bank.

"Johnny, you okay over there?!" Garrison shouted to Jenkins.

"I'm cut up from all that damn glass, but nothing serious," he replied.

"Good, because we need to get the hell out of this bank," Garrison told him.

"We don't stand a chance out there! They'll gun us down as soon as we step foot out of here," Watkins objected.

"I don't think so," Garrison insisted. "I don't think they even know that we're still alive in here. Those shots were just to break the glass so they could throw the torches in and light the place up. Besides, we can't stay here. Unless of course, the idea of being burned alive appeals to you," he added with a wink.

He was rewarded with a brief glimpse of the boyish grin he had become accustomed to seeing from Watkins. "Well, when you put it that way…" the young man said and then added, "lead the way, Boss."

"Alright, on the count of three, then," Garrison told him. "We hitched the horses right outside this window, so we'll go out that way," he added. Garrison counted down in his head, gave Watkins the 'go' signal, and both men leaped through the busted-out window with their pistols drawn.

What they saw brought both men to a sudden stop. It was as though they had stepped into one of Dante's seven circles of hell. Lifeless bodies were strewn everywhere. Panicked civilians were running this way and that in a fruitless effort to find safety. Men in Confederate uniforms were indeed shooting at anything that moved. Every structure seemed to be ablaze, including the homes set behind the main street. Billowing black smoke swirled about, making it hard to see more than a few feet in front of their shocked faces. The sounds of gunfire were punctuated by terrified screams. Despite his four years of experience on countless battlefields during the course of the war, Garrison had never seen anything so terrifying as what his eyes now beheld.

Neither man could comprehend what they were seeing. Why were the Confederates attacking their own town…slaughtering their own citizens? For a moment, Garrison considered the possibility that the men committing this atrocity might not really be Confederates. But then he thought about how his team had been lured here with what he now knew was faulty intel. No, this was clearly all part of a sinister plan. But whatever the end goal was, the scheme was simply too diabolical for Garrison to fathom what it might be.

Forcing himself to snap out of his reverie, Garrison took a step toward the horses only to again come up short. The horses were gone. He looked quickly toward the general store to check the status of the wagon Sexton and Jenkins had ridden into town in. Not only had the wagon been set ablaze but the mules hitched to it had been slaughtered.

"What do we do now?" Watkins asked. As Garrison turned to answer, the young man's head suddenly exploded, showering Garrison's face with blood and brain matter. In the same instant, Garrison felt a blossom of pain in his left shoulder as a mini ball tore a path through it.

Garrison looked toward the street and saw his assailants in front of the hotel, two men in confederate uniforms. They were just dropping their muskets and reaching for their side arms when Garrison spotted them. Garrison felt a deep seething hatred rise up from the depths of his soul.

With an enraged roar, Garrison opened fire on the two just as they began to fire on him. Garrison knew he had been hit again when he felt a sudden burning in his left thigh. He ignored the pain as he unloaded his two pistols, hitting both men multiple times.

Just as both pistols clicked on empty cylinders, the air was pierced by a shrill scream. Looking in the direction of the sound, Garrison's heart skipped a beat. There in the street, standing between him and the two men he had just killed stood a little girl. *She couldn't be any more than ten years old,* Garrison thought to himself. As Garrison watched, a dark red stain blossomed and spread across the front of the girl's sundress. Without another sound, the girl dropped to the ground.

Garrison holstered his weapons and rushed to her side. He dropped to both knees and pulled the girl into his lap. As he placed his hands beneath her, they were instantly coated with her warm, sticky blood. The round had gone clear through her body. It was impossible to know whether it was one of his rounds or one of his assailants' that had struck her. It didn't really matter. In Garrison's mind, he would forever be responsible for her death. In his rage, he just hadn't seen her standing there.

She lay in his arms as her life's blood slowly drained from her body. A bloody froth appeared upon her lips and Garrison knew her struggle was almost over. He looked into her eyes, which were a vibrant blue. They were fixed upon his face as if imploring him to tell her why this had happened. As he watched, the light slowly faded from her eyes and then she was gone.

As Garrison eased her body to the ground, he felt another round hit him, this time from behind. The round struck his right side just above his hip. Enraged by the death of this little girl and his role in it, Garrison again ignored the pain. He stood and whirled around to face his attacker, drawing the Le Mat from the cross over holster on his left hip as he did so.

The man was on horseback racing down the street toward him. He fired as he rode but his shots were wild, and they sailed harmlessly past Garrison. Garrison waited until the man was almost on top of him and then opened fire, emptying his weapon. At this distance, every round found its mark and the man was driven backward off his horse by the force of the impact.

The horse continued to barrel toward Garrison. As the horse came past him, Garrison reached out, grabbing the reigns while simultaneously lifting his right foot into the stirrup. He let the horse's momentum lift him from the ground and then swung his left leg over and came to rest perfectly in the saddle. It may have looked easy to an observer, but it was not, especially given the fact that Garrison had suffered three wounds and was losing blood.

Garrison pulled up on the reins as he saw more uniformed men massing on the end of town he was headed toward. He quickly guided the horse to turn around and then kicked hard, spurring the horse into a gallop. Garrison sighed with relief as the horse cleared the edge of town. He had done it; he had made it out of that hell alive. Little did he expect that there would come a time when he would wish fervently that he hadn't.

Chapter Nine

Rural Georgia (West of Bent Pines) – May 1864

As Matthew Garrison made his way through the Georgia countryside, he could feel the darkness closing around him as night began to fall. It was a new moon, so he would have only the light of the stars to guide him. As he looked skyward, they appeared to him as a thousand tiny pinholes piercing the darkness that enveloped him. All around him, he could hear the myriad sounds of nocturnal creatures as they began to stir.

He was no longer sure how far he had traveled from Bent Pines. He was growing weak from blood loss and could no longer think clearly. It was as if the darkness around him had somehow penetrated his mind, obscuring his thoughts.

He could only hope that he was heading in the right direction and nearing his destination. His right hand clung desperately to the map Watkins had given him, even though it was now useless. Thoroughly coated in his own blood, it was no longer legible. Still, he rode on into the gathering darkness.

The darkness of night was now complete, but Garrison rode on oblivious to it. He could no longer keep his eyes open as he drifted in and out of consciousness. He had wrapped the reins tightly around his wrists in hopes that it would be enough to keep him in the saddle. He knew with certainty that if he fell, he wouldn't have the strength to remount. He would die here, alone in the mud.

And that just wouldn't do. Despite the pain and blood loss, the will to live burned deeply within him. He had to survive this. He was the only one who could tell the world what really happened this day. He owed it to his men and the innocent men, women, and children that had died needlessly that day in Bent Pines.

Garrison's eyes fluttered open. He had lost all track of time during his seemingly endless journey. He could no longer sit up in the saddle and found himself draped over the horse's neck. All his strength had left him, and he knew he was running out of time.

As the horse rounded a bend in the road, Garrison could just barely make out a light up ahead. Garrison whispered a prayer of thanks. With the last of his strength, he spurred the horse forward, praying that he could stay in the saddle long enough to reach the light.

As he drew nearer, he could see that the light came from a small farmhouse. In the gloom, he could just make out the shapes of other buildings set around the house in a semicircle. There was a large structure that his clouded mind told him could be a horse barn. As his horse entered the property, he could hear the sounds of other horses neighing as they approached. He had made it. He was certain of it. A faint smile crossed his face just before he pitched to the side and fell off the horse face-first into the mud.

Chapter Ten

The Watkin's Ranch, Georgia – May 1864

"Welcome back to the land of the living," Garrison heard when he opened his eyes. Garrison blinked his eyes several times as he tried to get his bearings. The first thing he became aware of was the throbbing pain in his head. Pushing the pain aside, he tried to take in his surroundings.

He was lying on a soft bed under what appeared to be a mountain of blankets. The room was small and rustic. There was a cedar wardrobe on the wall opposite the bed and a small nightstand next to the bed. Two curtained windows allowed a moderate amount of sunlight to filter into the room.

The only other piece of furniture in the room was a high-back chair in which sat the man who had spoken to him. Garrison took in his appearance with blurry eyes. He was a large man with broad shoulders. His height was hard to judge from his sitting position. He had a large, round face. His head was covered with thick, wavy hair so blond that it was almost white. His face was clean-shaven with ruddy cheeks. He had the same sparkling brown eyes as Johnny Watkins. *This had to be the kid's father,* Garrison reasoned.

Garrison opened his mouth to speak but the only thing that came out was a dry, rasping sound. The man stood quickly and made his way to the nightstand. "Here, let me get you some water," the man said as he poured water from a pitcher into a glass that he then held up to Garrison's cracked lips. The water was cool and soothed Garrison's parched throat.

"Thank…thank you," Garrison told him as he struggled to extract his arms from beneath the blankets so that he could sit up.

"Don't you be moving around too much now," the man said sternly. "It wouldn't take much to open those wounds back up," he added. "Your head is probably splitting but that's because we've been pouring whiskey down your gullet for three days now, trying to break that fever. It'll pass," the man told him.

"Thank you again," Garrison said, "for everything." He finally asked, "Are you Mr. Watkins?"

"Jonathan Watkins Sr.," the man answered. "And thanks to this," he said, holding up the letter Johnny had given him for safekeeping, "I already know who you are. Since you're here and he isn't, I'm assuming that my son is…" His strong voice trailed off as he struggled to say the word aloud.

"I'm afraid so," Garrison answered, knowing what the man was trying to ask.

"No doubts?" the big man asked, a glimmer of hope in his eyes.

Garrison hesitated before answering. He saw the look in the older man's eyes, and he didn't want to be the one to crush that hope. At the same time, he wouldn't give the man a false hope either. "No sir," Garrison said. "He died standing right next to me," Garrison added with emotion in his voice as the image of Johnny Watkin's head exploding flashed in his mind. "There's absolutely no doubt," Garrison said with finality.

Watkins Sr.'s eyes had reddened as Garrison spoke. Now he spoke through the lump in his throat, "I thought as much, but I had to ask. Well, I need to get back to my chores, so I'll leave you to rest," Watkins said. "I'm sure the ladies will be in to check on you momentarily."

"Ladies?" Garrison asked.

"My wife, Elenore, and daughter, Olivia," Watkins said with a smile. "They've been tending to and fussing over you since the night you rode in here. You were awful delirious with fever, so you might not remember seeing them," he said.

Garrison smiled. He did remember them now that he thought about it. "I thought they were angels," he said sheepishly.

Watkins smiled, "That they are my boy, that they are."

Chapter Eleven

A week had passed since Garrison awoke to find himself in the care of the Watkins's family. He hadn't seen Jonathan Watkins again since their first meeting. The Watkins women, on the other hand, had been his near constant companions. There was rarely a moment when one or the other of the two women had not been in the room with him.

In the moments before full consciousness had returned, in his feverish state, he had thought that the two women were angels come to carry him into the next life. Their actions since he had come to had served to convince him that they were indeed angels, even if not from the heavenly realm. They changed the dressings on his wounds and brought him food at regular intervals, feeding him by hand until he was able to sit up and feed himself. And much to his chagrin, they emptied his bedpan without complaint. He was fairly certain that the two took turns sitting with him while he slept, for every time he woke, he found one or the other sitting in the chair by his bed, watching over him.

Elenore Watkins was not a particularly beautiful woman, although Garrison thought that she may have been in her younger years. A life of toil had taken its toll and showed in the wrinkles that lined her face. She had the calloused and rough hands of someone accustomed to manual labor. Despite this, her hazel eyes were vibrant and shone with an obvious love for life.

She was a kind woman with a soft and soothing voice. In the moments that she sat with him, while he was awake, she sought to engage him in conversation. She asked about his past, particularly his experience growing up around horses. Garrison found that he genuinely enjoyed his conversations with her and looked forward to her visits.

Oliva Watkins was the polar opposite of her mother. She was stunningly beautiful with soft features, long blond hair, and the same sparkling brown eyes as her father and brother. The differences between the mother and daughter extended beyond just their appearance. Whereas her mother had a pleasant and engaging personality, Olivia Watkins' demeanor was distant and aloof. She seldom spoke and ignored all of Garrison's attempts to engage her in conversation. The girl was cold as ice, plain and simple. More than once, he had awoken to find her gaze fixed on him with an icy-cold stare and obvious dislike. The look would disappear the moment she realized that Garrison was awake. Garrison silently resolved himself to break through her icy exterior.

Chapter Twelve

Early morning sunlight was streaming through the windows when the door to Garrison's room opened. To his surprise, it was Jonathan Watkins who entered. In his arms he carried a large bundle of clothes. "It's time we get you up out of that bed," Watkins said with a smile. "Thought you might like to take your breakfast at the table this morning," he added.

Garrison smiled back. "That sounds really good," he said. He had been getting up and down to relieve himself over the last couple of days but had not ventured out of bed beyond that. He was more than ready to get up and moving.

Watkins dropped the bundle of clothes onto the chair in the room. "We scrounged together an assortment of clothes. Hopefully you can find something here to fit you. Just come on out once you're decent." With that, the big man left the room, closing the door behind him.

After considerable trial and error, Garrison finally managed to put together a passable outfit. He settled on a simple homespun cotton pull over. Although a little short in the sleeves, it fit his torso adequately. His simple denim pants weren't a perfect fit either, but they would do. Fortunately, his own boots had been salvaged, so footwear was not an issue. Garrison paused with his hand on the doorknob as he realized that for the first time in recent memory, he was about to venture forth without his assortment of six guns. He suddenly felt naked and vulnerable. Shaking off the unsettling feeling, he turned the knob, opened the door, and stepped through.

Breakfast had been simple but delicious. Fresh biscuits covered in thick gravy accompanied by fried potatoes and thin-sliced, salt-cured ham had all been washed down with fresh brewed coffee. As Elenore and Olivia rose and began collecting the dirty crockery, Jonathan looked across the table at Garrison and said, "Let's you and me take a walk. I'll show you around the place."

As the two men stepped out onto the porch, the older man reached into the front pouch of his bib overalls and produced a corncob pipe and cloth pouch containing tobacco. The two men stood in silence as Watkins prepared and lit his pipe while Garrison simply took in his surroundings. Although much smaller than the horse ranches Garrison had grown up on, he was, nonetheless, impressed by what he saw.

The ranch was set well away from the main road. The buildings were arranged in a semicircle with the house at the center. Directly to Garrison's right were the stables. Next to it was another large building. *Most likely used for storage,* Garrison presumed. Several other buildings stretched out beyond this. Looking to his left, Garrison saw a chicken coop, hog pen, and hay barn. Behind the buildings on his right was open land as far as Garrison could see. Behind the buildings on his left were even more outbuildings and a small garden. In the center of the circle formed by the buildings was a large horse corral.

Watkins finally managed to puff the pipe to life, and he held it out toward Garrison, who declined with a simple shake of his head. The older man merely shrugged and moved toward the steps. Garrison quickly moved to join him. "We'll start with the buildings on the left here and work our way backwards around the circle so that we finish at the stables," Watkins told Garrison.

They had moved well away from the house and were nearing the hay barn when Watkins came to a stop. He fixed Garrison with a hard stare. "It's time you and I had a serious talk, son," he said. "I know from Johnny's letter why you were at Bent Pines and there's lots of horrific rumors going around about what happened there. Now I need to hear it from you. What really happened there?" Before Garrison could form any words, Watkins added, "And don't be leaving anything out to spare an old man's feelings. I need to know what happened and how my son died."

Garrison took a deep breath and then launched into the story of what happened at Bent Pines. He left nothing out this time. He told Jonathan Watkins how well his son reacted when the trap had been sprung on them and later how the young man's blood had splattered across his own face when Johnny's head had exploded. Garrison told of how in a rage he blindly opened fire on the men who had killed him. He told of how a young girl, probably hit by one of his shots, had died in his arms.

When Garrison finished, he found himself nearly out of breath. There were tears in both men's eyes. Watkins found himself momentarily unable to speak. He placed a large hand on Garrison's shoulder and gave him a reassuring squeeze. With that, he turned to continue the tour and motioned for the younger man to follow him.

Chapter Thirteen

As they entered the stables, Watkins headed toward the closest stall and began to tell Garrison about the horse occupying it. His voice trailed off as he realized that the younger man was no longer beside him. Looking around, his eyes widened when he spotted the young man all the way at the other end of the stables.

For his part, Garrison had been drawn to the horse standing in the last stall at the opposite end of the stables. It was the most magnificent animal he had ever seen. The words 'massive' and 'beautiful' simultaneously popped into his head as he admired the beast, a stallion he realized as he approached. Standing at least eighteen hands high, he was the size of a draft horse but had the muscle structure of a thoroughbred. He was truly beautiful, solid in color, and his coat a shade of gray so light as to be almost white. His mane and tail were just a shade darker.

"Don't get too close to…" Watkins began to shout but then trailed off as he saw that Garrison had placed his hand upon the horse's head. As he watched in amazement, Garrison placed both hands under the animal's head and touched his own forehead to the horse's face. As Watkins approached, he could just barely hear Garrison whispering to the horse, although he could not make out what was being said. "Well, I be damned," the older man said to himself as he increased his pace.

"I see that you've met Diablo," Watkins said as he came to stand at Garrison's side.

Garrison gave him a quizzical a look as he asked, "Why Diablo?"

"Johnny named him that," Watkins answered. "On account of the fact that he acts like he's got the devil in him, at least around most people. Johnny raised that beast and until today he's the only person that horse has allowed near him. Hell, I can't tell you how many times I've nearly got my head kicked off just trying to feed the bastard. How did you do it?" Watkins finally asked, the amazement evident in his voice.

"I don't really know," Garrison answered. "I guess I've just always had a special connection with horses. Is he fast?" Garrison asked.

"Like a bat out of hell," Watkins answered with a smile.

"Can I ride him?" Garrison asked.

Now Watkins's face took on a look of consternation. "Son, it really ain't up to me but you can try," he finally answered.

"What do you mean?" Garrison inquired.

Watkins smiled again. "Diablo decides who can ride him. Again, you can try, but I've gotta warn you; he's never let anyone other than Johnny saddle and ride him. But then again, he's never let anyone else this close to him before either."

"I want to try," Garrison told Watkins.

"Alright. Wait here while I fetch Johnny's saddle from the tack room," Watkins said as he moved across the building. When he returned, Watkins was carrying a beautiful black leather saddle. "Leatherworking is a bit of a hobby of mine and I made this saddle for Johnny," he said with pride.

"It's beautiful," Garrison said as he took the saddle from him and made his way toward Diablo's stall. Watkins watched in silent amazement as the animal stood stock-still while Garrison saddled him. After cinching the saddle down tight, Garrison next placed the bridle on the animal's head. He took the reins in his hand and led the horse from the stall and out toward the corral.

There was no obvious reaction from Diablo when Garrison swung himself into the saddle. With a soft clicking noise, Garrison spurred the horse into motion. They began with a slow walk that built toward a steady trot. The horse and rider seemed to be in perfect synch and within minutes, they were galloping around the corral.

An hour later, Diablo was back in his stall and the two men were preparing to return to the house. "Just a minute," Watkins said as he again disappeared into the tack room. When he reemerged, he was carrying Garrison's gun belts. "I thought it best to lock these up until we got a chance to talk. Johnny trusted you. That horse clearly trusts you. That's good enough for me," Watkins told Garrison as he handed the weapons over to him.

Chapter Fourteen

Another two weeks had passed. Garrison spent his mornings helping Jonathan with his daily chores around the ranch. The work proved to be just what he needed to rebuild his strength and stamina. Most afternoons, he saddled Diablo and went for a ride, exploring the countryside. He was careful to stay off the roads and skirted any homesteads he stumbled upon. The last thing he wanted to do was run into any of the Watkins's neighbors which could create an awkward, perhaps even dangerous, situation for the Watkins's family.

On his second day of explorations, Garrison stumbled upon an isolated meadow located in a small valley surrounded on three sides by heavy forest. A stream meandered its way diagonally through the meadow, its path twisting and turning in snakelike fashion. The stream was deep, its water cold and crystal-clear. Wildflowers in a dizzying array of colors covered the valley floor.

There was a number of large pine trees spread sporadically around the meadow. Garrison thought they would make perfect makeshift targets as he worked to rehab his firearm skills. Beginning the very next day, Garrison visited the meadow each day and spent several hours practicing drawing and firing with both hands. He felt confident that in time he would once again be lightning-fast and deadly accurate with both hands.

"It looks like you've just about made a full recovery," Jonathan Watkins said to Garrison. "You, given any thought to what you'll do next, where you'll go?" he asked. "Not that you're not welcome to stay here for as long as you like, of course," he added quickly.

Garrison eyed the older man from the opposite end of the table. He supposed it was inevitable that Jonathan Watkins would eventually ask about his intentions. He was surprised though that he had chosen to bring it up now as the family sat for supper. Garrison could feel the eyes of the two Watkins women on him as he contemplated his answer.

"I'm going to have to work my way east and try to link up with the 3ʳᵈ Brigade. I don't know if Benjamin is still in command or what may have changed in my absence, but it's the only thing I can think to do," Garrison told the family.

Jonathan Watkins sighed heavily. "I thought you might say something like that, but have you really thought this through? You've heard the rumors and you've seen the papers. They're saying that you and your men attacked Bent Pines and slaughtered all those people. Lincoln's come out and condemned the attack, calling you and your men a rogue unit made up of deserters."

"That's why I have to go back," Garrison told them. "I've got to set the record straight and tell everyone what really happened."

Watkins wasn't giving up easily. "Right now, everyone thinks you're dead, that there were no survivors. Why not take advantage of that and start your life over? As I understand it, you don't really have any family to go back to, so there's nothing holding you back."

At the mention of his family, Garrison shot a sharp look at Elenore Watkins. Having been born and raised in Virginia, Garrison's father had been a staunch supporter of the Confederacy despite the fact that Kentucky had remained in the Union. When Garrison had refused to resign his commission and join the Confederate army, his father had accused him of being a traitor to his heritage. The old man had disowned Garrison and forbade him from ever returning to the family home. Other than Jack Garnett, Elenore Watkins was the only other person Garrison had shared that painful memory with. Clearly, she had decided to share it with her husband. Elenore couldn't meet the young man's gaze, casting her eyes downward instead.

"That's precisely why I have to go back. My name is all that I have left, and now it's been smeared. I've got to do whatever I can to clear my name, not to mention that of your son and my other men," Garrison insisted.

Watkins sighed again. "From what you've told me about this Benjamin fellow, I can't imagine you'll even get a chance to tell your side of the story. He's the one who sent you in there, but his name's never come up in the papers. Do you really think he's going to let you tell everyone that the whole thing was his idea? No! You know what you'll be when they find out you're alive? You'll be their scapegoat!"

Garrison looked at Jonathan Watkins with growing affection. He knew the man had come to care for him and was only speaking out of concern.

"Be that as it may, I've got to try," Garrison said with resignation. "I don't think I could live with myself if I didn't," he told them.

"I understand," Watkins said at last. Neither woman spoke, although Garrison noted that Elenore seemed to be struggling to hold back tears. Olivia Watkins's face was an unreadable mask.

Chapter Fifteen

Garrison awoke the next morning to the sound of loud voices coming from outside his room. He struggled to make out what was being said. He quietly slipped out of bed and crept forward, putting his ear to the door.

The first voice he heard was that of Olivia Watkins. "Daddy, you were practically begging him to stay," she said in exasperation. "Why can't you see that having him here is dangerous? He said he didn't kill all those people, but how do we know he's telling the truth?" Olivia said, her voice growing louder as she spoke.

"Because I can tell when someone is lying to me, and I can tell that he isn't," Jonathan said, his own voice louder than normal.

"I think you're just blinded by your grief. You've lost your son and now you're trying to latch onto this man that you barely know. He isn't Johnny and he'll never be Johnny!" She screamed. "At best, he got Johnny killed. For all we know, he might have killed Johnny himself," she added.

"Olivia!" her mother said sharply.

Her father's voice was harsh when he spoke. "You are way out of line, young lady."

Olivia decided on another tactic. "What if a rebel patrol comes through here and finds him? He's not exactly hiding, you know. He's outside every day and who knows where he goes when he rides off on Diablo. What do you think will happen to us if anyone finds out we're harboring a Yankee? And not just any Yankee but the Butcher of Bent Pines!"

Before Watkins could answer, the door to Garrison's room swung open. All heads turned in that direction. Garrison walked out fully dressed and wearing his guns. He carried the few extra pieces of clothing that the Watkins had given him in a haversack.

"Jonathan, Elenore, I'm grateful for all you've done for me but it's clearly time that I move on," Garrison said. "I appreciate you allowing me to take

Diablo. I don't know if I can ever repay you, but if I can, I will." He barely looked at Olivia as he made his way toward the door.

"Wait, wait, wait," Jonathan said. "There's no need to rush off like this."

Elenore Watkins was nodding her head vigorously in agreement.

"No, I don't want to be the cause of strife in your family. Besides, Olivia is right. My presence here puts you all in danger. I already failed your son; I couldn't bear it if something befell any of you on account of me." And with that, he strode out the door. As the door closed, Jonathan and Elenore Watkins glared at their daughter.

Garrison was halfway down the steps off the porch when he heard a soft voice say, "Wait." He paused momentarily but then continued on. He had just reached the ground when the voice spoke again.

"Please Matthew, stop!" Olivia implored him. "Please give me a chance to apologize."

Olivia Watkins expected to see anger on Garrison's face when he turned around, but all she saw in his handsome features was a deep sadness. And for reasons she couldn't explain, she felt her heart breaking at the sight. When he spoke, his words further widened the chasm.

"There's no need to apologize," he told her. "You have every right to hate me and no reason at all to trust me," he added.

"Oh, Matthew, I don't hate you," Olivia said as she descended the steps to stand in front of him. "I wanted to," she admitted. "That's part of the reason I've been treating you the way I have been, trying to keep my distance."

"And the other part?" Garrison asked softly.

Olivia hesitated before answering. "I guess I knew that you would be leaving sooner or later. I didn't want to let myself care about you and then have to watch you leave. It would be like losing Johnny all over again. I know that probably sounds silly…" She trailed off as the tears began to stream down her face.

"It doesn't sound silly at all," Garrison said as he reached out and gently wiped the tears from Olivia's checks. "I only knew your brother for a few days, but I genuinely cared about him. He was a good man," Garrison told her.

Olivia's shoulders shook as she sobbed, her grief finally overwhelming her. Before either of them realized what was happening, Olivia found herself wrapped in Garrison's strong arms. They stood staring into each other's face, their eyes communicating more deeply than words ever could. When their lips met, the rest of the world and all its worries seemed to simply melt away.

Chapter Sixteen

The Watkins's Ranch, Georgia – July 1864

It had been nearly two months since the fateful day that Matthew Lloyd Garrison had ridden into the town of Bent Pines. He had never intended to stay with the Watkins's family this long, but everything had changed the day that he and Olivia had shared their first kiss. While he still spent his mornings helping Jonathan with his chores, he soon found himself spending more and more of his afternoons and evenings enjoying Olivia's company.

After supper each evening, the two of them would head to the front porch to sit and talk as they watched the sun set. Before long, they began to take afternoon walks around the ranch together before supper. Just a week ago, Olivia had surprised him by suggesting they go riding together once his chores were through. They had packed a blanket and picnic basket before setting out for the secluded meadow that Garrison had discovered and utilized for his target practice. Upon arriving, the food was quickly forgotten as their passion ignited and they had made love for the first time.

Garrison supposed that even a blind man would be able to see that the two were falling in love. The subject of his leaving seemed to have been forgotten by everyone in the Watkins home. In fact, Garrison had begun to give serious thought to Jonathan's suggestion that he let the world continue to think that Matthew Lloyd Garrison was dead so that he could start a new life with Olivia.

That was when the nightmares began. Each night, he found himself once again in Bent Pines, reliving the horrors that he had experienced there. Garrison found himself waking in a sweat each morning with images of Johnny Watkins's exploding head and a young girl dying in his arms filling his mind.

With each passing day, the nightmares grew worse, lasting longer and becoming more and more graphic. Last night had been the worst yet. Instead of re-experiencing the events as they unfolded, Garrison found himself walking through the town in its aftermath. The fires were out but the buildings still smoldered. Dead bodies covered the ground.

In his dream, Garrison approached a corpse. As he stood looking down at it, the head turned toward him as its eyes flew open. The corpse's mouth opened and screamed a single question at him over and over, "Why?" Every lifeless body he approached would do the same thing, adding its voice to the chorus until there were hundreds of voices screaming the accusatory question at him.

Garrison had awoken breathless and covered in sweat. He lay there in the dark for what seemed like hours, unable to go back to sleep. Finally, he could lay there no longer, so he got up and got dressed. He moved slowly through the house to avoid waking anyone as he made his way out of the house and headed to the stables.

As he placed the black leather saddle on Diablo's back, he admired its recent additions. Jonathan had crafted two holsters designed to hold a revolver and placed them so that they would be just behind the rider's legs. In addition to the five revolvers he wore, Garrison could now carry two more pistols into battle. Garrison was uncertain as to why the old man had decided to do this and when he had asked, Jonathan had shrugged it off saying only that he had some extra leather lying around that he needed to do something with. Perhaps the older man had already come to the same conclusion that Garrison himself was just now arriving at. Garrison had to go back and confront Benjamin. And when he did, he would need all the firepower he could carry.

Chapter Seventeen

The sun was just beginning to rise in the east as Garrison rode away from the Watkins's homestead. He had hoped that some early morning target practice might help him cope with the nightmare images still lodged in his brain. Arriving at the secluded meadow, Garrison wasted little time getting started.

With each shot, Garrison's resolve strengthened. He knew what he had to do just as he knew that doing it would break Olivia's heart. His own soul ached at the thought of hurting her. In his heart of hearts, he wanted nothing more than to stay with her forever, or maybe take her out west to start a new life together. But deep in his soul, he knew that his guilt would continue to eat away at him and spoil any chance he and Olivia might have at being happy. He had to report back to the army and try to set the record straight about what really happened at Bent Pines.

Garrison had just emptied his last pistol for the second time and turned to begin the laborious process of reloading them. As he did so, he glanced back in the direction of the Watkins's ranch. What he saw froze him in his tracks.

Thick black smoke rose high into the air. Garrison had seen this before and for a moment he was back in Bent Pines, watching the town burn as thick black smoke swirled through the street. His mind was drawn back to the present as he thought he could hear gunfire in the distance. His ears were still ringing with the sounds of his own shots, so he couldn't be certain, but he wasn't taking any chances.

With his heart thundering in his chest, Garrison hurried to reload his weapons. His hands were trembling as his mind raced with thoughts of what might be happening at the ranch and this slowed him down considerably. With his weapons finally reloaded, Garrison swung himself into the saddle and spurred Diablo toward the ranch at a gallop.

Chapter Eighteen

For the second time that day, Garrison found himself in what he had come to think of as his meadow. But this time, he hadn't come for target practice. Using a large piece of tree bark as a makeshift shovel, he set about digging three graves. As he worked, tears ran down his face and he replayed in his mind the scene that had greeted him upon arriving at the Watkins's ranch.

He had ridden in hard, a pistol in each hand, ready to do battle with whoever was attacking the ranch. But there was no one there. Whoever had done this had done their dirty work and moved on.

Garrison sat in shock upon his horse as he surveyed the scene before him. Every single building had been set ablaze, producing the thick black smoke that was now tickling Garrison's throat and stinging his eyes. The only sound was the roar of the fire as it quickly consumed everything in its path. The silence filled him with dread as he thought through its ramifications.

Where were Jonathan, Elenore, and Oliva? He shouted their names as he leaped from the saddle. There was no answer and deep down, Garrison knew that the worst had come to pass. Still, he had to be sure. He was about to race headlong into the burning house when a glance toward the horse corral stopped him in his tracks.

Garrison stumbled toward the corral as shock began to set in. He fell to his knees in front of what was left of the Watkins's family. Jonathan Watkins lay face-down in the dust. Garrison quickly flipped him over, intending to check to see if he was breathing. He stopped when he saw the ragged hole in the man's forehead. A few feet away lay the body of Elenore. She appeared to have been beaten to death, her face almost unrecognizable.

Garrison turned last to Olivia. Her clothes had been torn from her body, leaving little doubt as to what she had had to endure in the final moments of her life. Her face was bruised and battered. Blood still trickled from her nose.

When they had finished with their fun, they had shot her in the head just as they had her father.

Garrison wept uncontrollably as he held her lifeless body. Mixed with his grief was an overwhelming sense of guilt. *If only I had been here, I might have prevented this,* he thought to himself miserably.

Garrison kneeled in front of the three fresh graves. With only his makeshift shovel of tree bark, it had taken most of the day to get the holes deep enough to hold the bodies. He had lugged stones from the stream and used them to cover the graves. He was determined to prevent scavenging animals from further desecrating the bodies of the people he had come to think of as family.

Garrison made crude crosses using fallen tree branches to mark the graves. With this task done, there was only one thing left he could do for the Watkins's family. There were no tears on his face now as Garrison kneeled before the graves one last time. Sorrow had been replaced by an ice-cold hatred that shone forth from his icy blue eyes. He silently vowed to find and punish those responsible for the slaughter of the Watkins's family. He stood and strode resolutely toward Diablo, a cold, hard expression of determination upon his face.

Garrison was an excellent tracker, although he hardly needed to be. The culprits had made no effort to cover their tracks. Surveying the scene once more as the sun began its slow decent in the west, it didn't take Garrison long to pick up their trail. He had little doubt that he would catch up to them before night fell. They would be moving slowly, since they had absconded with the Watkins's horses and other livestock. Garrison doubted that the culprits would even bother trying to hide their tracks, as they had no reason to suspect any retribution for their heinous act. They would soon discover just how wrong they were.

Chapter Nineteen

Lieutenant Dillon Cole and his men sat by their campfire passing a whiskey bottle back and forth. A contented smile crossed Cole's face as he thought about his situation. He loved foraging duty, as did his men. It gave them free reign to ride through the countryside, taking whatever they wanted.

He smiled again as the bottle made its way back around to him. This fine whiskey was just one of the prizes they'd found today. They'd raided a ranch early that morning looking for horses. Cole had heard rumors about a massive stallion being there and thought it would make an impressive gift for his commanding officer. Cole always made it a point to find something special for the man while out on these forays. It ensured that he would continue to get these choice assignments in the future.

A frown crossed Cole's face as he thought about this. They'd met with disappointment when the rumored horse was nowhere to be found. But the raid hadn't been a total waste. They'd found five better-than-average horses along with other livestock.

And then there was the girl. Cole smiled again as he thought about how her body felt and the defiant look in her eyes as he had his way with her. Her father had tried to intervene and had been shot in the head for his troubles. The girl's mother had wailed so much that his men had begun to kick and beat her in an effort to shut her up. By the time he'd finished with the girl, the mother had been beaten to death. He'd let each of his men have a turn with the girl and then he had put a bullet in her head.

'*Yes, it had been a good day,*' Cole thought to himself as he took another swig from the bottle and passed it to the man on his right. As he did so, he looked up from the fire and the smile faded from his face. Standing in the road not ten feet from the campfire was a massive horse, light gray in color. The man sitting upon the stallion held a Colt revolver in each hand and wore an expression of cold hatred upon his face. Cole felt a chill run up his spine.

Chapter Twenty

Matthew Garrison, sitting atop Diablo, looked down upon the carnage he had wrought. As he suspected, it hadn't been difficult to find the men responsible for the Watkins's deaths. The men were carefree and careless. Their security was nonexistent, and he'd spent several minutes just observing them.

He hadn't been sure what he would find when he had set out from the Watkins's ranch on the trail of their killers. He was shocked and disgusted when he had finally come upon their camp and saw their blue uniforms. Union soldiers, clearly a foraging party, had slaughtered the Watkins's family. This discovery served only to further fuel the seething anger boiling unseen beneath the surface.

Garrison had waited nearly ten minutes sitting silently upon Diablo, watching the men pass a bottle around as they laughed and joked with one another. Finally, one of them looked up and saw him. This was what Garrison had been waiting for. He wanted at least one of them to see him coming.

As the smile on the man's face was replaced with a look of fear, Garrison spurred Diablo forward toward the camp as he opened fire. Caught off guard, some of the men died where they sat without ever realizing what was happening. Several jumped to their feet, reaching for their own pistols but were gunned down before they could draw. The man who had looked up and been the first to see him jumped to his feet and tried to flee.

Garrison spurred Diablo forward in pursuit of the man. They gained on him quickly and Garrison allowed the horse to plow into the man who was sent flying by the force of the impact. Garrison turned Diablo around and brought him to a standstill next to the man. Dillon Cole's eyes were filled with terror as he begged for his life. Garrison let him beg while he slowly and deliberately reloaded his two pistols. When this task was complete, he holstered his left-hand Colt while he took slow and careful aim with the one in his right hand.

Garrison looked the coward in the eye as he pulled the trigger, then pulled it again and again until it clicked on empty.

Garrison felt no remorse as he looked upon the bodies of the men he had just killed. They had earned their fate as far as he was concerned. But he felt no satisfaction either. The men had been made to pay for their crimes, but it wouldn't bring the Watkins's family back. And while these men would never hurt another soul, Garrison knew that there were others out there who would.

Garrison felt the need to use these men to send a message to those others who would prey upon the weak if given a chance. Unfortunately, he was at loss as to how to best go about sending such a message. But then a memory of his time with the Watkins's family came unbidden into his mind. Every evening after supper and before retiring for the evening, the family sat down to read the Good Book together. Garrison had never been overly religious, but Jonathan Watkins had insisted that participation was not optional as long as he was under their roof. Now a particular passage came back to him and as he looked at the large tree the raiders had decided to camp under, Garrison knew just what to do.

Chapter Twenty-One

The sun had been up less than an hour, but the day was already blistering hot as Reverend Josiah Daniels made his way along through the Georgia countryside. He was a Methodist circuit rider doing his best to make his rounds despite the war that was ravaging the country. He spotted a large tree up ahead and thought it looked like a good place to rest and get out of the sun for a few minutes.

His eyes widened in shock as he neared the tree. Overcoming his shock, he spurred his horse ahead for a closer look. Hanging upside down from the branches of the tree were six male bodies, naked from the waist up. Reverend Daniels dismounted and approached the tree, covering his face with a handkerchief. The bodies appeared to have been hung there only recently, but the smell of death was already beginning to waft from them, and black flies buzzed all around.

As Reverend Daniels looked closely at the bodies and the tree from which they hung, he discovered a message written in what appeared to be blood. The message began on the chest of the first man and proceeded across the chest of the others and finally concluded on the trunk of the tree. Reverend Daniels sucked in his breath as he pieced the message together and recognized it as a passage from the Book of Revelations. *"I looked, and behold a pale horse, and he who sat on him was Death, and Hell followed with him,"* Daniels read aloud. The messaged was signed, *"The Pale Rider."*

Chapter Twenty-Two

Outskirts of Atlanta, Georgia – September 1864

Major Jack Garnett could not move. He was paralyzed by fear, his feet rooted in place. He was surrounded by utter darkness and could see nothing except the approaching horse and its rider. Garnett watched in terrified silence as the horse and rider came barreling toward him.

The horse was a massive white stallion. Flames flew up from its hooves every time they touched the ground. Smoke came from its nose in great white plumes. Where its eyes should have been were orbs of flickering flames.

As the horse bore ever closer, Garnett could finally see the rider clearly. The shock overwhelmed him when he recognized the rider as his best friend, Matthew Garrison. Just like the horse, flames flickered in the sockets where his eyes should have been.

As Garnett watched, Garrison stood in the stirrups and drew a pistol from each hip. The pistols were bigger than anything Garnett had ever seen before and they were pointed right at him. When the rider finally spoke, the voice was not that of Matthew Garrison. "It's time to die!" shouted the demonic-sounding voice just as Garrison opened fire. Flames erupted from the barrels of both guns and quickly engulfed Garnett.

Jack Garnett's eyes flew open as he bolted upward in his cot, the sound of his own screams still ringing in his ears. Garnett got to his feet, moved to the table by his cot, and poured himself a shot of whiskey. He felt the liquid burning its way down his throat as he tried to calm his rapidly beating heart and gain control of his breathing.

Garnett shook his head as he tried to clear it of the nightmare images that haunted him. He had been crushed by a nearly overwhelming sense of guilt when the news about the massacre at Bent Pines had reached him. Garnett had personally recommended Garrison to lead the covert mission to Bent Pines. In the aftermath of what had happened there, Garnett couldn't help but feel like he had sent his best friend to his death.

The Confederate authorities claimed that Garrison and his men had burned the town to the ground and slaughtered every living thing there including men, women, and children. Not even the animals were spared. Garnett had known Matthew Garrison his entire life and he still couldn't believe that the man was capable of such butchery. He desperately wanted to hear his friend's side of the story, but that would never happen. According to reports, a small detachment of Confederate infantry had arrived too late to save the town but just in time to engage and kill all of the men attacking the town

That night, Garnett dreamed of burning buildings and murdered children. His subconscious mind created images of Garrison gunning down screaming women and children with an expression of ecstasy on his face. They were images that, once created, he could not expel from his brain. As time passed, his mind created new images with which to haunt him. Many nights, he watched his friend die over and over. Garnett feared that these nightmares would plague him for the rest of his life.

And just when Garnett thought things couldn't get worse, the rumors of strange killings began filtering through the lines. According to the rumors, small groups of soldiers were being attacked and slaughtered by an unknown assailant. In every instance, the bodies were found with a paraphrase of Revelations 6:8 written in their blood, the messages signed by: *"The Pale Rider."* Most puzzling was the fact that both Confederate and Union units had apparently fallen prey to this mysterious Pale Rider.

The rumors had been enough for Garnett's overactive subconscious to create a whole new series of terrifying images with which to torture him. Tonight's nightmare had been the worst yet. Garnett had steadfastly refused to consider that Matthew Garrison might be the one perpetrating these attacks, but his subconscious clearly thought it was a possibility.

Garnett's thoughts were interrupted when a breathless young soldier barged into the tent unannounced. The young man stood to attention and snapped off a quick salute. "Sorry for the interruption, sir. I've been sent to fetch you; we've got to go right now."

Garnett did not move. He fixed the young man with a hard stare. "Sent by whom? What's happened?" he asked.

The young corporal could barely contain his excitement. "Garrison's alive, sir!"

Garnett felt like he had just been punched in the gut. "What? Are you sure?" he asked.

"Yes sir. He's here, sir! He turned himself in to the pickets and asked to see Benjamin. He's being escorted to the Lt. Col.'s tent now. Benjamin wants you there too and sent me to get you. We have to go, now!" the soldier pleaded.

Garnett felt like the whole world had just been turned upside down. "Does Col. Murray know about this?" Garnett asked. General Kilpatrick had made a swift recovery from the wound he had received at Resaca and had resumed command of the division. As a result, Colonel Murray had returned to his previous post commanding the 3rd Brigade. This had bumped Benjamin back to second-in-command.

The corporal hesitated for a moment. "I don't really know, sir," he admitted.

"Okay, you go back to Benjamin. I'll be there momentarily," Garnett instructed. He had every intention of riding straight to Murray's tent. The man would want to be present for this. Plus, the Colonel had always thought highly of Garrison. Garnett had once heard him refer to Garrison as the finest soldier he had ever commanded. It couldn't hurt to have someone with such a high opinion of Garrison there either.

The young man fidgeted uncomfortably. "Sir, I was instructed to bring you straight to Benjamin's tent myself. You need to come with me, now please."

Garnett just stared at the man for a moment. He knew in his gut that something wasn't right about this situation. Without a word, he grabbed his hat and uniform jacket. "Let's go," he said as he strode past the young man and out into the night.

Chapter Twenty-Three

As he neared Benjamin's tent, Garnett noted that there were two horses already hitched outside it. One of the animals looked like every other horse used by the cavalry unit. Garnett thought the other one might just be the most magnificent beast he'd ever seen. The animal was massive in size and light gray in color. The saddle on the animal's back appeared to be made of hand-stitched black leather. Garnett noted the two pistol holsters on the saddle with interest.

The army sure didn't have any animals like this at their disposal. No, this had to be the horse that Garrison had ridden in on. A giant, pale-colored horse no less. Could Garrison be the Pale Rider after all? Garnett was unable to suppress a shiver as the nightmare image of a demonic Garrison bearing down on him flashed through his mind. "Behold a pale horse" Garnett mumbled under his breath. He tried to push the image away as he hitched his own horse outside Benjamin's tent. The corporal, having completed his assignment, turned his horse and headed back the way they had come.

As Garnett stepped into the tent, he quickly surveyed the scene before him. The interior of the tent was lit by a single oil lamp that sat upon a small field table. Turned to full brightness, the lamp cast a circle of light in the center of the tent but left the far corners hidden in darkness. Benjamin sat on the other side of the table. Standing on Garnett's side of the table were Matthew Garrison and a soldier that he didn't recognize. Garrison's gun rigs and weapons had been piled on the table.

Garnett looked closely at his friend and found himself disturbed by what he saw. Garrison's hair was longer than the last time Garnett had seen him. Brushed straight back, it now hung to his shoulders. Garrison's cheeks and chin were covered by several days' worth of stubble. He had lost some weight and it showed particularly in his face. But what concerned Garnett the most was the expression on his friend's face and the general aura that emanated from him. Garnett could describe it only as being stone-cold.

"Glad you could join us, Major," Benjamin said in his gravelly voice. Turning to the other soldier, he said, "You may leave us now."

The soldier hesitated, clearly uncertain about leaving his charge alone with the two officers.

"It'll be fine," Benjamin assured him. "The prisoner has been disarmed and is in irons. Besides that, the Major is armed and I'm sure he's more than capable of defending us should it become necessary."

"Yes sir," said the soldier with a nod before turning and leaving the tent.

With the soldier's departure, a tense silence settled over the three men. Garrison locked his gaze on Benjamin, who simply stared back at him. Garnett fidgeted restlessly as he observed the two men. He had a million questions he wanted to ask but felt it best to let Benjamin take the lead.

Several minutes passed before anyone spoke. Benjamin was carefully observing the man standing before him and he didn't like what he saw. The situation was eerily similar to the first time he and the young officer had met, but something was different this time. The officer who stood before him nearly four months ago had been nervous and filled with anxiety.

The man who stood before him now showed no fear as he met Benjamin's gaze with his own unblinking stare. There was a cold confidence about the man that put Benjamin on edge. If anything, Garrison should be more nervous now than at the first meeting. The man was facing charges of treason and murder, for God's sake! It was at that moment that Benjamin realized that he was dealing with a man who was far more dangerous than he initially thought.

"So, the Butcher of Bent Pines lives," Benjamin said with false bravado. He could feel the icy cold fingers of fear reaching out to grip him, but he refused to let it show.

Garrison made no reply. He just continued to stare Benjamin down. Unlike at their first meeting, Garrison was the one in control this time, even if Benjamin had yet to realize it.

"Well?" Benjamin finally broke the silence, exasperation clearly evident in his voice.

"Well, what?" Garrison replied.

Benjamin rolled his eyes and gave an aggravated grunt. "Everyone thought you were dead. You could have just disappeared, but you didn't. You decided to come back here, and I can only presume it wasn't just so you could stand there and stare at me."

"I came back to clear my name," Garrison said.

Chapter Twenty-Four

For a moment, Benjamin just stared at Garrison, his expression unreadable. Then without warning, his eyes widened, and he let out an amused laugh. "To clear your name, really? You are either incredibly naive or incredibly stupid. The whole world thinks you slaughtered an entire town. Are you really going to stand there and tell me that you didn't?" Benjamin asked incredulously.

Garrison stared at Benjamin for a moment, his contempt for the man obvious. "We rode into a well-planned trap," he finally said. He went on to describe every detail of what had happened at Bent Pines. But he didn't stop there. He told them how he had made his way to the Watkins's ranch, how they had nursed him back to health, how they had been brutally murdered by Union soldiers, how he had tracked down and slaughtered those soldiers, and finally that he was the Pale Rider.

Garnett could do nothing but stare as Garrison told his story. Guilt threatened to crush him. It was all his fault. None of this would have happened if he hadn't recommended Garrison for the mission. Because he had, his friend had suffered terribly. And that suffering had changed Garrison irrevocably.

Garnett could hardly believe what he was hearing. Matt Garrison, his best friend since childhood, was the Pale Rider. Had anyone else been telling this story, he wouldn't have believed a word of it. But Garnett knew Garrison and he believed every word.

Benjamin was not so easily convinced. "That's some story. You expect us to believe that the Confederates slaughtered their own people. It's absolutely preposterous," he concluded.

"Almost as preposterous as the idea that they had twenty million in gold hidden away and planned to pay the French to intervene in the war," Garrison responded coldly. "The only difference is that my story is true, while theirs was just a ruse designed to lure us there," he added.

Garrison continued, not giving Benjamin a chance to speak. It was time for the man to take a dose of his own medicine. "A ruse that you fell for, I might add. You really did believe all that gold was sitting there, didn't you?" His voice was openly mocking now.

Jack Garnett watched the exchange between the two men in shocked amazement. He'd been an aide to Benjamin for several years now and he had never heard anyone speak to the man the way Garrison was now. Benjamin was accustomed to using his rank to bully and belittle those below him, but Garrison was having none of it today.

Garrison kept up his barrage of questions. "Why did you report us as being AWOL? Who approved the mission to Bent Pines? Did you even tell anyone else about the gold? What happened to the captured courier?"

"Enough!" Benjamin shouted. "Who the hell do you think you are talking to me like this? What exactly are you trying to accuse me of?" Benjamin asked defensively.

"I'm the man you set up to take the fall for the theft of the gold at Bent Pines," Garrison said calmly. "Only you never considered the possibility that the whole thing was a setup, that there never was any gold. I'm pretty sure that either Sexton or Jenkins was supposed to kill the rest of us once we had the gold. I don't really care which one it was; they're both dead. Whichever it was, he would bring you the gold and you would, no doubt, shoot him in the back the first chance you got. Does that sound about right?" Garrison's voice was strong and confident. He'd had a lot of time to think this over and was certain he had it right.

Benjamin jerked backward in his chair as if he had been physically struck. But he recovered quickly, a wicked grin spreading across his face. There was an evil glint in his eyes when he spoke. "You think you're so smart, don't you? You think you figured it all out, but you're wrong about one thing." Benjamin fell silent then, waiting for Garrison to take the bait. And take it he did.

"Yeah, what's that?" Garrison asked. His confidence was beginning to fade. He could feel Benjamin slowly regaining control of the situation.

"I didn't trust either one of those idiots you mentioned. Watkins was my inside man," Benjamin announced with a cruel smile on his face.

Chapter Twenty-Five

Garrison's mind was reeling. Benjamin had just named young Johnny Watkins as his inside man. Watkins was the one man in the group that Garrison had trusted, cared for even. It couldn't be true. Benjamin was lying. He had to be.

Benjamin could see the torment on Garrison's face as he tried to process this new information. The older man laughed with glee. "What's wrong?" he asked with mock concern. "He's just as dead as Sexton and Jenkins, so it really shouldn't matter, right?" Benjamin was thoroughly enjoying himself now.

"No. You're lying. I don't believe you," Garrison insisted. But even he could hear the doubt in his voice. It was like he was trying to convince himself.

Garrison was suddenly struck by another chilling thought. What if Benjamin wasn't lying? If Johnny was the traitor, did the rest of the Watkins's family know about it? Did Olivia? Was that why she had been so cold toward him when he first arrived? Was that why Johnathan had tried so hard to talk him out of coming back to confront Benjamin?

"Yes, you do," Benjamin said with confidence. "You don't want to believe me, but you do. I can see it in your eyes. The boy got to you, didn't he? Earned your trust? Just as I knew he would. Why do you think I chose him?" Benjamin berated.

"You're a son of a bitch!" Garrison said through gritted teeth.

"Maybe," Benjamin admitted. "But you, Lieutenant, are out of your league if you think you can match wits with me."

"Did his family know?" Garrison asked, not sure if he really wanted to know.

Benjamin smiled. The question meant Garrison had accepted the truth. But the young man was in for another shock. "I honestly don't know, but I couldn't take that chance."

"What?!" Garrison asked, his voice sharp.

"Oh, come on, Lieutenant! Do you really think that foraging unit just happened to wander out to the Watkins's ranch?" Benjamin asked.

Garrison could hardly breathe. Was Benjamin saying what he thought he was?

"You sent them there to kill the kid's family?" Garrison asked.

"Oh, I hardly had to send them. I merely nudged them in that direction. All I had to do was mention that Goddamn horse the kid was always bragging about. Well, that and his sister. Those men never pass up an opportunity at a hot piece of ass," Benjamin taunted.

Garrison's face had turned red with rage. He eyed the guns that were piled up there on the table. His hands were chained in front of him. If he could reach the table, he could certainly make use of the weapons. Could he get there and gun Benjamin down before Garnett stopped him? Would Garnett try to stop him? He had to find out.

"I knew what would happen when those boys got there. They never leave any witnesses behind. I didn't count on you still being alive, or that you would avenge the family. I guess I should thank you for cleaning up a loose end for me," Benjamin continued to gloat.

"Enough. Just tell me one thing. Was he in on it with you?" Garrison asked, a note of desperation in his voice. He couldn't take one more betrayal.

Chapter Twenty-Six

Jack Garnett was having a hard time keeping up with the conversation. His mind was blown. The shocking revelations were coming too fast for him to process.

First, Garrison had admitted to being the Pale Rider, while insisting that the Confederates had been the ones behind the slaughter of Bent Pines. Benjamin admitted that he had intended to keep the gold himself. He had recruited Johnny Watkins to take out the rest of the team once they had the gold. Benjamin was behind the murder of the Watkins's family too.

Now Garrison was asking if someone else had been in on it. With a start, Garnett realized that Garrison was talking about him.

He looked his friend in the eye and said, "Matt, I recommended you lead the mission and I hate myself for doing it, but I swear to you that I thought the mission was sanctioned. I didn't know anything about the rest of this. How could you think that I would do that to you?"

"Oh, come now, Major. There's no point denying it at this juncture. You might as well come clean," Benjamin spoke up.

"What?! What are you talking about? I didn't have anything to do with your plans!" Garnett insisted. Turning to Garrison, he said, "Matt, you have to believe me."

Garrison stared into his friend's face, looking for any hint of deceit. Garnett met his gaze without flinching. Garrison was good at reading people and felt confident that Garnett was being truthful.

"I believe you," Garrison finally said.

"I've heard enough," Benjamin growled. "You can't prove a single thing you've said. Not about me and not about what happened at Bent Pines. You've accomplished nothing by coming here, except your own demise," he threatened.

"I'll take my chances at court martial. I believe that the truth will win out," Garrison insisted.

"There you go being naive and stupid again," Benjamin said with a cruel smile. "You'll never stand before a tribunal. Here's how your story is going to end. You came back here determined to kill me for some unknown reason. Luckily, the Major was able to gun you down before you could reach your weapons."

Garrison's eyes narrowed. He hadn't expected Benjamin to play it this way. Perhaps he was a bit too naïve.

Garnett just stared at his commanding officer. He was sure that he must have heard Benjamin wrong. But the man's next words made any doubt impossible.

"Well, Major, what are you waiting for? Shoot the man!" he ordered.

"Why on Earth would you think that I would do that?" Garnett asked in disbelief.

"Self-preservation, of course," Benjamin answered. "Sure, he says he believes you now, but that's just so he can use you against me. Once he gets me out of the way, he'll kill you. He's the Goddamned Pale Rider, for Christ's sake! He'll probably string you up with a fucking Bible verse painted on your chest! In your own blood, of course!" Benjamin added.

Garnett looked from Benjamin to Garrison. Could his friend be lying to him? Would Garrison kill him once Benjamin had been dealt with? One thing was certain. Benjamin was proving to be a master manipulator. Garnett would take his chances with the man he'd known all his life.

Looking at Benjamin, Garnett said, "Unlike you, Matthew is a man of his word. I'm not doing your dirty work."

Benjamin stood to his feet, his face a red mask of anger. With a look of exasperation, he drew his own weapon and leveled it at Garrison. "Fine, I'll do it myself and deal with you later," he said in disgust.

Garrison stared straight into Benjamin's face as he waited for the man to pull the trigger. He refused to give him the satisfaction of showing any fear. Despite his resolve, Garrison couldn't help but flinch when the gunshot rang out. He waited for the pain and eventual darkness to overtake him but neither came.

Looking back up at Benjamin, Garrison saw a look of surprise on the man's face. As Garrison watched, Benjamin's face went slack. The pistol fell from his hand as he sank heavily back into his chair. Garrison turned his eyes toward Garnett who stood to his right, the smoke still curling from the barrel of his pistol.

Chapter Twenty-Seven

The sudden silence was almost as deafening as the gunshot. Garnett was looking at the pistol in his hand as if he wasn't sure how it had gotten there. He wore a shocked expression on his face when he turned to look at Garrison. "I just reacted…I didn't think…" he said by way of explanation.

For a moment, the two friends just looked at one another, both caught off guard by this turn of events. The sounds of yelling voices and running feet brought both men back to the present. As a member of the 3rd Brigade's command staff, Benjamin's tent was set apart from the main camp with only the tents of the other command staff officers nearby. This meant that this initial response to the gunshot would be limited to a dozen or so men. That was the good news. The bad news was that they would still be outnumbered at least six to one.

"We've got to go," Garrison said.

"Go? Why? He was about to commit murder; the shooting was justifiable," Garnett insisted.

Garrison gave Garnett an incredulous look. "Jack, you just killed your commanding officer. And the only witness who can corroborate your story is the guy everyone thinks killed hundreds of civilians and burned a town to the ground. We either make a run for it now or we end up swinging from the end of a rope later."

Garnett didn't respond. He was frozen in place by fear and indecision. Garrison could wait no longer; he knew they were fast running out of time and options. "Okay, Jack, you do what you think is best, but I'm getting out of here," he told his friend.

It was only when Garrison began moving that Garnett was finally able to break free from his trancelike state. "I'll get the key to your irons," he told Garrison as he moved toward Benjamin's body. "Start grabbing your gear," he added.

Garrison moved toward the table and looked at the weapons piled on it. He should be able to get the gun belt around his waist, but the shoulder holsters would have to wait until Jack found the key and unlocked his irons. Garrison was just finishing tying down the holster on his right thigh when Garnett stood up holding the key out before him like a prize. Once his hands were free of the irons, Garrison quickly slung his shoulder holsters on. He drew the Colt from his right hip.

"Now what?" Garnett asked.

Garrison signaled him to be quite as he listened to the sounds coming from outside the tent. It sounded as if at least a few men had reached the tent. Garrison could just barely hear their whispers as they debated whether or not to go into the tent or wait for someone to come out.

Garrison looked around the tent until he finally spotted Benjamin's sword. Grabbing it, he quickly unsheathed it and headed toward the rear of the tent.

"Good thinking," Garnett commented as he realized what Garrison intended to do. "We can slip out the back and away from the camp without anyone even realizing we're gone."

Garrison used the sword to cut the back wall of the tent in half. Turning to Garnett, he said, "No, that won't work. The horses are hitched in the front."

"We can procure a couple of horses once we're away from here," Garnett objected.

"I can't leave Diablo," Garrison told him.

For a second, Garnett just stared at Garrison dumbly. "You named your horse after the devil?" he asked rhetorically as he shook his head in wonder. "Never mind that. What's so damn special about the horse that you'll risk your life for it?" Garnett asked sincerely.

"It would take too long to explain," Garrison told him. "Look, you can slip out the back and disappear if you want to. I'm getting my horse," Garrison said stubbornly.

"I presume that you have a plan?" Garnett asked.

Garrison flashed him a smile. "Yeah, I do. Wait here," he instructed as he grabbed the oil lamp, turned it down until the flame was barely visible, and slipped out the hole he'd cut into the tent.

Chapter Twenty-Eight

Standing in the near darkness, Garrison took in his surroundings. Benjamin's tent stood alone, but to his right, Garrison could see the cluster of tents belonging to the junior officers assigned to Benjamin's staff. He estimated that they were no more than twelve to fifteen feet away. Garrison took a deep breath and hurled the oil lamp in the direction of the tents.

The lamp landed in the midst of the tents just as Garrison had intended. It broke on impact, spilling its flammable contents. The once-small flame burst to life as it followed the path of the oil streaming across the dry ground. The oil carried the flame straight to the tents which went up like dry kindling. In a matter of seconds, a roaring conflagration lit up the night sky.

The fire had its desired effect, thought Garrison as he heard the startled shouts coming from the men who had been waiting in front of Benjamin's tent. The shouts were followed almost immediately by the sound of trampling feet as the men raced toward the burning tents. Garrison smiled with satisfaction as he slipped back through the rear of the tent.

"It's time to go," Garrison told Garnett as he carefully picked his way through the now-darkened tent. Garnett followed him through the tent flap but pulled up short when he saw the inferno blazing its way across the camp. "Jesus, Matthew, what'd you do?" Garnett wondered aloud.

"I created a diversion," Garrison responded. Looking toward the fire, he saw that the flames had begun to spread across the open ground. What he had intended to be a small diversionary fire was on the verge of engulfing the entire camp. It filled him with regret, but he pushed all thoughts of this aside.

Garrison and Garnett had just climbed on their horses and turned them to head around the opposite side of the tent, away from the burning camp, when a gunshot rang out. Garnett was nearly knocked out of the saddle as the ball crashed into his right side. Turning toward the sound of the shot, Garrison saw

Benjamin, a look of rage on his face, standing in the tent entrance. One hand clutched his bleeding side, while the other held his side arm.

Pure hatred emanated from Benjamin's eyes as he struggled to pull the hammer back for a second shot. Garrison drew the Colt from his right hip and fired at Benjamin. The big man went down hard, but Garrison kept firing. He was determined that the bastard wouldn't get back up this time.

The junior officers attached to the command staff of the 3rd Brigade were halfway to the burning tents when the sound of gunfire caused them to whirl back around toward Lt. Col. Benjamin's tent. They turned just in time to see Garrison gun the man down. As one, they raced toward their fallen commander, firing their side arms as they ran.

Garrison was struggling to get a hold of the reins of Garnett's horse when they began taking fire from the junior officers. With great effort, Garnett sat up straight in the saddle and took the reins himself. He could taste blood in his mouth and struggled to draw in a breath. He knew he had been mortally wounded. He could almost feel his lungs filling with blood. Drawing his pistol, he looked at Garrison. "I'm not going to make it," he said simply. "Ride away. I'll try to buy you some time."

Before Garrison could object, Garnett whirled his horse toward the oncoming soldiers and kicked his horse into a gallop. Firing blindly as he went, Garnett charged toward their attackers. The soldiers kept coming and as the two sides drew closer, Garnett felt round after round slam into his chest. The force lifted him from the saddle, and he stood in the stirrups as the balls continued to strike him.

Garnett's horse took multiple rounds as the dozen soldiers emptied their weapons at the approaching rider. The beast eventually crashed to the ground, throwing Garnett's lifeless body through the air. The soldiers stopped their advance, certain they had seen both men go down. Gun smoke swirled through the air, obscuring their view.

The men stood idle as they waited for the smoke to clear. They were in no hurry to reload. As the smoke cleared, the men were chilled by what they saw. Sitting calmly upon his massive stallion was Matthew Lloyd Garrison, a pistol in each hand. With fear-induced trembling, each man raced to reload his pistol.

Garrison knew that he should have ridden out like Garnett had wanted him to, but he couldn't bring himself to do it. When he saw his friend go down, the icy rage that had become his constant companion began to take hold. He waited for the gun smoke to clear, gambling that the soldiers would be complacent about reloading.

As the smoke cleared, Garrison saw that he had been right. As the soldiers scrambled to reload their pistols, a grim smile crossed his face. Garrison charged the men firing his Colts as he came at them. When one pistol clicked on empty, he holstered it and drew another until all five pistols had been emptied. The air was once again filled with gun smoke. This time, it cleared to reveal the lifeless bodies of all twelve soldiers.

Sitting atop Diablo, Garrison looked down on the dead men sprawled across the ground around him. He looked up to see that the fire had spread to engulf the entire camp. Panicked screams mingled with shouted commands as the entire unit set about the task of bringing the raging inferno under control. The commotion around Benjamin's tent seemed to have been forgotten.

Garrison smiled, knowing that he now had time to send a proper message. He scavenged the dead bodies, taking whatever might be useful. He took two pistols and placed them in his saddle holsters. Finally, he rode back to Benjamin's tent and, using the dead man's blood, scribbled the words of Revelation 6:8 onto the side of his tent. He signed his message: *"The Pale Rider."* He then mounted Diablo and rode off into the darkness.

Chapter Twenty-Nine

Western Kentucky – November 1864

Matthew Garrison was a full day's ride from his destination when he stopped to make camp. He had traveled hundreds of miles over the past two months. His route had been circuitous by necessity. He often found himself backtracking and taking indirect routes in order to avoid both Union and Confederate forces as he made his way out of Georgia, through Alabama, into Tennessee, and ultimately on to Kentucky.

He'd fled Atlanta with nothing but the clothes and weapons he was wearing and the contents of his saddlebags. The one thing he had in abundance was time to contemplate his circumstances. Garrison found it impossible not to harbor a certain amount of bitterness. His loyalty to the Union had cost him his family. That loyalty had been repaid by betrayal and he now found himself branded a traitor and mass murderer.

In reality, it was only his commanding officer who had betrayed him, but Garrison couldn't overlook the fact that his government had never given him an opportunity to prove his innocence. If he were to be captured now, Garrison knew there would be no trial. He had been pronounced guilty in his absence and now there was nothing he could do to change the verdict. If Garrison allowed himself to be captured, he knew he would end up swinging from the end of a rope.

He had only made things worse by going back to try and clear his name. Garrison had been forced to kill Benjamin in self-defense. The fire Garrison had set as a diversion had swept through the camp, causing hundreds of unintended casualties. Worst of all, Garrison had gotten his best friend killed.

In anger, Garrison had slaughtered the men who killed Jack Garnett. He deeply regretted that now. They were only doing their duty in attacking the men they saw kill their commanding officer. They couldn't have known that

Benjamin had tried to kill Garrison and Garnett and that the two men were merely defending themselves.

Sadly, Garrison knew that it wouldn't be the last time he would kill honest men who were simply trying to do their duty. Riding away from Atlanta that fateful night, he had made a vow to himself that he would never allow them to take him alive. Because of the charges against him, and his own actions that night, Garrison knew that the authorities, both civil and military, would never stop coming after him. Whenever they caught up to him, he would have to fight for his life if he wanted to keep his vow and avoid the gallows. Garrison would have to become, at least to a certain extent, exactly what he was accused of being: a stone-cold killer.

Garrison sat close to the campfire in an attempt to ward off the cold as night began to fall. He had very little in the way of provisions and settled on a can of beans for dinner. He ate them cold straight from the can. As he stared into the flickering flames of the campfire, his thoughts turned once again to the events of that night just outside of Atlanta. He supposed it would always be this way, with his past creeping out of the shadows to haunt him when he least expected it.

He had to admit, albeit grudgingly, that Benjamin had been right about his naivety. Garrison had been a fool to go back, and not for the first time, he wished he had taken Jonathan Watkins's advice. If he had, his circumstances would be different and Jack Garnett would almost certainly still be alive.

Garrison knew that it was his sense of guilt over his friend's death that had ultimately led him back to Kentucky. Because of him, not only was Garnett dead but he too had been branded a traitor. Garrison couldn't undo the past and bring Garnett back, but he could at least let his family know that the man was no traitor. Perhaps knowing that would offer at least some measure of relief to Garnett's grieving family.

Garrison also knew that he was taking a grave risk in coming this close to home. The authorities would almost certainly be expecting him to go home at some point. They wouldn't know about his falling out with his family. But Jack Garnett had ridden willingly to his death so that Garrison could escape, and for that, Garrison felt he owed him a debt that he could never fully repay.

Finishing the last of the beans, Garrison discarded the empty can. He used water from his canteen to rinse his spoon and then packed his supplies back into his saddlebag. Unfurling his bedroll and using his saddle for a pillow, he prepared to turn in for the evening.

As he lay by the fire staring up into the night sky, Garrison felt utterly alone. He knew that it would always be this way. Because of his newfound notoriety, he was forced to avoid the main trails and skirt around towns. He knew that every time he encountered other people, there was a risk that someone would recognize him and try to collect the reward that had been placed on his head. Entering a town meant risking an encounter with the authorities. In either case, blood would be spilled, and he already had enough blood on his hands.

With a deep sigh, Garrison acknowledged to himself that he was at least partially to blame for his notoriety. Writing out the passage on Benjamin's tent and signing it 'the Pale Rider' had been a colossal mistake. When he'd done that after killing the men who slaughtered the Watkins's family, there had been a good reason. He wanted to send a message to deter other foraging parties from preying on the weak. He left the same message when he killed those who didn't heed his warning. But he still couldn't say for sure why he had decided to leave the same message after killing Benjamin. All it had accomplished was to identify him as the Pale Rider and link him to numerous other killings. It no longer mattered. Now it was just one more regret that he was going to have to learn to live with Garrison thought to himself as he closed his eyes and drifted off to sleep.

Chapter Thirty

The Garnett Estate, Kentucky – The Next Day

Stuart Jackson Garnett was alone in the stables. He was doing the dirty work of mucking the stalls. It was menial work and he could have left it to one of the hired hands. He should have left it for one of them. That was what his wife would have told him just a few weeks ago. But since they had learned of Jack's death, she hardly spoke at all, to him or anyone else. She had simply shut down, overcome with grief at the loss of her only son. Now she barely left her room.

Stuart understood. He hadn't been the same since his son's death either. That was why he was out there alone, doing a job he had once hated. He couldn't say why but hard work and solitude somehow provided him with a sense of solace. Like his wife, he didn't want to be around people either, but he couldn't simply shut down and lock himself away. So instead, he worked hard every day, taking on the most grueling of chores himself.

Lost in thought, Stuart nearly jumped out of his skin when he heard the voice from behind him. He whirled around to see Matthew Garrison stepping out of the shadows.

"Your son was no traitor," Garrison said again.

For a moment, Stuart could do nothing but stare. He felt as if he was seeing a ghost. Without even realizing it, he held his pitchfork up to his chest as if he was ready to use it as a weapon. He could feel the heat rising in his cheeks as he stared at the man he blamed for his son's death.

"You son of a bitch!" Stuart spat. "How dare you come back here after what you've done?"

"I wanted you to know the truth about what happened to Jack," Garrison said, keeping his voice as calm as he could. The last thing he wanted was a physical confrontation. He had come to ease the man's suffering, not make it worse.

"I know the truth," Stuart asserted. "You got my son killed! That's the truth!" The man could barely contain the rage he was feeling inside.

"Jack died trying to save my life. That much is true. But it was his choice."

"Oh, so now it's his fault?" Stuart asked.

Garrison sighed. He never was good with words. He didn't know how he was going to get through to Stuart Garnett, but he wasn't ready to give up yet. "That's not what I meant," he said.

"I don't care what you meant. I want you off this property!" Stuart shouted.

"I'll go," Garrison told him, "but not until you've heard what I have to say."

The two men stared at each other for what felt like an eternity. At long last, it was Stuart who finally broke the silence. "Well, let's have it then. The sooner you say your piece, the sooner you'll be away from here."

"Look, I know you've heard that I did some terrible things in Georgia. I also know that you've known me my entire life. You should know, just as Jack did, that I'm not capable of the atrocities I was accused of."

"War changes a man. I don't know what you're capable of!" Stuart barked.

Garrison ignored the interruption. "I was sent to Bent Pines by Lt. Col. Benjamin. He thought that the Confederates were hoarding a stash of gold there that they intended to use to get the French to attack the Union. He wanted me to lead a group of four other men into the town to steal the gold. It was a trap; there was no gold. Most of my men were gunned down within minutes of entering the bank. But that was only part of the trap. The Confederates burned the town to the ground and killed everyone living there."

"Why would they do that?" asked an incredulous Stuart Garnett. He was curious in spite of himself.

"I can't say for sure, but I think they hoped that by blaming the massacre on the Union, they could entice one or more countries in Europe to intervene in the war on their behalf. They probably expected a more official campaign to capture the town by uniformed Union soldiers. They didn't count on a weasel like Benjamin being the one to intercept their courier."

"What do you mean?" Stuart asked. His curiosity had gotten the better of him.

"Benjamin never reported his captured intel up the chain of command because he wanted to keep the gold for himself. One of the men on my team was meant to kill the rest of us after we got the gold. I have little doubt

Benjamin would have then had that same man kill your son, since he was the only other person who knew about the gold. Benjamin probably would have shot that man in the back afterward so he wouldn't have to share the gold with anyone. He was a greedy son of a bitch and a coward."

"But you said there was no gold," Stuart reminded him.

"That's right. It was a trap. One that none of us were supposed to survive," Garrison told him. "Only, I did survive. Eventually, I put all the pieces together and figured out what Benjamin was up to. Instead of letting the world think that I was dead, I went back to confront Benjamin. That was a mistake and it's what got your son killed. Benjamin had the two of us brought to his tent. When I told him that I knew what he was up to, he ordered Jack to kill me. When Jack refused, he decided to do it himself. Jack saved my life by shooting Benjamin first. We thought he was dead, but we were wrong."

"Who killed my boy?" Stuart asked.

"As we were about to ride away, Benjamin came out of the tent and shot Jack. I put Benjamin down for good, but it was too late. The gunshots alerted a group of nearby soldiers and they came after us shooting as they came. Jack knew he had been mortally wounded, so he charged the men to give me time to escape. They finished him off."

The two men stood in silence for a moment or two as Garrison gave Stuart time to absorb everything he had been told. It was Garrison who broke the silence this time. "You're right; I did get your son killed. I never should have gone back. It was foolish of me to think that I could clear my name. Look, I didn't come here for forgiveness. I just wanted you to know that your son was no traitor." With that said, Garrison turned to leave.

"Wait," Stuart called after him. "There's something I need to tell you. With everything that's happened, your father and I haven't been on speaking terms for some time now. But I heard from a mutual acquaintance of ours that your mother has fallen ill. She's dying, Matthew. I thought you should know." Stuart told him, his voice almost a whisper.

Garrison never turned around. He didn't want the man to see the tears that had suddenly welled up in his eyes. "Thank you," he said in a choked voice just before disappearing through the doorway.

Chapter Thirty-One

The Garrison Estate, Kentucky – The Next Day

Garrison could scarcely believe his good luck. He had managed to make it all the way to the front porch of his childhood home without being detected. He paused at the front door as a wave of memories, both good and bad, flooded over him.

Shaking his head, he opened the door and peered inside. With no one in sight, he figured that the coast was clear. He quickly stepped inside and turned to quietly pull the door shut behind him.

Garrison had just closed the door when he heard a door slam somewhere behind him. He spun around, his hand instinctively reaching for the pistol on his right hip. What he saw caused him to freeze in place.

Standing at the other end of the entrance hall was a large, colored woman. She stood stock-still in front of the door she had just come through. Her wide eyes stared at him in shock and then began to fill with tears.

Garrison smiled as the woman rushed toward him. Reaching him, she threw her stubby arms around him and squeezed so tightly that for a moment he could barely breathe.

"Oh, my sweet, sweet baby's done come home! Let me look at you," she said as she pushed him away and then held him at arm's length. She frowned. "You're too skinny!" she exclaimed.

"Hi, Nana," Garrison said. He was fairly certain that that wasn't her real name, but it was the only name he knew her by. A slave in title only, she had been his nursemaid when he was a boy. In reality, she had played a far larger role in raising him than either of his parents had.

Her frown deepened. "Boy, what are you doing here? It's too dangerous for you here now. Oh Lawdy, I don't even want to think about what your father would do if he seen you."

"I didn't do all those things they said I did," Garrison told her.

She reached up with both hands and gently cupped his face. "My sweet Matthew, I knew when I heard it that it wasn't true. Not my sweet boy."

Feeling suddenly uncomfortable, Garrison gently extracted himself from the woman's embrace. He was far from the sweet boy she remembered, but he didn't have the time to explain that to her now. He looked her in the eye and said, "I've come to see Mother."

Chapter Thirty-Two

Garrison looked down at the woman in the bed before him with a frown. He barely recognized her. Four years had passed since the last time he saw his mother, but she looked as if she had aged at least ten. Her once-lustrous black hair was now stringy and streaked with gray. Her face was drawn and gaunt. Her eyes were closed, and her breaths came in short gasps. Nana had tried to prepare him, but he was still shocked by the sight and overcome with grief.

Garrison was about to sit in the chair that had been placed by her bed when the door to the bedroom crashed open. He spun toward the sound, his hands automatically reaching for his weapons. His fingers curled around the handles of his guns, but he made no attempt to draw either weapon.

Jefferson Thompson Garrison stood in the doorway. His face was red with rage, his blue eyes filled with hate. In his outstretched right hand, he held a cocked revolver. His hand trembled with rage as he pointed the deadly weapon at his youngest son.

Seeing Garrison's hands resting on the handles of his own weapons, the elder Garrison shouted at him, "Do it! Draw those guns! Please, just give me a reason."

Matthew Garrison stepped to his right, away from his mother's bed. He moved his hands away from his guns, holding them out to his sides, palms open toward his father. As he looked his enraged father in the eye, he couldn't help but think about the last time the two had met.

They had argued bitterly over Matthew's decision to fight for the Union. Although the family had relocated to Kentucky when Matthew was still a young boy, the elder Garrison had been born and raised in Virginia. He insisted that the Garrisons were distant relatives of General George Washington, although Matthew harbored serious doubts as to whether or not this was true. He wasn't sure why it should make any difference one way or the other.

But the elder Garrison was a Southerner at heart and an ardent supporter of state's rights. Even though Kentucky stayed in the Union, Jefferson Garrison's loyalty lay firmly with his birth state and he thought the same should be true of his sons. Matthew's older brother had made their father proud when he journeyed to the Confederate capital in Richmond to join the fight against the Union. Matthew knew the old man would be disappointed with his decision to fight for the Union, but Jefferson's reaction had been far worse than anything Matthew could have imagined.

"Sorry to have disappointed you by surviving," Matthew said to his father now, thinking of the last words the man had said to him four years ago. When Matthew left home to report for duty, his father had called him a traitor and wished him a painful death upon the battlefield. The old man's words had hurt Matthew more than his father would ever know.

"At least now you can have the satisfaction of rectifying the situation yourself," Matthew told his father now. "Go ahead, pull the trigger," he said softly. "Do it!" he said louder. "Somebody's bound to gun me down eventually. It might as well be you," Matthew added, egging his father on.

"It was bad enough that you betrayed your heritage by siding with the Yankees, but how could you stoop so low as to massacre a town full of innocent people? Do you despise your southern heritage that much?" Jefferson asked his youngest soon. The look of rage on his face now tempered with disappointment.

Matthew had harbored a great deal of anger toward his father after the man had disowned him. In truth, he felt as if he was the one who had been betrayed. It was as if his father's love for Virginia was greater than that he felt toward his own flesh and blood.

That anger had shown clearly upon Matthew's face the moment his father had barged into the room. But now, upon hearing the man's latest words, the anger melted away. In its place was a look of immeasurable sadness.

"If you really believe everything that they're saying about me, believe I'm capable of slaughtering innocent women and children, then you really should go ahead and pull that trigger," Matthew told his father, the look of sadness on his face mirrored by the tone in his voice.

Jefferson Garrison just stood there for a moment staring at his son. He wanted to believe it, believe his son had committed every heinous act he had been accused of. If it were all true, the anger and hatred he felt toward his son would be justified, and he wouldn't have to feel guilty about feeling that way. But deep down in his soul, Jefferson knew better.

"What are you doing here anyway?" he finally asked. "Those damned blue belly patrols ride in here at least once a week and tear the place apart looking for you. I guess they didn't believe me when I told them you weren't welcome here."

This was news to Garrison. His timing really had been fortunate, since he had managed to miss the patrols. "I got word that Mother was ill," he answered.

The older man's features softened just slightly. "She's not ill, son; she's dying," he said.

"I know. I came to say goodbye," Matthew told his father. "And that's what I'm going to do," Matthew said resolutely. "Shoot me or don't. I don't really care either way." With that, he returned to his mother's bedside, sat in the chair, and took the dying woman's hand in his own.

Jefferson stood there a moment longer, the revolver still trained on Matthew. Finally, he lowered it. "I'm going out to the stables. Do what you came for and get out. You best be gone when I come back because the next time I see you, I won't hesitate to pull the trigger."

Chapter Thirty-Three

Despite the tense confrontation with his father, and the grief he felt over his mother's impending death, Garrison was glad that he had decided to make this quick but risky visit home. Seeing Nana had been an unexpected but pleasant surprise. She had another surprise waiting for him, he recalled with a smile.

He had descended the stairs after visiting with his mother to find Nana waiting for him by the door. Sitting on the floor before her were a large saddlebag and another large canvass rucksack. In her arms, the woman held a bundle of clothes.

"What's all this?" Garrison had asked.

"You didn't think I was gonna let my sweet baby leave this house in those rags, did you? Why, they're so threadbare. I can almost see straight through them," she said with a smile. Before Garrison could express his thanks, Nana continued, "I told you when you came in that you were too skinny. Well, I aim to do something about that. The saddlebags are full of food. Salted meats in one side, canned vegetables in the other. It's probably not enough to get you through the winter but it's a good start. The canvas bag has got some warm clothes for winter. I can't let my boy freeze to death, now can I?"

At a loss for words, Garrison had simply wrapped his arms around her and held her tight. This time, it was Nana who had to extract herself from Garrison's embrace. "You best be going now, honey," she had said with tears in her eyes.

"Your father could be back any minute now. And don't you worry about your mother. She'll be heading on to a better place real soon now that she's seen you." Nana gave him one last hug and said, "You take care of yourself now, and know that I love you. I'll be thinking about you and praying for you."

Chapter Thirty-Four

One Mile from the Garrison Estate, Kentucky – Later That Day

Garrison was still lost in thought, thinking about his final encounter with Nana as he rode away from his childhood home for what he knew would be the last time. Rounding a bend in the road, he pulled up short as he almost collided with a group of four riders coming from the other direction. Equally startled by the near collision, the other riders pulled on their reins, bringing their horses to a halt as well.

For a moment, the two parties regarded each other. Garrison noted with a rising sense of alarm that the four men all wore the blue uniform of a Union soldier. This close to his home, he had little doubt that they were one of the patrols that his father had mentioned.

The fresh clothes that Nana had brought him had included one of his old cavalry hats and an officer's jacket. He whispered a silent 'thank you' to the woman, as the hat cast a significant shadow over his face, while the jacket hid his shoulder holsters. He hoped this would be enough to keep the men from recognizing him.

"My apologies, gentlemen!" Garrison said. "I'm afraid I was lost in thought and not paying a bit of attention. It was quite careless of me, and I'm just grateful that we managed to avoid disaster. I'll just be on my way and let you get on with your journey," he added as he made to move around them.

At a signal from one of the men, the others spread out across the road, effectively blocking Garrison's way.

"Now just a minute," one of the men, the ranking officer Garrison assumed, spoke up. "What's your name?" the man asked.

"Benjamin Lloyd," Garrison answered quickly, not really sure how he had come up with that answer so quickly.

"You just come from the Garrison place?" the man continued to question him.

"That's right," Garrison answered. The man was obviously suspicious, and Garrison had a sinking feeling that this wasn't going to end well. The last thing he wanted to do was get into a gunfight this close to his home. The authorities would almost certainly assume that his father had been harboring him there all along.

The Union officer smiled at him. "Would you mind removing your hat, sir?" he asked. "I like to look a man in the eye when I'm speaking to him," he added.

With a resigned sigh, Garrison removed the hat with his left hand. He held the hat in his lap in such a way that it hid his right hand. As he looked the officer in the eye, he slowly reached his right hand back toward the pistol holstered on the saddle behind his leg.

When the officer's eyes widened in obvious recognition, Garrison didn't hesitate. Tossing the hat to the side, he drew the pistol with lightning-fast speed and opened fire. Each of the four Union soldiers went down with a single bullet wound between his eyes. It was over before the men even realized what was happening.

Garrison felt a twinge of regret, but deep down, he felt that he'd had no choice. It was either him or them and he was determined to fight for his freedom for as long as he could. He retrieved his hat and quickly turned his attention to the problem before him. He couldn't let the bodies be found this close to his home.

He quickly loaded the bodies on their horses and tied the reins together so that he could lead all four horses. He mounted Diablo and left the road, looking to find a secluded place to bury the bodies. He traveled as far from the Garrison Estate as he dared; it wouldn't do to be spotted toting the bodies through the countryside.

Finding a suitable spot, he used one of the soldiers' trenching tool to dig the four graves as quickly as possible. Before burying the men, he went through their pockets, scavenging anything he thought might be useful. Aside from some tobacco and a flask of whisky, there wasn't much.

He repeated the process with the saddles before also burying them. His search of the saddlebags proved far more profitable, as he found additional rations as well as a significant amount of ammunition. All four men had been carrying Spencer carbine rifles in their saddles and Garrison helped himself to two of them, storing them away in his own saddle. The remaining weapons he buried with the saddles.

With this task completed, he now had to figure out what to do with the horses. He couldn't turn them loose and risk them making their way back to whatever camp they had come from. After some searching, he finally found a wooded area that would suite his purpose. He hated what he was about to do but felt he had no choice. He tied one horse to a tree and then moved about a hundred feet away before hitching the next horse to another tree.

Once all four horses were hitched, roughly a hundred feet away from one another, he shot the last horse he had hitched in the head. The single well-placed shot brought instant death. He repeated the process with each horse until all four lay dead. He didn't have time to bury the bodies but hoped that scavenging animals would make quick work of the carcasses before anyone discovered them. He had selected the woods to be their final resting place in hopes that the trees would keep the vultures from detecting the carcasses. A large flock of scavenging birds would almost certainly bring unwanted attention and lead to the discovery of the bodies.

With remorse and guilt eating away at him, Garrison mounted Diablo and prepared to ride away. He silently prayed for forgiveness for what he'd done today, to both the men and animals, and hoped that the steps he took to conceal the deaths would prevent any ramifications from befalling his father. The man may have come to hate his own flesh and blood, but the feeling was not mutual. With that final thought, Garrison spurred Diablo forward and continued his journey westward.

Chapter Thirty-Five

Southeast Missouri – February 1865

Garrison sat by the fireplace, enjoying the warmth after his meal of freshly killed rabbit meat. Outside, the ground was covered with a thin layer of snow. A bitter cold wind howled around his tiny shelter. He had made his way west after the altercation outside his father's home without any further trouble. Halfway between the state's southern border and Saint Louis, he had stumbled upon this abandoned homestead.

It was in a sad state of disrepair and he guessed that it had probably been abandoned sometime near the beginning of the war. Even in such a state, it would provide far better shelter against the bitter cold of winter than anything else he was likely to find. The house was little more than a shack, but the stone fireplace seemed to be in good shape. There was a small barn that would provide shelter for Diablo. The surrounding trees would provide adequate fuel for the fireplace.

After giving it some careful thought, Garrison had decided to hole up here for the winter. There seemed little risk that the owners would return to find him squatting on their property. He was hesitant about using the fireplace, worrying that someone might see the smoke and come to investigate. He had done some reconnoitering around the area and found no indication of any other settlements nearby. This eased his worries to a certain extent. Ultimately, it was purely a matter of survival. Without a fire, he was going to freeze to death. He would just have to take his chances.

He needn't have worried, for he had not seen another soul since he had settled in for the winter. This thought had no more crossed his mind than he heard a commotion coming from outside. He could hear the hoof beats of multiple horses, softened by the snow but still audible. Just barely audible were the sounds of multiple voices, too soft to be intelligible.

Garrison had learned to live in a constant state of readiness. His weapons were always loaded and nearby. He was holstering the last of his five pistols and reaching for one of the Spencer rifles when a loud male voice rang out, "Hello, the house!"

Garrison threw his winter coat on and grabbed both rifles. He peered through a crack in the door. Ten mounted men were spread across the front of the property, evenly spaced. The men were heavily armed and had a hard look about them. *Most likely Missouri guerrilla fighters,* Garrison thought.

"Anyone home!?" the voice cried out again.

Garrison opened the door to reveal himself but refrained from stepping outside. He stood there concealed in shadow with a rifle in either hand. Standing just inside the doorway, he could dive either to his left or right for cover should things go sideways in a hurry. "Yeah?" Garrison hollered by way of reply.

The man mounted in the center of the group gave a friendly wave. "I don't suppose you'd have room for a few frozen freedom fighters in there by the fire, would you?" the man asked in a congenial voice.

Freedom fighters my ass, Garrison thought to himself. *Murderers and rapists more likely.* Aloud, he said, "Afraid not. You best move on." There was a cold edge to his voice.

The mounted man reacted as if he had been smacked. "You may want to reconsider that, friend. My name's Bloody Bill. You might have heard of me." The once-congenial voice was now openly menacing. The man clearly wasn't accustomed to being refused.

There were probably a dozen men using that name these days, Garrison knew. He remained silent as he weighed his chances of winning a standoff against that many men. The one thing in his favor was that they would be reluctant to burn him out, since it was his shelter they were seeking in the first place. Garrison's real concern was that he didn't know if this was all of the men. For all he knew, they could have him surrounded.

The silence was broken by Bloody Bill. "You got a name, friend?" he asked.

Garrison thought over his response for a moment. The man wanted to namedrop to inspire fear. Maybe he could do the same thing.

"Yeah, you might have heard of me, too. They call me the Pale Rider," he finally called out.

A round of nervous laughter rippled through the men, but the man calling himself Bloody Bill seemed unperturbed. "Is that right?" he asked in mock wonder. "I thought you was a myth," he added.

While the man had been speaking, Garrison had quietly set one of the rifles down, leaning it against the doorframe. With an almost superhuman suddenness, he brought the other rifle up to his shoulder and fired.

The hat flew from Bloody Bill's head when the round struck it.

"I'll bet that felt real enough, didn't it?" Garrison called out. "The next one goes between your eyes. Your men may eventually get me, but you won't be around to see it!" Garrison hollered out before the man could respond.

Every one of the mounted men had a hand on his pistol as they waited for Bloody Bill's response. The man was red-faced with anger. Normally, he wouldn't stand for anyone to humiliate him in front of his men like that. But the man was no fool either, and he had no desire to die. The man that could shoot the hat off his head like this one had done would be more than capable of making good on his threat.

Bloody Bill raised his hand to halt his men from doing anything stupid that might get him killed. "It's not worth it," he said to his men. "We'll move on, but you best hope that our paths don't cross again!" he yelled aloud for Garrison's benefit.

As should you, Garrison thought to himself as he watched the men ride off, never taking his aim off the man calling himself Bloody Bill. He fully expected them to come back after nightfall to surprise him. Garrison didn't sleep for two full days, as he awaited an attack that never came.

Chapter Thirty-Six

Saint Louis, Missouri – April 1865

Garrison was on edge, his nerves nearly frayed. He'd spent so much time deliberately avoiding other people that suddenly being surrounded by them again was nearly overwhelming. But he was only here out of necessity.

Other than his encounter with Bloody Bill and his men, Garrison had spent an uneventful winter hunkered down in the abandoned homestead. He had stayed there through March wary of getting caught in a late winter snowstorm. By April, he figured that the chance of snow was slim, so he had packed up and resumed his journey.

The long winter had nearly depleted his provisions and the journey north toward Saint Louis had finished off what little had remained. While he could hunt for fresh meat, he knew from experience that even a skilled hunter often went considerable time between kills. It would be essential to have a supply of dried meats to fall back on. And then there were all the things that just couldn't be procured out on the trail, things like canned vegetables, coffee, and tobacco, all of which he was nearly out of.

Fortunately, Nana had also secreted a wad of cash in his saddlebags before he left home. He'd only discovered this when unpacking everything at the homestead. He could only smile and shake his head. That woman never ceased to amaze him.

And so, here he was in the bustling city of Saint Louis. He had considered trying to resupply in one of the smaller towns along his route but ultimately had decided against it. He hoped that the larger population here would make it easier to blend in. With a little good luck, he just might be able to get in and out without incident.

Garrison had arrived that morning to find the city abuzz with the news of Lee's surrender at Appomattox. Amidst the excitement was an undercurrent of tension, and this no doubt contributed to Garrison's general feeling of unease. Missouri had been split just about evenly when it came to secession and there had been considerable violence between the two factions to decide which side the state would take in the war. Garrison had heard somewhere that at one point, there were two governments, one pro-South, the other pro-Union, vying for control of the state.

It was no wonder then that the news of Lee's surrender received such a mixed reaction. Garrison felt conspicuous in his Union cavalry hat and officer's jacket. He could probably discard the hat, but the jacket would still be a problem. The jacket concealed his shoulder holsters and he feared that he would be even more conspicuous walking around openly carrying five pistols. In the end, all he could do was try to go about his business as quickly as possible. He had every intention of being on his way by the afternoon.

Chapter Thirty-Seven

It was early afternoon and Garrison was quite pleased with himself. He had found everything he needed at one of the general stores in the city. Other than some uncomfortable questions from the shopkeeper, Garrison had managed to limit his interaction with the townsfolk. He was just finishing up with securing all of his purchases in his saddlebags and would be ready to head out in a matter of minutes.

That was when he heard the commotion behind him. Risking a glance over his shoulder, he saw a group of five men emerging from the saloon across the street. One of the men was pointing at him and the entire group seemed to be headed his way. "Hey, Yankee!" The pointing man called out.

Garrison ignored the man, concentrating instead on securing the last of his purchases. Just another minute or so and he'd be ready to ride out. Apparently, it just wasn't meant to be.

"I said, 'Hey, Yankee,'" the man repeated. "Don't you go trying to ignore me neither, you blue belly bastard. I bet you're the one that kilt my brother," the man accused.

With a resigned shrug of his shoulders, Garrison turned to face the men. They had spread out to form a loose semicircle around him with the speaker in the middle. The townsfolk were quickly clearing the street.

Great, Garrison thought to himself. Even if he could somehow manage to talk his way out of this, he was almost certain that someone was, even now, on his or her way to alert the authorities. If the law got involved, there was a good chance he would be recognized. If that happened, there would be no avoiding bloodshed.

"Well? What you got to say for yourself?" It was the same man who had spoken before. He was clearly drunk. He was slurring his words and as he stood between his friends, he swayed back and forth constantly. If the man's friends were drunk, they gave no outward sign. Each of the five men wore a pistol on his right hip.

"Look, I don't want any trouble," Garrison told them. "I was just about to head out of town, so there's no need for this. Besides, all my fighting was done back east. I'm sorry your friend lost a brother, but I seriously doubt it was me that killed him." He directed his words toward the man's friends. He knew better than to try to reason with a drunk.

"You might not have kilt his brother, but I bet you kilt somebody's brother. Hell, I bet you kilt a bunch of folks," one of the other men finally spoke.

Garrison had had enough. He deliberately tucked the edges of his coat behind his hip holsters. "As a matter of fact, I have," Garrison admitted, his voice turning cold. "And to tell you the truth, I really don't have a problem killing five more, if that's what you want."

Garrison watched as understanding dawned on the faces of the four sober men. His harsh words had awakened them to how serious the situation had become. He felt certain they had set out only to enjoy a little harassment, never expecting it to become a matter of life and death.

Now Garrison's only concern was whether or not they could get their drunk friend under control before he did something stupid. The question was answered a split-second later.

"Well, let's do this!" the drunk slurred as he reached for his pistol.

Garrison's reaction was instantaneous and, in less time than it takes to blink, the drunk lay dead in the street. Garrison cursed silently to himself at the needlessness of it all. He slid his pistol back into the holster on his right hip but left his fingers curled around the grip. His left hand hovered above the pistol on his left hip as he waited to see how the dead man's friends would react.

Each of the four men had reached for his gun when they saw their friend go down. But they each halted short of drawing, almost as if waiting to see what the others would do. Each looked at the other while Garrison waited in tense silence.

As if on some unseen signal, all four men drew at the same time. In that same instant, Garrison drew a pistol from each hip. Once again, he was lightning-quick and deadly accurate. Only one of the four men even managed to get a shot off, but it went wide. Garrison fired four times, each shot dropping a man to the dusty street.

Without wasting another second, Garrison unhitched Diablo and swung himself up into the saddle. "Let's go!" he commanded the horse. Diablo took off like a shot. It was almost as if the animal understood the urgency of the situation.

The city marshal stepped out of his office just as Diablo and Garrison raced past. The horse and the rider were moving so fast that he perceived them as little more than a gray and black streak. In the marshal's experience, a man only rode like that if they were trying to get away from something, and he was about to mount his own horse and set off in pursuit.

He was just about to take off when a murmur went up among the gathering crowd. Just then, a near breathless man that the marshal didn't know pushed his way through the throng. For a moment, he simply stood there in front of the Marshal panting in an attempt to catch his breath.

Finally able to speak, the man said, "I seen the whole thing, Marshal. He did it, the man on the gray horse. He killed them all!"

This gave the marshal a pause. "All? How many men did he kill?" he asked the witness.

"Twas five men that drew down on him, but he killed them all. Twas the damnedest thing I ever did see," the witness reported, still gasping for air.

'Perhaps it had been a bit premature of him to race off in pursuit of this man alone,' the marshal thought to himself as he stepped down from his saddle. The marshal was a survivor and he wasn't about to go it alone against a man capable of doing what this one had just done. As fate would have it, the marshal would go on to live a long and rewarding life, never knowing just how close he had come to a fatal encounter with the Pale Rider.

Chapter Thirty-Eight

Western Missouri – May 1865

Rodney Swanson, his vision blurred by tears, stared in helpless horror as he watched all of his hopes and dreams literally go up in smoke. He and his wife, Sarah, had left a life of squalor back east to chase their dreams of a better life. It had taken them a year to save up the money to buy this place. They had arrived to find the fields overgrown with weeds and the buildings barely standing. It had taken Rodney another year of hard work to make the house livable and the barn usable. Then the fields had been cleared, plowed, and seeded. Their very first crop would have been ready for harvest soon.

Rodney and Sarah had just sat down to breakfast when the riders arrived. There were ten of them in total. They were rough-looking men with hard eyes and bearded faces, every one of them toting a gun on his hip. Even the simplest-minded of men would know with a single glance that these men meant trouble. And Rodney Swanson was far from simpleminded.

He grabbed his shotgun, checking to make sure that both barrels were loaded. After a quick peek to ensure that the coast was clear, Rodney sent Sarah out the backdoor to the barn to hide. He was filling his pockets with extra shells for the shotgun when a loud voice rang out.

"Hello, the house!" one of the riders called out.

Rodney stepped out onto the porch, the shotgun held across his chest. He wanted the men to know that he was prepared to defend himself, but he had no desire to escalate tensions by pointing the shotgun at them. "Mornin," he called out, "what can I do for you folks?"

"There's some mouth-water'n smells coming from that chimney," the rider said in a pleasant voice. "We would sure appreciate you sharin' a bit of that with us," he added.

"Sorry, but it's been a bad winter and I barely got enough for myself," Rodney told the men.

The rider frowned. "I was afraid you was going to say that," he told Rodney. "I tell you what. Why we don't, we just take a look for ourselves." He gave a nod toward his men and they dismounted and began heading toward the house. The speaker remained on his horse.

As the men approached the house, they spread out, effectively surrounding the porch. Rodney aimed the shotgun at the two men in the center of the formation as they neared the steps. "I don't want to use this, but I will," he warned.

The men halted and glanced back toward their leader. He gave them another nod and they moved forward again. The two men in the center of the formation began climbing the steps as the other men closed up rank behind them. When the two reached the top of the stairs, Rodney fired both barrels. At such a close range, the effect was devastating, nearly cutting the two men in half.

Rodney scrambled to reload as the remaining men reached for their pistols.

"I want him alive!" yelled the leader. His men held their fire as they continued to rush the porch, determined to reach the top before the shotgun was reloaded. The first man to reach the top swiped at the shotgun, knocking it from Rodney's hands. The second man to the top, just seconds behind the first, struck Rodney across the face with his pistol. Rodney crashed down, all the fight leaving him in an instant.

"Bring him down here. One of you'll have to guard him. The rest of you tear the place apart. Grab anything of value and when you're done, light it up. The fields too," the leader instructed. "I'm going around to check the barn," he added.

Rodney Swanson was on his knees, a gun held to his head as he watched the men ransack his home. He balled his fists in impotent rage when the men began to set fire first to the house and then his fields. Just then, a woman's scream came from somewhere behind the house. It was followed almost instantly by a cry of pain.

Rodney tried to rise to his feet but was instantly sent back to the ground as the man guarding him struck him across the shoulders with his pistol. A moment later, the leader emerged from around the house practically dragging Sarah Swanson by her long red hair. The right side of her face was beginning to bruise, and blood trickled from her nose. "Look what I found hiding in the barn, boys!" he shouted.

"Leave her alone!" Rodney screamed.

The leader cast an amused look at the enraged man at his feet. Eyeing the pile of valuables and provisions that his men had removed from the house before setting it ablaze, he said, "It looks like you were holding out on us."

Rodney just stared at the man with unconcealed hatred in his eyes.

"Just for that, I think I'll make you watch us have some fun with this beauty before I kill you," the leader said with a cruel smile upon his face. He then positioned Sarah in front of him. "On your knees," he commanded.

With a defiant gleam in her green eyes, Sarah resolutely shook her head and stood stock-still.

Without warning, the man backhanded her hard across her left check. "Bitch! I said get on your knees!" he shouted.

With tears streaming down her bruised cheeks, Sarah slowly dropped to her knees. With a triumphant glare at Rodney, the man began to undo his belt buckle. He was unbuttoning his pants when a gunshot rang out. A look of confusion crossed the man's face as he looked down at the crimson stain slowly spreading across his shirt. As the truth slowly dawned on him, he fell backwards, landing with a thud.

Chapter Thirty-Nine

Matthew Garrison was lost in thought as he traveled through the western part of Missouri. He still regretted what had happened back in Saint Louis, but he had given the men every chance to walk away. Once they pulled iron, he had no choice but to put them down.

At least he had managed to get clear before the law got involved. Garrison had circled back on his own trail a couple of times to see if he was being pursued. To his surprise, the posse he kept expecting to encounter never came.

In another sign that perhaps his luck was improving, Garrison had managed to avoid any further trouble as he made his way west. The heavily wooded countryside had forced him to stick to the roads, so he considered himself particularly fortunate. Although he had no particular destination in mind, he had decided to try his luck in Kansas.

Garrison had never seen a buffalo except in pictures. He thought he might try his luck hunting the beasts. He'd heard that there was good money to be made, selling the hides and the money Nana had secreted in his saddlebags was running dangerously low.

Garrison had just crested a hill when he spotted black smoke curling up into the sky from the valley below. Memories of Bent Pines and the Watkins's ranch flooded his mind. On instinct, he almost spurred Diablo toward the smoke, before thinking the better of it. Instead, he moved off the road until he found a spot that allowed for a better view of the valley below.

Making good use of the spy scope he had picked up in Saint Louis, Garrison was able to see the tragedy unfolding below him with great clarity. A small house had gone up in flames. Seven armed men were gathered around the front of the house. Another man, the homesteader Garrison assumed, lay sprawled on the ground at their feet.

As Garrison watched, another armed man came around from behind the house. Garrison's grip tightened involuntarily at the sight of the young woman the man was pulling along behind him by her hair. Thoughts of Olivia Watkins crashed down upon him with terrifying force. He was certain that this woman was about to suffer a similar fate.

He focused on the man and cursed under his breath. Garrison had seen him before. He had called himself Bloody Bill when he and his men had confronted Garrison at the old homestead a few months back. The other men with him now were probably the same ones who had been with him that day.

Garrison felt a sudden twinge of guilt. If he had killed the man back then, perhaps the couple down there wouldn't be going through this ordeal now. *Of course, he'd probably be dead too,* Garrison realized. He wouldn't have been able to hold off the other nine men from inside his shack that day. But today was a different day and he had the advantage this time.

Garrison zoomed out to see that Bloody Bill was forcing the woman to kneel in front of him. He closed the scope, having seen enough. Even on a horse as fast as Diablo, it would take Garrison several minutes to arrive on the scene and a lot could happen in that time, none of it good for the man and women in the clutches of the killers below.

Fortunately, he had another option. The hill he was on provided the perfect field of fire and was well within rifle range. There was a large outcropping of rock that would provide decent cover should any of the men down there happen to have a rifle. Garrison knew he would be out of range of their pistols.

Garrison raced back to Diablo, grabbed both Spencer rifles, and hustled back to his vantage point. Bloody Bill was just about to drop his pants as Garrison carefully took aim. Pistols may have been Garrison's preferred weapon, but he was no stranger to the long gun. He had been hunting since he was a child. The key, his father had taught him, was to aim for center mass. A head shot might be a kill shot, but it could just as easily be a miss, especially at this distance.

With this in mind, Garrison lined the sight up on the center of Bloody Bill's chest. He took a deep breath, expelled it slowly, and gently squeezed the trigger. The roar of the rifle sounded deafening in the silence. Before Bloody Bill's lifeless body hit the ground, Garrison was already taking aim at his next target. Only one of the other men had a weapon already out, so Garrison dropped him next.

The remaining men quickly drew their pistols and were looking all around, clearly unsure of where the shots were coming from. Garrison fired again, taking another one of the men down. *Three down, five to go,* Garrison thought to himself.

One of the men must have finally spotted the smoke from his rifle, because he was now franticly pointing in Garrison's direction. The men opened fire, but Garrison was well out of their range. There was no cover in front of the house, so the only option for the men was to try to mount their horses and ride away.

One by one, Garrison picked them off. Only one of the men survived long enough to mount his horse. Garrison promptly shot him out of the saddle. Having dispatched the attackers, Garrison stowed his rifles, mounted Diablo, and headed toward the homestead.

Chapter Forty

Rodney and Sarah Swanson clutched tightly to each other as they kneeled in the dirt in front of their burning home. All around them lay the bodies of the men who had just moments ago been threatening their lives. Their circumstances had changed so quickly that neither of them could fully comprehend what had just happened.

The sound of hoof beats drew their attention toward the road. Approaching slowly was a single rider sitting upon a massive light gray stallion. He wore a tattered cavalry hat and what appeared to be a Union officer's jacket over a simple white shirt. His pants were black denim. The rider's dark hair hung to his shoulders and his face was covered by a full beard of the same color. Across his lap lay a rifle.

To Rodney, he didn't look all that different from the men that had nearly killed him and raped his wife. With that thought in mind, Rodney quickly extracted himself from Sarah's arms and scrambled to pick up one of the pistols lying on the ground near him. He had just wrapped his fingers around the pistol's grip when the rider came to a stop and spoke.

"You won't be needing that, at least not for me," Garrison told the man before him. "I just wanted to check and see if you folks needed any help."

The man and woman just stared at him for a moment. Garrison figured they were still in shock. And who would blame them after what they just experienced? As Garrison watched, the man stood up and pulled the woman to her feet beside him.

"Did you do…all this?" the man finally asked, holding his hands out toward the carnage that littered the yard.

Garrison replied silently with a simple nod of his head as he dismounted. He stowed his rifle away and turned to regard the man and woman a little closer.

Rodney now looked upon this stranger with a growing sense of awe. "Thank you, for what you did," he said sincerely as he walked up and offered Garrison his hand. "I'm Rodney Swanson and this is my wife, Sarah," Rodney said as he shook Garrison's hand.

"My name is Matt," Garrison said simply.

"Forgive me, but I've got to ask; why did you help us?" Rodney asked.

After a moment's hesitation, Garrison finally answered, "I had a run in with this bunch myself a few months back. I gave their leader a bit of a scare, but I made a mistake by letting them live. Seeing what they were putting you through, I kind of felt I owed it to you to right that wrong," Garrison told them. He glanced toward the burning house and added, "I'm sorry I didn't come around in time to save your home."

Rodney and Sarah exchanged a brief glance. When Rodney spoke, his voice was choked with emotion. "Buildings can be rebuilt. Things can be replaced. But what you saved, both our lives, Sarah's virtue? Once gone, they're gone forever. You were just in time to save what really matters."

Garrison thought that just might be the nicest thing anyone had ever said to him. Hell! That was probably the nicest thing anyone would ever say to him. "Thank you," he said with true sincerity.

Looking around at the bodies scattered around the yard, Garrison frowned. "I know this hit you folks out of the blue and you're both still reeling from it. But you need to give some thought to what you want to do now," he told the couple. "And we've definitely got to do something with these bodies," he added, pointing skyward where a large flock of buzzards was already circling.

"If you want me to leave you two alone to figure things out for yourselves, I'll be glad to do that. But I'm also willing to stick around and help with the bodies. You just need to let me know what you want me to do," Garrison told the couple.

Chapter Forty-One

After some back and forth, it was decided that Rodney and Sarah would check on the status of the barn and spend some time there, figuring out what they wanted to do. In the meantime, Garrison decided to busy himself with the task of searching the saddlebags and bodies of the dead ruffians. After hitching the horses to keep them from wandering off, Garrison searched through the saddlebags. Between the ten sets of saddlebags, Garrison found a significant amount of ammunition and canned goods. After removing what he wanted from the saddlebags, he tossed each, along with the saddle it accompanied, into the Swanson's burning home.

Garrison next turned his attention to the bodies littering the ground. He quickly decided he wouldn't bother with the two Rodney had killed with his shotgun. Anything of value in their pockets would have been destroyed by the shotgun blast or so coated in blood as to be worthless. He started with Bloody Bill and quickly worked his way through the others. His efforts proved to be wasted as he recovered only a few dollars in Confederate currency and a couple of pouches of tobacco.

Garrison was standing staring into the dying flames when Rodney and Sarah finally reappeared. He looked at them expectantly as he waited impatiently for them to speak. It was well past midday and there was a lot of work to be done if they were going to bury ten bodies before nightfall.

"Good news!" Rodney finally said. He went on to explain, "The barn was left untouched, as was our wagon and both draft horses."

"That's great," Garrison agreed. "The barn may not be the most comfortable place you've lived, but at least you'll have a warm, dry place to sleep until the house is rebuilt. The draft horses will come in handy for clearing away the remains of the burned…" Garrison's voice trailed off as he noticed the looks that Rodney and Sarah were giving each other. "Is something wrong?" he asked.

"We're considering heading back east," Rodney replied.

"Okay," Garrison said, nodding his head. "This kind of life isn't for everyone."

"It's not that," Rodney objected. "This place was a wreck when we first arrived. We repaired the house and barn with our own hands. The fields were overgrown, but we cleared them. We plowed them. We seeded them. We loved this life and we were scratching out a good living here!" Rodney exclaimed with passion. "Until today, that is," he added, hanging his head as if in defeat.

"We're just scared," Sarah said. It was the first time Garrison had heard her speak. Her voice was soft and had an almost musical quality to it. "We're afraid that what happened today could happen again. Do you think that's likely?" she asked Garrison.

Garrison hesitated for a moment. He thought he knew what they wanted to hear from him, but he wasn't going to be anything less than truthful. "Yeah, I think it's very likely," he told them.

"And just why is that, do you think?" Sarah asked.

"The war may be over, at least in the east, but it's left a lot of devastation and bitter feelings in its wake. And it turned a whole bunch of farmers and tradesman into killers," Garrison told her.

"Well, I guess most men would have to kill in a war, but as you said, the war is over now," Sarah protested.

Garrison admired her spirit. Despite what had nearly happened to her today, she was clearly in favor of staying. Her husband must be the one with concerns about a repeat of today's events. And Garrison didn't blame him either or think him cowardly. The man had a beautiful wife and a duty to protect her. The man had killed two of the attackers before Garrison had arrived, so he was clearly no coward. No, today had simply taught him that there were situations in which he wouldn't be able to protect his wife like he wanted to.

"The problem with killing is that some men, once they get a taste of it, they can't get enough," Garrison told the couple.

"Are you one of those men?" Sarah asked pointedly.

"Sarah! This man saved our lives!" Rodney objected.

"I meant no offense," Sarah quickly stated. "But you did kill a lot of men today," she pointed out.

"None taken," Garrison told her. "I kill when I have to. Men like that," he said, pointing toward a corpse, "they kill because they like it. They didn't come here today for provisions. They came to rape and kill. You could have welcomed them in and fed them, and they would still have killed you," he said, looking at Rodney. Turning his gaze to Sarah, he continued, "And they still would have tried to rape you. And it's not just because you're pretty. If you looked like a hag, they still would have done what they tried to today. It's just who they are. And thanks to the war, there's a whole lot more out there, just like them."

For a moment, Rodney and Sarah just stared at Garrison. Finally, Sarah turned to Rodney and, in the soft voice of defeat, said, "Let's go home."

Chapter Forty-Two

With the difficult decision out of the way, everyone realized it was time for action.

"So, about those bodies?" Rodney asked Garrison.

Garrison considered for a moment. "If you two are leaving, there's no real need for concealment," Garrison thought aloud. "Have you got any rope in that barn?" he asked Rodney as an idea sprang to mind.

"Plenty of it. Why?" Rodney asked.

Garrison ignored the question. He didn't think either Rodney or Sarah would appreciate what he had in mind. "Leave the bodies to me," he said instead. "I'll take care of them once we get you two on your way," he added.

Rodney and Sarah exchanged a quick glance. With a sheepish grin on her face, Sarah said, "Actually, we were hoping we could convince you to escort us, at least part of the way."

Garrison just looked from one of them to the other.

"We would sure feel a lot safer with you along for the ride," Rodney added.

"Do you have a plan?" Garrison asked the couple.

"We figured we would load the provisions that were spared into the wagon. We'll use it to travel to Independence. From there, we'll catch a train going east. We should have just enough to get two tickets," Rodney explained.

"Unfortunately, we can't pay you. But we thought it might be just as well if we left you the wagon, horses, and any provisions that don't get used on the way. The horses and wagon should fetch a decent price if you sell them," Sarah chimed in.

Garrison gave a resigned sigh. "Okay, I'll ride with you as far as Independence," he told them. "But I don't think money will be a problem," he added with a sly smile.

"What are you saying?" Sarah asked.

"We have ten healthy horses to sell," Garrison said with a smile, pointing toward the horses he had hitched together earlier. "But we do need to get a move on," he said with a little more urgency.

Looking at Rodney, he said, "Let's go get that wagon hitched up. You can drive it up here and we'll load the provisions. Then you two can get a head start and I'll catch up once the bodies have been dealt with."

Garrison waited until the wagon had carried Rodney and Sarah out of sight before he set about the task of dealing with the bodies of the dead raiders. The two had looked a little nervous as they rode off without him. Perhaps they feared that he wasn't going to meet up with them as planned.

He had no intention of abandoning the couple now. He had told them that he would escort them to Independence, and he had every intention of doing just that. Garrison just didn't want them to see what he was going to do with the bodies and, more importantly, the message he intended to leave with them. Not only would they most likely find it disturbing but they would also know who he really was.

Now that the couple was gone, Garrison wasted little time. Using the rope from the barn and the dead men's own horses, he dragged the bodies to the barn. Using the heavy beam that ran lengthways down the center of the barn, Garrison hung the eight men that he had killed upside down.

Because the men had already bled out, using their blood to write a message wasn't an option. Fortunately, the barn had a dirt floor. Garrison knew that he could scratch the Bible verse into the dirt. The indoor setting would preserve the message until someone stumbled upon the bodies. With great patience, Garrison scratched out the words from Revelation 6:8 into the dirt. As always, he signed the message from the Pale Rider.

When he was done, Garrison closed the barn doors and prepared to ride after Rodney and Sarah. Garrison figured he only had a couple of hours of daylight left by the time he set out with the newly acquired horses in tow. He caught up with Rodney and Sarah far quicker than he had expected to.

Perhaps one or the other of them had to stop to relieve themselves, Garrison thought to himself. After what they had been through, Garrison wouldn't be surprised if either, or both, of them was experiencing some stomach trouble. Despite his initial curiosity, he quickly forgot the incident as the three of them continued the journey together.

Chapter Forty-Three

Much later that night, Garrison sat by the campfire, using his saddle as a backrest. He could hear snoring coming from the wagon where the Swansons slept a few feet away. He could hear the horses as they milled about, just beyond the circle of light cast by the fire.

He had told the Swansons that he would stand watch, but it was hardly necessary. Garrison was a light sleeper and he always kept his weapons within reach. The truth was that he had come to dread falling asleep. Whenever sleep did come, it always brought the nightmares with it.

Earlier in the day, he had told Sarah Swanson that he wasn't offended when she'd called him a killer. There was no two ways about it; that's exactly what he was. But he realized now that he hadn't been totally honest when he said that he only killed when he had to. He didn't have to kill the men who slaughtered Olivia Watkins and her parents, although he still felt justified in doing it. He didn't have to kill the men who killed Jack Garnet, and he was just as certain that in that instance, he had been wrong.

But Garrison had been telling the truth when he said that he didn't like killing. It was true that he hadn't felt a shred of remorse for most of the killing he had done. He certainly didn't feel any remorse over the men who were even now hanging by their feet inside the Swansons' abandoned barn. But their deaths hadn't brought any pleasure either.

But there were many deaths that did haunt him. In several instances, he hadn't even been the one to pull the trigger, but he still felt responsible. Whenever sleep came, it was the faces of the Watkins's family, Jack Garnet, a nameless little girl in a green dress, and many more that would haunt his dreams. Even the four horses he had killed outside his father's estate made an occasional appearance in his nightmares.

And so, this night, like so many before it, he sat wide awake well past midnight. That was how he heard her approaching well before she stepped into the light cast by the fire. She had a blanket wrapped around her shoulders and her hair was a frizzy mess. Even so, Garrison had to admit she was a beautiful woman.

"Couldn't sleep?" he asked as he looked up into Sarah Swanson's bright green eyes.

"Not really," she said with a frown as she came around to sit on the ground at Garrison's side.

She looked at him with great intensity for a moment and then said, "I wanted to apologize for the way I acted earlier."

Garrison started to say something, but she cut him off, "No, let me finish, please."

Garrison closed his mouth and waited for her to continue.

"I know that I escaped a fate worse than death today. And the only reason I did is because you had the…well…the…whatever it took to kill those men. Whatever else you may have done in the past, you did a good thing today. I didn't mean to sound like I was judging you," she explained.

Without warning, she leaned over and kissed him on the cheek. As she moved back, she whispered in his ear, "Thank you, Mr. Garrison."

Garrison jerked back as if he had been shot. Sarah's green eyes sparkled in the firelight and a mischievous smile played across her lips. She was obviously pleased with herself and the reaction she had caused.

"I figured it out when I came back to the barn and saw what you did with the bodies," she explained.

Garrison was speechless.

"I made Rodney stop the wagon so that I could sneak back and see what you were up to. He didn't want to, of course, but I can be quite persuasive when I want to be," Sarah explained.

That explains how I caught up with the two so quickly, Garrison thought to himself. Aloud, he asked, "You're not upset?"

"I was at first. I've heard about all the terrible things the Pale Rider has supposedly done. Based on the stories, he would have to be a monster. But I don't see a monster sitting in front of me. I see a man who's haunted by his past but not a monster. Regardless of how others see you, you'll always be a hero to me," she said with a smile.

She leaned over and gave him another peck on the cheek. Standing, she said, "Good night. Your secret is safe with me." She assured him before heading back to the wagon and her sleeping husband.

Chapter Forty-Four

Garrison was dangerously close to losing his temper. When he and the Swansons had reached the outskirts of Independence, Garrison had sent the couple on into town to the train station while he took care of selling the extra horses that they had acquired. Now he had been standing here arguing with the livery owner for what felt like hours. The Swansons had to be wondering what was taking him so long. They might even be wondering if he had decided to double-cross them and keep all the money for himself.

"I am sorry, young man, but for the last time, I simply cannot buy horses if I don't know where they came from. In my experience, an undocumented horse is a stolen horse. I have a reputation to uphold and I simply cannot take the risk of buying undocumented horses," the livery owner insisted in a nasally voice. It was at least the third, maybe even the fourth, time Garrison had heard him say the same thing.

"I have half a mind to alert the sheriff to the possibility of stolen horses in town," the livery owner added, hoping it would scare the overly persistent cuss standing in front of him and prompt him to leave.

Garrison's eyes blazed for a moment, and his voice went cold as he fixed his gaze upon the livery owner. "That would be a mistake," he said.

"Then take these horses and get out of here. I'm a busy man and I don't have any more time to waste with you," the livery owner spat.

Garrison determined to try one last time. "Look, these horses belonged to a group of marauders led by somebody calling himself Bloody Bill. They raided a homestead three days' ride south of here and nearly killed the owner and tried to rape his wife. Those two lost everything and I'm just trying to get them some cash to help them start over."

The livery owner now wore a shocked expression on his face. "Oh dear, that's awful. Bloody Bill, you say? The Bloody Bill?" he asked Garrison.

"Hell, if I know," Garrison admitted. "Lots of fellas are going around using names like that to try to scare decent folks."

"If the horses belonged to this Bloody Bill and his men, how did they come to be in your possession?" the livery owner asked.

Garrison gave the man his most intimidating look. He hated doing this, but it always seemed to get better results than honesty alone did. "I killed them," Garrison said simply. "Dead men don't have much use for horses, so I helped myself," he added.

The livery owner gulped as he looked at the man in front of him with new appreciation. He noted for the first time the pistols the man wore on each hip. He wore another across his midsection. The livery owner could just barely see the grips of two more pistols hidden beneath the man's jacket. Holstered in the man's saddle were two more pistols and two rifles. The livery owner broke out into a cold sweat as he realized for the first time that he was standing in the presence of a killer.

"You killed Bloody Bill and nine others all on your own?" the livery owner asked skeptically.

"The homesteader got two of the bastards before I got there, so I only had to kill eight of them. He nearly cut his two in half with a shotgun at close range. My eight are hanging by their feet in the barn," Garrison explained.

"Do you have a name, mister?" the livery owner finally asked. The mention of dead men hanging by their feet reminded him of the stories he had read in the papers from back east about a mysterious killer calling himself the Pale Rider. 'This couldn't be the same man, could it?' the livery owner wondered to himself fearfully.

"Not one that you need to know," Garrison told him, his voice hard as steel. "Now are you going to buy these horses or not?" Garrison asked as he casually placed a hand on the grips of the pistols he wore on each hip. He had no intention of doing anything if the livery owner told him no, but the man was clearly frightened of him and Garrison intended to use that to his advantage.

After a moment's hesitation, the man finally stammered, "I could give you fifty dollars per horse."

"Make it a hundred per horse," Garrison said in a voice that would brook no argument.

A few minutes later, Garrison rode away from the livery with a smile on his face and a thousand dollars in his pocket. He now hurried to catch up with Rodney and Sarah. He hoped that they hadn't run into any trouble, or already left. He had every intention of giving them all the money from the sale of the horses. They could make better use of it than he could. After all, they had a future and he didn't.

Chapter Forty-Five

Garrison couldn't help but feel good about himself. Rodney and Sarah had greeted him with genuine smiles when he finally met up with them at the train station. Those smiles had only broadened when he handed them the wad of cash that he had obtained from selling the horses. Garrison had tried to give them all of it, but they had insisted on splitting it with him.

When he arrived, the train was already at the station. It was steadily building a head of steam and would be departing any minute. This had necessitated a quick goodbye with the couple, and that suited Garrison just fine. Rodney had shaken his hand and thanked him profusely for what he had done for them. Sarah had given him a hug and a quick peck on the cheek.

Garrison was still smiling as he watched the train disappear in the distance. He had done a good thing in helping those two and it made him feel good. He knew that it could never make up for all the bad that he had done, but it gave him something positive that he could cling to when the nightmares came to haunt him again.

Perhaps it was these good feelings that kept him from feeling the usual sense of trepidation that came with being in a town. For the first time since being branded an outlaw, he wasn't worried about being recognized and wasn't in a hurry to leave. The poor livery owner looked as though he would faint when Garrison had gone back there to sell the wagon and two draft horses that the Swansons had left behind. There had been no reluctance or haggling this time, and Garrison left with another two hundred and fifty dollars in his pocket.

With a total of seven hundred and fifty dollars unexpectedly at his disposal, Garrison had decided to treat himself to a hot bath before leaving town. He had no idea what was so special about the 'special touch' bath the place offered but had splurged the extra dollar on it anyway. Garrison had just lowered his naked body into the soothing hot water when there was a knock upon the door.

Garrison was reaching for his nearest six-gun when the door opened to reveal a stunningly beautiful woman. He quickly removed his hand from the pistol grip as she stepped into the room.

"You ordered the special touch, hun?" she asked with a smile.

Garrison just nodded as he took in her appearance. She had a pretty face framed with long, dark hair that shone luxuriously. She wore a black corset trimmed in red lace. It pushed her cleavage up to such an extent that only the woman's nipples were left to Garrison's imagination.

"Just sit back and relax," she said as she kneeled beside the iron tub. "I'll take good care of you," she said with a seductive smile. She proceeded to wash Garrison's body from head to toe. He let out a gasp when she wrapped her delicate fingers around his manhood.

"What do we have here?" she said with a giggle as she began to stroke him. Garrison hadn't felt a woman's touch in nearly a year. He felt a twinge of guilt as he thought of his last time with Olivia Watkins. It was just days before she had been brutally murdered. Forcing those thoughts from his mind, he closed his eyes and leaned his head back, determined to enjoy what the woman was doing for him.

After the bath, Garrison paid a visit to the town barber. When he left, his hair was just slightly longer than he had worn it while in the army and his cheeks were bare. He felt more like himself than he had in nearly a year.

Chapter Forty-Six

With the extra money at his disposal, Garrison had decided it was time to update his wardrobe. He still recalled the trouble that the remnants of his Union uniform had caused back in Saint Louis. He figured that anti-Union sentiments were likely to be even stronger where he was headed, so he would avail himself of this opportunity to replace them.

He found the local tailor without much trouble and purchased several suits of clothes. He replaced his cavalry hat with a simple black hat in a style the tailor had called a 'gambler.' He purchased button-down shirts in white, black, and red. The tailor managed to talk him into three vests, one red, one black, and one brown, and even a gold pocket watch. Garrison decided on a couple of frock coats, one in black and one in gray, and a brown duster. He added three pairs of sturdy workpants to his wardrobe in black, gray, and brown.

Garrison's last stop had been the general store. He had decided to load up on nonperishable provisions while he had the money. He splurged on a sack of sugar cubes for Diablo. The faithful horse had more than earned the simple treat.

With all of this accomplished, Garrison decided it was past the time that he head out of town. He had managed to get all of his purchases secured and loaded on Diablo and now he couldn't help but take one last look at his reflection in the storefront window. He wore the black pants and shirt with his brown vest. The brown duster effectively hid all of his weapons except for the Le Matt holstered across his midsection.

He was so focused on his own reflection that he failed to see the reflection of the lawman approaching behind him. As such, he was startled when a loud, strong voice called out his full name. With a sigh, he turned to face the man.

Standing in the street was an older man. His face was sunburned and weather-beaten. A bushy white mustache covered his upper lip, but his cheeks were bare. The man wore a gold star on his vest and held a nickel-plated Colt in his right hand.

"Raise those hands and step down here," the man commanded.

Garrison stepped off the boarded sidewalk to stand in the street, just a few feet away from the lawman. His hands remained at his side.

"I told you to raise them hands," the man commanded again.

Garrison felt a genuine sadness wash over him as he eyeballed the man. He slowly reached down and tucked the edge of his duster behind the holster on his right hip, making his intentions clear.

The old lawman's eyes narrowed. "Don't be a fool now, son. I got the drop on you; you've got no chance. I don't want to kill you, but I will shoot if you force me to," he said.

"I don't want to die today either," Garrison said with sincerity, "but better to die today at your hand than swing at the end of a rope later. I'm going to skin leather and I hope you do shoot," he told the lawman. "Because if you don't, I will," Garrison added quietly.

A bead of sweat broke out on the lawman's brow and his gun hand trembled just slightly. He'd been a lawman for most of his adult life, but in all that time, he'd never had to shoot a man. He'd always been able to talk a man into tossing his weapon aside. One look into this man's eyes told him that wasn't going to happen today.

He wasn't sure he could bring himself to pull the trigger and, for a moment, he considered holstering his gun and letting Garrison go. The townsfolk had begun to gather to see what would happen and the lawman's pride wouldn't allow him to look weak in their eyes. It would surely be the end of his career. So instead, he stood there, weapon aimed, waiting for the man to make a move.

"Last chance," Garrison said.

"I was just about to say the same thing," the lawman said with a confidence that he didn't feel.

With a sigh, Garrison made his play. His hand flashed like lightning and he didn't hesitate to fire. As he had feared, the old man stood there either unable or unwilling to fire. The Colt slid from his lifeless fingers to land in the dirt, only to be joined a second later by the sheriff's body.

The townsfolk stood in silent shock as they watched the sheriff die right in front of them. No one made a move as the stranger slowly holstered his pistol, mounted his horse, and rode away. Garrison rode away knowing that all the good he had done in helping the Swansons had just been wiped away in a split-second. No one would forget or forgive what he had just done, least of all himself.

Chapter Forty-Seven

Central Kansas – June 1865

Garrison slowed as he approached the town, if indeed the cluster of hardscrabble buildings ahead could be classified as a town. *Someone apparently thought so,* Garrison mused as he rode past a hand-painted sign on a piece of rough-hewn timber welcoming travelers to Abilene, Kansas. This was the place he was looking for, but it certainly wasn't what he had expected to find.

The settlement was split by a small creek running through the center. On its west bank sat a compound consisting of two log houses, a log stable, and a horse corral. A sign out front advertised: *'The last square meal east of Denver.'*

Directly across from this compound on the east bank of the creek sat another large structure. According to a sign in front of the building, it served as a way station for the Short Line Stage Company. Several hundred feet east of the creek, Garrison spotted what he presumed was some type of mercantile called the Frontier Store. Also set back from the trail, and in the midst of a prairie dog town, was Old Man Jones saloon.

Garrison counted a dozen simple log houses scattered along the east bank of the creek. Amazingly, there were no streets and prairie grass grew tall in the spaces between the houses. *This place makes Bent Pines look like a bustling city by comparison,* Garrison thought. *No, Bent Pines is nothing more than a pile of rubble and dry bones now,* he thought as a dark, brooding look momentarily crossed his face.

Garrison was hungry and could hardly wait to find out if the food offered on the west bank of the creek really lived up to the claims made about it. But his first stop would be the stable. Garrison knew, just as any true horseman did, that the care of one's horse always came first.

After making arrangements for Diablo at the stable, Garrison made the short walk to the building offering 'the last square meal east of Denver.' He felt his stomach growl as the savory smells of roasted meat wafted toward him. Garrison hadn't tasted fresh cooked meat in months, but he hadn't realized just how much he had missed it until his nose had been assaulted by the titillating aroma.

Stepping inside the building, Garrison found himself in a large open space dominated by a large stone fireplace. On one side of the fireplace, there was a smattering of rough-hewn tables. On the other was a sitting area with a couple of leather couches and several rough-hewn chairs arranged around a long, low table where guests could relax and mingle. There was a counter to the left of the fireplace where, Garrison assumed, one could order their food.

He stood just inside the doorway for a moment as he let his gaze travel from one end of the room to the other. Only a few of the tables were occupied, as were two of the chairs on the opposite side of the room. All the occupants were men and Garrison noted that at least two of them had a Colt hanging from their hips. Overall, the atmosphere was subdued.

A couple of the men looked up when he entered. They gazed upon him with curiosity for a brief moment before turning their attention to their own pursuits. Relieved that he had not attracted any undue attention, Garrison moved toward the food counter.

Chapter Forty-Eight

Garrison leaned back in his chair fully sated as he pushed the now-empty plate, his second, away from him. He couldn't recall the last time he'd had a meal of this quality. A fresh slab of beef accompanied by roasted potatoes and corn had been washed down with a cold beer. Living life on the run, he couldn't be sure when his next hot meal might come, so he had indulged himself with a second platter. Now he was so full that he felt like he could barely move.

Garrison looked around to see that the other diners had finished their meals and moved on. Some had moved over to the other side of the building and were lounging by the fire. The others had presumably retired for the evening. *That might not be a bad idea,* Garrison thought as he felt his eyelids growing heavy.

Movement caught Garrison's eye and he turned to see an old, colored man approaching the table. His spine was bent, and he walked with a limp. Despite his infirmities, there was a smile on his face when he spoke. "Scuse me, sir, you mind if I take these now?" he asked, pointing at the dirty dishes on Garrison's table.

"That's fine. I'm all done," Garrison told him with a smile.

"Was everything alright, sir?" the man asked him.

"It was the best meal I've had in a long time," Garrison said sincerely. "Mind if I sit awhile longer and have a smoke?" Garrison asked.

"That'd be fine," the old man said.

Garrison reached into his jacket and removed his smoking kit. As he went about rolling a cigarette, he asked the old man who he needed to talk to about getting a room for the evening.

"I'll take care of it for you," the man offered.

Garrison thanked the man and then watched as he retreated behind the counter with the dirty crockery. Garrison lit his cigarette and blew a cloud of smoke into the air. He puffed on it occasionally as he sat in silent contemplation of his life.

Garrison took in his surroundings and wondered, not for the first time, *What the hell am I doing here?* Looking back on the past year, he couldn't recall a single time when he had encountered other people and no one had died. After what happened in Independence, he had sworn to himself that he would avoid towns no matter the cost.

Yet, here he was not even a month later, sitting in a rooming house with a stomach full of food. Even worse than that, he was really pushing his luck by staying in town overnight. It would be the first time he had slept in a real bed since he rode away from the Watkins's ranch.

Some people might think that after roughing it for so long, they deserved a night of sound sleep in a real bed. Garrison wasn't one of them. He knew better than most that the world didn't work that way.

Sure, there were days when he felt like life owed him something in exchange for all that had been taken away. His loyalty to the Union had cost him his family. He'd seen countless brothers in arms die on the field of battle. He'd found love with Olivia Watkins only to have her taken away. Between Benjamin's scheming and the Confederacy's plotting, he'd lost his good name, his freedom, and his life.

Some might argue that he was both free and alive. But this wasn't real freedom. He couldn't go anywhere he wanted or do anything he wanted. He had to be constantly on guard, always watching over his shoulder for the men who constantly pursued him.

And this wasn't the life he would be living if circumstances hadn't conspired against him. His was a solitary existence by necessity. He could never hope to stay in one place long enough to build relationships. There would be no settling down with a good woman and raising a few kids for him. He would be alone until the day his luck ran out. And he started each day knowing that it could very well be the day when that happened.

Garrison's melancholic thoughts were interrupted when the stooped old man returned. "Room's ready, sir," he said. "Top of the stairs, second door on the right. You can settle your bill in the morning," he added.

Garrison thanked the man, crushed out his cigarette, and stood up to leave. He had just reached the stairs when a thought occurred to him. Turning back to the old man, he said, "I think I'll try one of those cigars. A bottle of whiskey and glass would be much appreciated, too," he added. With the dark thoughts swirling through his mind, he didn't expect sleep to come anytime soon or without some help.

Chapter Forty-Nine

The room was small. The bed sat against one wall, opposite the lone window. There was a tiny nightstand next to the bed. A high-back chair sat by the window. A chamber pot sat in the corner. A single oil lamp stood on the nightstand. Noticeably absent was a dresser. This wasn't the kind of town one was expected to spend more than a day in. It was just a stopping point on one's way to somewhere bigger and better.

Garrison sat in the chair with his feet propped on the bed. The lamp was turned down low, leaving the room in gloomy shadow. The whiskey bottle he asked for sat on the floor beside him. In his left hand, he held a glass containing the amber liquid. He raised it to his lips occasionally, taking small sips.

Garrison liked the taste of whiskey, but he wasn't a heavy drinker. He never allowed himself more than a single glass. Any more than that could dull a man's senses. Garrison couldn't allow himself to fall into that kind of state. He knew that a man who lived by the gun had to be sharp at all times.

Thick smoke curled from the cigar in Garrison's right hand. He supposed it was good, but he really wasn't one to judge. According to the old man downstairs, the cigar was handmade in Cuba. *It could have been rolled with prairie grass from outside and I wouldn't know the difference,* Garrison mused.

As he sat in near darkness nursing his drink and puffing on his cigar, Garrison's mind continued to wander along the dark path of self-reflection. He could wallow in self-pity at the hand he had been dealt, but he refused to. As much as he sometimes wanted to lay all the blame on fate, he knew that it was his choices that had brought him to this point.

He had chosen loyalty to the Union over his family. It hadn't been forced on him. He could have given in to his father's demands and resigned his commission, but he hadn't. He stood by his decision even when he knew what it would cost him.

Garrison didn't know what he could have done differently about Bent Pines. At the time, he thought he was following a legitimate order from his superior officer. But after it all went to hell, it was his decision to go back and try to clear his name. Jonathan Watkins had warned him and tried to talk him out of it. But once again, Garrison had made his mind up and he wouldn't be swayed.

Downstairs, Garrison had asked himself what he was doing here in Abilene, Kansas. But the real question should have been simply, 'what the hell am I doing?' There was no set destination and no grand plan. He was simply heading west in the foolish hope that he could somehow outrun his own notoriety. But deep down, he knew it didn't matter how far or fast he ran; his past would eventually catch up with him. It always did.

There was still a part of him that wanted to decry the unfairness of it all. As far as the world was concerned, he was the notorious Butcher of Bent Pines. He may be innocent of that particular crime, but that didn't make him an innocent man.

But the hard truth was, once again, that his own actions had contributed to his current plight. He couldn't put all the blame on fate. He was the one who had decided to leave warning messages written in the blood of his enemies signed in the name of the Pale Rider. He was the one who made that name and his own synonymous by leaving the same message on Benjamin's tent.

He couldn't deny that he was a killer. He had been since the first battle of the war. But he had never felt bad about killing until the night he killed to avenge Jack Garnett's death. Those dozen men had been doing their duty based on what they had been told about him. So had the four soldiers he killed in Kentucky. The same was true of the sheriff he killed in Independence. All had died only because Garrison refused to allow himself to be captured, because that meant hanging.

Garrison hadn't been lying when he told that sheriff that he hoped he would shoot when Garrison made his play. That would have been a merciful ending to what was becoming an unbearable existence. Garrison feared that it wouldn't be the last time he was forced to kill a good man just to avoid the hangman's noose. He could kill men like Bloody Bill all day, every day, without a second thought. But every time he killed a good man like that sheriff or those soldiers, a little piece of his soul died with them.

Garrison cursed out loud at the sudden pain he felt in the fingers of his right hand. He quickly dropped the remnants of the cigar into the tin ashtray on the nightstand to avoid any further burns. He had been so wrapped up in his thoughts that he had let the thing burn right down to his fingers. He just shook his head and downed the remaining whiskey in his glass.

Garrison left the bottle and empty glass on the floor. He wedged the back of the chair under the doorknob. It wouldn't keep anyone from coming in, but it would make enough noise to wake Garrison and give him time to grab a gun. His gun belts hung over the bedpost within easy reach. He sat on the edge of the bed and tugged his boots off and then lay back on the bed fully clothed. He closed his eyes and waited for the demons that haunted his sleep to descend upon him once more.

Chapter Fifty

It was after noon the next day, and Garrison found himself still in the small settlement of Abilene, Kansas. He knew he was pushing his luck, but he was looking for information, and he didn't want to leave until he got it. He knew exactly where he should look, but he didn't relish going there.

Despite his misgivings, here he was standing in front of Old Man Jones Saloon. Saloons were dangerous places where violence could erupt without warning. Not that everyone who frequented one was a bad man or troublemaker, but when you mixed combustible elements like gambling, booze, and women together, even the most levelheaded of men could become raving, murderous lunatics.

Garrison also knew that they were frequented by the type of men who would be pursuing him. Bounty hunters, lawmen, and soldiers always seemed to find their way to the local watering hole sooner or later. This thought was what made Garrison feel uneasy.

If he encountered any of the three inside, gunplay would almost certainly be the result. It wasn't the idea of having to kill or be killed that frightened Garrison so much as the danger it posed for the other patrons. Garrison still had nightmares about the little girl who died in his arms after being caught in the crossfire at Bent Pines. He didn't think he could bear the guilt if another innocent life was lost because of him.

Despite his concerns, Garrison had made up his mind that he was entering this particular saloon. In reality, there was risk involved no matter what type of building he was entering. If there were people in it, there could be a confrontation. Garrison also consoled himself with the fact that given this saloon's humble setting, it was far less likely to be the kind of happening place encountered in larger towns or cities.

He was prepared to make a hasty exit, nonetheless. He had already retrieved Diablo from the stable and had the horse saddled and ready to go.

Normally, Garrison would hitch the horse right outside before entering this type of establishment but that wasn't practical here. Old Man Jones sat right in the middle of a prairie dog town and Garrison feared that the horse might step into a hole and break a leg, especially if they had to ride out in a hurry.

Garrison stopped just inside the saloon, as was his habit, letting his eyes survey the surroundings, looking for any sign of trouble. He saw no badges and no uniforms, so that was a good sign. In a packed saloon, bounty hunters were harder to spot but the only other person Garrison saw was the bartender. He was an older man with a potbelly and a bald head. Confident that he posed no danger, Garrison approached the man.

The bartender eyed the stranger as he approached the bar. He counted five pistols on the man and cast a quick glance toward the shotgun he kept beneath the bar. He hoped he wouldn't need it, but the man approaching him sure looked like trouble. When the stranger took a seat in front of him, the bartender forced a welcoming smile and asked, "What can I get you, stranger?"

"Whiskey," Garrison answered. He didn't like the look the man had given him as he approached. He had swapped his duster for a black frock coat and realized now that the sight of his weapons may have unnerved the old man. "Relax. I'm just here for a drink and friendly conversation," he told the man.

The bartender placed a glass in front of Garrison and then poured a generous amount of whiskey in the glass. "There you go," he said to the stranger. "My ma named me Ezekiel, but most folks just call me Zeke. You got a name?"

"You can call me Matt," Garrison said with a smile as he raised the glass to his lips.

"Nice to meet you, Matt. Can I get you anything else, a cigar maybe?" Zeke asked.

Garrison made a show of looking around as he lit the cigar and then turned back to Zeke. "It's kind of dead in here, Zeke," he commented. "I hope, for your sake, it's not like this all the time."

"It's just the time of day is all. Mostly immigrants living around here, trying to eke out an existence. They won't be in until the sun sets. Got two stage lines come through every few days, but again it's too early for that," Zeke explained.

Garrison just nodded. Silence filled the room for a moment as he sipped on his whiskey and took a puff of the cigar.

"Now if you want to see this place packed, just wait until the hunting outfits come in," Zeke said with a big smile. "I make good money then," he added, his eyes bright.

The statement peaked Garrison's interest. "Buffalo?" he asked.

"Yeah, lots of them use this as a jumping off place. Then they always stop here on the way back to the railhead to ship the skins back east. Mighty thirsty by the time they make it this far."

"Zeke, it's funny you brought that up. The only reason I came in here was to find someone that could tell me about the buffalo. I've never seen one and I've got an itch to do a little hunting," Garrison explained.

Zeke gave him a big smile. "Well, if you hang around a few days, I'm pretty sure you could hire on with one of the outfits. It's a big business, you know?"

Garrison was leery of staying in one place much longer but that was the only reason he had come to Abilene in the first place. He decided he would wait a week to see if any of the hunting outfits came through. If not, he would just have to strike out on his own.

Chapter Fifty-One

The Great Plains, Kansas – July 1865

Garrison had waited impatiently in Abilene for several fruitless days. He had all but given up on connecting with one of the established hunting outfits. In fact, he was preparing to head out on his own when a large contingent of wagons and men on horseback came riding in from the east.

Zeke had been true to his word and introduced Garrison to the outfit's leader, a man who went by the name Tully. The man was just slightly shorter than Garrison and appeared to be about ten years older with a slight build. His hair was sandy brown in color and his eyes were hazel. Tully's face was sunburned and weather-beaten. Thick, dark stubble covered his face and neck.

Tully was soft-spoken and practical in his speech. Garrison liked him almost immediately and hoped the feeling was mutual. Once the introductions had been made and Zeke headed back behind the bar, Garrison decided to get straight to the point.

"Zeke mentioned that you might be hiring," Garrison said, "but that's not really necessary. I'd be content if you just allowed me to tag along. I can pay my way if need be."

Tully had leaned back in his chair to take a better look at Garrison. His eyes lingered for a moment on the pistols that Garrison carried. He blew a cloud of smoke in the air and asked, "So, what's your story?"

Garrison shrugged as he responded. "I fought in the war," he said simply. "I don't really have anything or anyone left back east, so I decided to head west. I've heard stories about the buffalo and decided I want to see them for myself," Garrison had explained.

Tully sat for a moment in silent contemplation. Then he asked, "You wouldn't happen to be on the run, would you?"

For a moment, Garrison feared that perhaps Tully had seen his face on a 'wanted' poster and recognized him. But his instinct told him that that wasn't the case. Tully's expression and tone hadn't changed since Garrison sat down. He was calm, most probably just curious.

"We're all running from something, aren't we?" Garrison had responded. He stood and said, "I appreciate you taking the time to talk to me, and I understand if you don't want to bring a stranger along with you. I'll be fine on my own."

"I'd advise against that," Tully told him. "The plains can be a dangerous place for a man on his own. You got three different tribes out there taking scalps right now," Tully warned.

"I'm pretty good at taking care of myself," Garrison replied.

Tully chuckled. "I'll bet you are," he said. "Now sit down and finish your drink. You're welcome to ride with us," he said as a broad smile spread across his face. Pointing toward Garrison's guns, he said, "I'm assuming you know how to use those things and if that's the case, we could use a man like you out there if we do run into trouble with the redskins."

After that had been worked out, the conversation flowed easily. Later that evening, Tully had introduced him to the other members of the outfit. There were twenty men in total and Garrison was surprised at just how big an operation hunting buffalo could be. Each man had a specific job to do once they located a herd and the hunt began. Tully was the hunter and did all the shooting. Others were assigned as skinners, gun cleaners, teamsters, cartridge re-loaders, and wranglers. There were two blacksmiths among the group. The cook was a man they called Beans. His was the only name that Garrison could remember aside from Tully.

After the introductions had been made, everyone headed off to get a good night's sleep. Tully instructed everyone to meet at the wagons by five the next morning. They would have a quick breakfast and plan to be underway before daybreak.

Chapter Fifty-Two

They had been on the range for a week and a half without any sign of buffalo in the vicinity. The mood in camp was growing darker with each passing day. But everything had changed the day before. It was just before dark when Tully and Garrison had come upon the tracks of what appeared to be a very large herd.

The tracks were relatively fresh, no more than a day old. Buffalo moved slowly as they grazed, so a single day's advantage could be easily overcome by the hunting party. Tully had decided to make camp there and then start out on the herd's trail at first light. Beans and some helpers would go about setting up a more permanent encampment while the others tracked the buffalo.

Tully and Garrison rode out well in advance of the others. Thus, they were the first to lay eyes on the herd. Garrison's breath caught in his throat. They had just crested a small hill and there below them was the herd spread out as far as the eye could see. *There must be hundreds, maybe thousands, of the beasts,* Garrison thought to himself. It was like an undulating wave of brown rolling slowly over the prairie.

Garrison quickly pulled the spy scope from his saddlebag so that he could get a better look at one of them. He focused in on one of the animals and studied it closely. The animal was massive, close to two thousand pounds if Garrison had to guess. It was light brown in color and far less shaggy than he had anticipated. Its hide appeared smooth except for around the animal's head where the fur was shaggy and darker in color. Large curved horns protruded from either side of the massive head. Garrison guessed that each was nearly two feet in length. Just behind the head was a rounded hump. Even standing still, the animal just seemed to exude power.

"Well, what do you think?" Tully asked.

Garrison could feel the smile spread across his face. He felt like a little kid, but he couldn't help himself. "Magnificent," he heard himself say. It was the one word that he could think of to describe the exhilaration he felt. "Not as shaggy as the pictures I've seen," he added as an afterthought.

Tully smiled. "It's summer," he explained. "The shaggy coat you're thinking of is the winter coat. They start shedding that in the spring. A good summer coat will fetch three dollars apiece. I can get fifty dollars each for a good winter coat."

Garrison didn't know how to respond to that, so he just remained silent. Tully turned back to the rest of the team and signaled for them to join him. Once they arrived, he would give out last-minute instructions and then the hunt would begin.

While they waited for the others, Tully turned to Garrison. "Matt, you're with me today. This is your chance to see the buffalo up close. Starting tomorrow, I want you to remain in camp to provide security."

Garrison gave him a puzzled look. "Okay," he said. "But what exactly am I supposed to be protecting the camp from?" he asked.

"This is a lucrative business, but it's hard work. There are always a few unscrupulous hunters that would rather steal from others than do the work themselves. One look at you with all those guns and that kind of man will pass right on by us and look for an easier target," Tully said with a smile.

"And if they don't?" Garrison asked.

"Then you use those pistols," Tully replied. "The other threat is the redskins. If they come, they won't be interested in stealing anything. They will try to destroy the pelts we've got along with the rest of the camp. They won't be deterred so easily as the thieves. You'll have to use your guns just to stay alive."

Before Garrison could respond, the rest of the men arrived. The excitement in the air was almost palpable. Everyone brought their horses in close so that Tully could be heard without raising his voice enough to disturb the herd. With the last-minute instructions out of the way, the group separated, each man heading off to do his part.

Chapter Fifty-Three

Garrison and Tully had remained on the hill. Tully estimated that they were right around a hundred yards from the edge of the herd. This was the perfect distance, he assured Garrison. Tully removed the two fifty-caliber rifles, wrapped in cloth, from his horse and spread the cloth out on the ground. He then instructed Garrison to move the horses about a hundred yards in the opposite direction. He didn't want them getting spooked when the shooting started.

Garrison returned to find Tully lying on his stomach as he looked down the sights of one of the rifles. He looked over his shoulder at the sound of Garrison's approach. He quickly waved him over. Garrison lay on his stomach near Tully, the spare rifle between them.

"Okay, Matt, here's how this is going to work," Tully said in a whisper.

"Bison ain't like most other animals. If you see a herd of deer and shoot one, the others are going to take off. The buffalo don't do that. Once I drop the first one, the herd will gather around it. They'll stay that way awhile before they sense danger and stampede. I should be able to drop twenty to thirty of them before that happens," he explained.

Garrison was stunned. He could never have imagined that they would be able to kill that many in a single day. "You drop them with one shot? A headshot?" he asked.

"One shot to drop them, yes, but not a head shot," Tully replied. "The skulls are too thick; the lead slug flattens on impact and won't penetrate. You want to hit them broadside, through the lungs," he further explained.

"Now, Matt, this is important. Once I start shooting, I will get into a rhythm and I don't want to break that rhythm once I've found it. You count my shots and be ready to hand me the other rifle as soon as I fire the last from this one. Then you need to reload the first as quick as you can. We'll repeat that process until the bison take off. Got it?" Tully asked.

Garrison just nodded.

"Okay, here we go then!" Tully exclaimed as he lined up his first shot.

Chapter Fifty-Four

Garrison was silent as he and Tully rode toward the bison carcasses that littered the ground. Tully had exceeded his own estimate, dropping thirty-four of the majestic animals before the herd became spooked and stampeded. And he did it all in less than two minutes.

Garrison hadn't seen this kind of slaughter since the battle of Gettysburg. He had been there, under Kilpatrick, before the unit was transferred to the western theater. He had watched from a distance as the Confederates attempted a frontal assault on Cemetery Hill and were slaughtered for their effort. Even though they were the enemy, he'd had a lump in his throat as he cursed their stupidity while simultaneously applauding their valor.

He couldn't really describe what he had felt that day. But whatever it was, he felt it again as he watched Tully slaughter the buffalo with such lethal precision. Now as they drew nearer, Garrison realized that, just like the men back at Gettysburg, many of the bison did not die when they dropped. He could hear a low, mournful rumble coming from somewhere deep inside several of the wounded animals. They now lay there in the gathering heat, suffering as they slowly expired.

Tully pulled up on the reins and dismounted well short of the wounded animals. Garrison followed his lead.

Turning to Garrison, Tully said, "Don't get too close to any of them. Even mortally wounded, these beasts can be deadly. If they get you with one of those horns, you're good as dead way out here," he warned.

Garrison barely registered the warning. "I hate to see an animal suffer like this," Garrison said softly.

If Tully heard him, he gave no indication. He was slowly moving among the dead and dying animals. When he found an animal that he was certain was dead, he waved his skinners over. As they set about their work, he removed a bundle of wooden stakes from the wagon and continued his tour of the carnage.

Whenever he came upon a dead animal, he drove a stake in the ground to alert the skinners that the animal was ready.

Garrison soon lost sight of Tully. He stood riveted with morbid fascination as he watched the skinners perform their work. Using a sledgehammer, they drove a spike through the first dead animal's nose. With that complete, they hooked up a horse team and used the horses to rip the hide from the carcass. The hide was then turned over to another team charged with dressing and prepping the hide while the skinners moved on to the next animal. The dressed and prepped hides were stacked in an empty wagon.

Garrison's thoughts were interrupted when Tully called out, "Pretty efficient operation, don't you think?" The man had a big smile on his face, clearly pleased with himself. He was puffing on a cigar as he approached Garrison. He held one out to Garrison, who declined.

"What about the rest of the animal?" Garrison asked.

Tully just looked at him for a moment as if he didn't understand the question.

"We'll leave the carcasses to rot right where they are. That's why we established basecamp all the way back at the beginning of the trail. A day or two in this heat and the smell will be nearly unbearable. We'll come back this way in a few weeks to collect the bones. We'll ship those back east. I hear that the chemical companies use them to make glue," Tully explained.

Garrison didn't say anything, but inside he was fuming. When he decided to join a buffalo hunt, he never expected anything like this. It was both barbaric and wasteful. No wonder the Native American tribes were opposed to this.

Tully took notice of the look on Garrison's face. "You okay?" he asked.

Garrison looked the man in the eye when he answered, "This isn't hunting; it's slaughter and I don't want any part of it. I'm riding back to camp," Garrison told him. He turned and walked away without waiting for a response.

Chapter Fifty-Five

Garrison couldn't get the images of skinned buffalo carcasses out of his mind. He had arrived back at the camp, still not sure what his next move would be. He had seriously considered riding on without stopping. But Garrison knew himself well enough to know that he was thinking with his heart rather than his head.

And so, he had returned to camp, determined to think it over for a night. He would make his decision in the morning. In the meantime, Beans and a couple of men whose names Garrison couldn't recall were still working on setting up the camp. Garrison jumped in to help, glad to have something to preoccupy his mind.

Garrison had a crate of canned beans in his hands when the sound of galloping hooves drew his attention. He looked up to see Tully riding toward the camp at breakneck speed. He galloped right into the camp and then pulled harshly on the reins to bring his horse to a quick stop. Jumping down from the saddle, he headed straight toward Garrison.

Garrison set the crate down. Tully was clearly angry, and Garrison had no idea what his intentions were. The man was wearing a Colt tied down low on his right thigh, so Garrison wanted his hands free, just in case.

In a matter of seconds, Tully was in his face, practically screaming. "What the hell is your problem?! We allowed you to join us so that you can see the buffalo, see what a hunt is like, and you're going to act like that?"

"Act like what?" Garrison asked.

"Like we're some kind of monsters. Like what we're doing is wrong. We're out here working hard to make an honest living. Who the hell are you to judge us?"

"I'm not judging you," Garrison insisted. A sardonic smile crossed his face. "Trust me, I am the last person who has any business judging you, or anyone else for that matter."

Tully stared hard into Garrison's face. "You sounded mighty judgy out there," he said, pointing in the general direction of the herd.

"I didn't mean to come across that way," Garrison finally responded. "But what happened out there today was akin to slaughter, not the hunting I'm used to doing. That doesn't make it wrong in the grand scheme of things. But it is wrong for me to be a part of it," he tried to explain.

"So what? You're just going to tuck tail and run?" Tully asked incredulously. He had genuinely liked this young man and thought he had found someone he could relate to as an equal out here on the range. Now he suddenly felt betrayed.

The conversation had helped Garrison make up his mind. "I'll be leaving in the morning," he told Tully.

"You son of a bitch! I told you I was counting on you to provide security here at the camp. Can't you at least do that much?!" Tully exclaimed.

"No, I'm afraid that if I did that, I would still feel guilty about being involved. I carry enough guilt on my shoulders as it is. I don't need to pile any more on top of it," Garrison explained. "I don't know how to explain it," he added.

"Well, try," Tully practically commanded.

"Between the war…and other things…I've just seen too much slaughter," he began to explain. "It doesn't matter that we're only talking about animals out here now. When we were out there earlier today, you just saw dead buffalo. Maybe a source of income for you and your men. For a moment, I was back at Gettysburg. It was bad enough the first time. I can't be around something that takes me back there again," he said, hoping Tully could understand where he was coming from.

The two men stood in silence for a moment. Finally, the anger drained from Tully's face. He wasn't happy, but Garrison's answer at least seemed to appease him. He put a hand a Garrison's shoulder, gave it a squeeze, and then turned and walked away without another word. Little did Garrison suspect that this would be the last conversation the two would ever have.

Chapter Fifty-Six

The next morning, Garrison rose early and did what he could to help Beans prepare breakfast. The men would be heading out at first light in search of the herd. To avoid tension the previous evening, Garrison had decided to help Beans prepare dinner and then clean up afterwards. It kept him busy and gave him an excuse to avoid the others most of the evening. He had actually enjoyed it, so he decided to help out again this morning before heading out.

Beans had seemed to appreciate the help. And it had given Garrison a chance to get to know the cook a little better. The man could best be described as short and round. At just over five feet, he was at a least a foot shorter than Garrison. Despite this, he probably outweighed Garrison by nearly a hundred pounds. He had round, chubby cheeks that seemed to be perpetually covered in peach fuzz despite the man being at least twenty years older than Garrison. A mop of unruly curly brown hair sat atop his head.

What Garrison appreciated most about the man was the fact that he always had a smile on his face. He had a cheery disposition no matter the time of day or the amount of work to be done. Despite being a prankster, he took his role as cook seriously. He saw it as his responsibility to take care of the men in the outfit, ensuring they had food that kept them strong and healthy.

Once the men were gone and cleanup had been completed, Garrison prepared to ride out. He would miss Beans and Tully, but he just couldn't stomach what was happening to the buffalo out there. He thought it best to be gone before Tully and the men returned. That way, he could avoid any awkward goodbyes with them.

The same could not be said of Beans. The man had followed him to the corral and watched as Garrison saddled Diablo and prepared to leave. Even now, the man wore a smile on his face, even if there was a hint of sadness in his eyes.

"I sure hate to see you leave like this. Especially on bad terms with Mr. Tully. You two seemed like you were on the way to being fast friends," Beans said.

Garrison just regarded the man for a moment. "We're not really on bad terms, Beans," he explained. "We're just not on good terms is all," he added with a smile.

"Well, whatever went on with you two, I know I'm going to miss you. It was real nice having some help for a while," Beans replied.

Garrison wasn't listening. He was focused on a low rumbling sound that seemed to be coming from a distance somewhere. As he stood listening, it grew in volume.

"Do you hear that?" he asked Beans.

Beans had turned to look toward the open range where the sound had originated. The rumbling was so loud now that it was hard to hear anything else. Now the ground beneath their feet began to shake. All of a sudden, a series of gunshots rang out, barely audible over the now-deafening rumble.

"What the hell?!" Garrison exclaimed.

When Beans turned back toward Garrison, his eyes were wide and the smile was gone from his face.

"Stampede!" he screamed.

"We got to get out of here right now!" Beans hollered as he came into the corral and began trying to mount one of the workhorses used to pull the chuck wagon. Garrison had already swung himself onto Diablo's back and now turned to check on Beans. He let out a curse as he jumped down and ran toward the cook. Without a saddle and stirrups, there was no way the man was going to make it onto the horse without help.

Garrison grabbed the horse's mane in an attempt to hold it steady. The animal was as spooked as they were. It wouldn't take much for the horse to rear and throw Beans to the ground.

"Goddammit, Beans! You better get your fat ass on that horse!" Garrison shouted.

The cook had managed to drape the upper half of his body across the animal's back, but his legs still dangled free. Taking a risk by releasing the horse's mane, Garrison ran around to the side, grabbed the man's chubby legs, and did his best to push him up onto the horse.

As soon as the man's wide bottom settled across the horse's back, Garrison yelled for Beans to hold on tight and slapped the horse on its rear as hard as he could. The animal took off like it was shot from a cannon. Garrison immediately mounted Diablo and set off after the cook.

Garrison was less than a hundred yards away when he risked a glance backwards. As he watched, a teaming mass of brown bodies crested the hill and came crashing down on the camp like a tidal wave. Tents were torn to pieces. Wagons were shattered. Supplies and gear sailed through the air before landing in front of the wild tide where they were subsequently trampled. It was one of the most terrifying spectacles Garrison had ever seen.

He had almost caught up with Beans. He waved for the man to follow him and hoped he had understood. He then turned Diablo ninety degrees to the left and urged the horse forward as fast as he could go. They were never going to outrun the stampeding herd. Their only hope was to reach the edge before the animals caught up with them.

Looking backwards, Garrison gave a quick prayer of thanks when he saw Beans just behind him. Focusing his eyes forward, he searched for the edge of the herd. Finally, he spotted it fifty yards ahead. *This is going to be close,* he thought to himself.

And indeed, it was. Bean had just cleared the edge of the herd when the first of the stampeding beasts passed them mere inches away. Both men brought their horse to a halt and sat watching the buffalo roar past. Both knew they were lucky to be alive.

Chapter Fifty-Seven

Garrison snapped his pocket watch closed as the last of the herd finally passed by and eventually disappeared into the distance.

"Thirty minutes," Garrison said as he looked over at Beans. The man's face was ghostly pale and his eyes so wide that one might think that they had been glued open. Garrison had no doubt that his own face mirrored that of the cook. He had experienced more than his fair share of close calls, but he couldn't recall any closer than that.

"You ever seen anything like that before?" Garrison asked.

"Hell no!" the cook exclaimed. "I've never even heard of anything like this, and I've heard every story there is to tell out here," he added.

Both men looked out in the direction from which the herd had come. Neither man said a word. They were thinking the same thing but neither wanted to be the one to bring it up.

"You think there could be any survivors?" Garrison finally asked, unable to bear the silence any longer.

Beans gave him a long sigh accompanied by a deeply saddened expression. "I don't see how," he said simply.

"We've got to check to make sure," Garrison told him.

"Hell, even if someone survived it, they won't have done it unscathed. There won't be a damn thing we can do to help them," Beans complained.

"There's always something that can be done," Garrison said grimly. At the very least, they could put a man out of his misery, just as Garrison had done for Barnes back in Georgia.

Slowly, the two men rode side by side back in the direction they had come from, both silently fearful of what they would find. As they rode, Garrison turned to Beans. "Beans, what would cause the buffalo to stampede like that?" he asked.

Beans shook his head in silence for a moment, as if to say he had no idea. This was followed by a deep breath before he finally replied, "I've never seen a herd stampede except when they're being hunted. But that's not what happened here," the cook added, his voice ringing with certainty.

"How can you be so sure?" Garrison asked.

"Because Tully was no greenhorn; he knew what he was doing," Beans answered. "Besides, we were trailing that herd. Tully would have come upon the tail end of it and he would have set himself up to drive the herd away from camp, not toward it," the cook explained.

"What about another hunting outfit? Maybe one coming from the other direction?" Garrison suggested.

"I guess it's possible," Beans said, but the look on his face said he didn't really think so. "I'm pretty sure we would have heard some gunshots…before the stampede started, I mean. Those big fifty-caliber rifles have quite a report," Beans went on to explain.

"Natural predators then?" Garrison asked.

Again, Beans looked doubtful. "Wolves maybe, but I've never heard of them trying to take down anything as big as an adult buffalo. They would have to be near starved to even attempt it. No, they typically prey on the outliers, the young, the old, or the sick that sometimes fall behind the rest of the herd. I don't think that would cause a stampede."

"Okay. Then what else?" Garrison asked.

There was deep note of exasperation in Bean's voice when he answered. "I have no goddamn idea! Nothing I can think of fits the facts. I mean, a prairie fire would do it, but we'd have seen the smoke from that long before the herd stampeded. A bad-enough thunderstorm could do it too, but again…" Beans paused to raise his hand toward the heavens. "…Just look, nothing but clear blue skies looking down on us," he finished.

The two rode on in silence, neither man able to think of anything else to say. They came upon the wreckage of the camp first. The debris was spread out across the prairie as far as they could see. At a quick glance, it looked as if nothing had survived.

Garrison looked over at Beans. "Why don't you search through this mess to see if there's anything salvageable?" Garrison suggested. "Keep your eye out for a shovel," he added as an afterthought. *We're going to need one,* he thought to himself.

"What are you going to do?" Beans asked him.

"I'm going to look for survivors," Garrison answered.

"God, forgive me, but I almost hope you don't find any," Beans said.

"I know," Garrison said simply. He knew what Beans was getting at. If anyone did survive, they would almost certainly be seriously injured. If that were the case, a quick death would be the only assistance Garrison could give.

"If you hear two gunshots, one right after the other, you'll know I found somebody that we can save. You come to the sound as fast as you can. If you hear a single shot…well, you know what that will mean," Garrison said grimly.

Chapter Fifty-Eight

Garrison rode on alone out into the sea of carnage. After the thunderous sounds of the stampede, the silence that had now settled over the plains was eerie and it had Garrison on edge. Every so often, the silence was shattered by an unearthly scream. As a horse soldier, Garrison had been around enough wounded horses to immediately recognize the sound for what it was. Even so, each time the sound reached his ears, he felt a shiver run up his spine.

It didn't take long to determine that there had been no survivors. Most of the men had been so trampled that they were unrecognizable. Skulls had been crushed and limbs twisted in directions they were never intended to go. Several of the men, probably the skinners, had been crushed flat, every bone in their bodies smashed to pieces. Large scavenger birds were already pecking and tearing away at the remains by the time Garrison found some of them.

The horses had fared no better. In some ways, seeing them had been worse than finding the mangled men. Some of the animals had been caught by the center of the herd and trampled just as thoroughly as the men. Others had been closer to the edges of the stampeding herd but couldn't escape the deadly horns that protruded from the skulls of both the male and female buffalo.

Some of these animals had survived and dragged themselves away from the stampede before collapsing. Garrison found them lying in pools of their own blood, their sides heaving as they slowly died. He had put down four of the unfortunate beasts.

Garrison had found one horse that was still alive but lacked the strength to ward off the scavenger birds. They danced around the animal pecking and tearing at its flesh even as the horse screamed in pain, unable to do anything else. Garrison had quickly killed the animal to end its suffering.

Even after he had accounted for all the men and horses, Garrison kept pushing forward, hoping to find some clue as to what had caused the stampede. Mile after mile, he continued onward across the prairie. *I have to be getting close to the stampede's starting point,* he kept telling himself. Cresting a small hill, he came to a sudden stop. Spread out across the plain below him was the answer he had been looking for.

Chapter Fifty-Nine

Spread out across the prairie were a dozen buffalo carcasses. Garrison pulled his spy scope from his jacket to get a better look. Focusing on one of the dead animals, Garrison counted over half a dozen arrow shafts protruding from the animal's rump and flanks. He examined each of the buffalo corpses through the lens of the spy scope and found them all to be in the same condition.

So, he'd been on the right track after all. The stampede had been caused by another hunting party. Only it was an Indian hunting party hunting with their traditional bow and arrows, which explained the absence of gunshots prior to the stampede. And they had driven the herd straight into Tully and his men. Was that just a strange twist of fate or had it been done intentionally?

Of more immediate concern was another question. Where were the Indians now? There was no sign of them on the prairie down below, just the dead buffalo. Could they be hiding, waiting to spring a trap on anyone who came to investigate? Garrison didn't think so; there was nothing but open ground as far as he could see. He decided to chance a closer look, but he drew a Colt from each of the saddle holsters just in case.

Garrison brought Diablo to a halt several feet away from the nearest dead animal. He approached it on foot, moving cautiously as he recalled Tully's warning from the day before. Once he was certain that the animal was dead, Garrison moved toward its flank and grabbed one of the arrows. He attempted to pull it free, but it was buried too deep into the animal's thick flesh. Using both hands and grunting with the effort, Garrison was finally able to snap the shaft. He hoped that Beans might be able to identify the tribe if he saw the arrow.

Moving along, Garrison briefly examined each of the dead buffalo. When he came to the last one, he pulled up short. This one was partially skinned. It looked as if they had just gotten started and then suddenly stopped, like they had been interrupted.

Garrison again wondered where the Indians could be. Something just wasn't adding up here. Native Americans didn't hunt like white men who often killed for profit and sometimes just for sport. When they killed, they used every part of the animal, not letting anything go to waste. There was no way they would just leave these corpses here to rot. Garrison looked again toward the partially skinned beast. Clearly, the hunters had begun to harvest the animal, but something had caused them to stop. What would do that?

And suddenly it dawned on him. He had caused the interruption. Garrison thought about the horses that he had put down. The Indians had to have heard those shots and had probably gone to investigate. If they had intentionally driven the herd toward Tully and the camp, they now knew that someone had survived.

Fortunately, Garrison had been crisscrossing his way across the prairie without any real pattern, which would make it harder for them to track his movements. That was probably the only reason that they hadn't found him yet. And then another thought occurred to Garrison. What if the Indians simply headed toward the campsite figuring any survivors would eventually go there? Beans wouldn't stand a chance.

Garrison practically leaped into the saddle and made a beeline toward camp. He knew it was risky; he could ride headlong into the hunting party without warning. But if he took his time, there was the risk that he would arrive at the campsite only to find Beans dead and scalped. He decided he'd rather risk his own safety than take that chance.

Garrison galloped into the destroyed camp at full speed, pulling hard on the reins to bring Diablo to a halt. Beans had been wandering aimlessly through the destruction, kicking debris out of his path, when he heard the sound of the approaching horse. He stood stock-still, watching the horse and rider approach and breathed a sigh of relief when they got close enough for him to recognize. That relief was short-lived, however. One look at Garrison's face and he knew something was very wrong.

"Mount up. We've got to go!" Garrison ordered, the tension in his voice palpable.

"Why? What's happened? Did you find survivors?" Beans asked hopefully.

Garrison shook his head. "There were no survivors, neither men nor horses."

"Then what's the damn hurry? Besides, we can't go nowhere until we bury them. I won't just leave them out there to rot," Beans declared.

"We don't have time to bury them, and we don't have time to argue about it either. Now get on your damn horse," Garrison ordered again.

"You're not making any damn sense, and I'm not going anywhere until you do," Beans stubbornly insisted.

Garrison pulled the broken arrow from his saddle and tossed it to Beans. "I found out what caused the stampede," he told Beans.

The older man's eyes widened in shock as he looked at the arrow shaft he now held in his hands. "This is a Cheyenne arrow!" he exclaimed. "Where'd you find it?"

"I pulled it out of a dead buffalo's ass," Garrison shot back in frustration. "Now will you get on that goddamn horse so we can get out of here before we end up with matching arrows sticking out of our backsides?"

"If we leave the boys out there, the Cheyenne will scalp them," Beans complained.

"I don't mean any disrespect, Beans, but they're dead. They're beyond caring about being scalped. The only scalps I'm worried about are the ones on our heads. I don't know about you, but I'd like to keep mine right where it is. So please, just get on that fucking horse!" Garrison was shouting now, his patience having reached its limit.

"Okay, okay," Beans muttered. "But you're going to have to help me get up there again."

"Fine," Garrison said as he dismounted. He held the horse steady while Beans tried his best to climb up on its back. Once he got his torso draped over its back, Garrison grabbed his legs and pushed him all the way up, just as he had when the stampeding buffalo had been bearing down on them.

"Now hold on tight and follow me," Garrison instructed as he mounted Diablo and gave the reins a snap. Together, the two men galloped away from the scene of destruction.

Chapter Sixty

Night had fallen and Garrison and Beans sat before their small campfire, each lost in his own thoughts as they stared into the flickering flames as if mesmerized. Garrison was glad that he had left the cook to search through the camp and spared him the sights that would now haunt Garrison's dreams for years to come. He doubted that he would sleep tonight, for every time he closed his eyes, the ghastly images floated there in his mind's eye.

Garrison looked across the fire at Beans. He was worried about the man. Until today, Garrison had never seen him without a smile on his face. After today, Garrison feared the man may never smile again.

Beans just stared into the fire, unaware of Garrison's concerned gaze. Garrison could only guess what was going through the man's mind. He hadn't shed a tear, but his grief was almost palpable. Garrison had only known the men for a few weeks, and he was saddened by their loss, particularly Tully. But they had all been like family to Beans, and now they were all gone.

Garrison finally stood and walked around the fire, plopping down next to Beans. He offered the man his flask. Beans looked at it blankly for a moment before accepting the offer. He took a long pull of the strong whiskey and handed the flask back to Garrison, wiping his mouth with the back of his hand.

"You going to be okay?" Garrison asked.

For a moment, Garrison didn't think he was going to answer. But then, Beans turned to face him, and Garrison saw that the tears had finally begun to fall. "I don't know," Beans answered, his voice barely above a whisper.

The two men sat in silence for a while longer before Beans spoke again, his voice choked with emotion. "I can't believe they're gone. All of them. Taking care of them was my life for so long. Now they're gone and I don't know what to do. I've never felt so alone in all my life."

Now Garrison placed a hand upon Bean's shoulder. Giving it a squeeze, he said, "You're not alone."

Beans wiped the tears from his face and contemplated what Garrison had said. "You were all set to ride out alone just this morning. Now you want an old cook tagging along with you?" he asked incredulously.

"I was leaving to get away from the hunt and what it reminded me of, not the people," Garrison explained.

"You really want me to ride with you? Where would we be heading?" Beans asked, starting to think the idea over.

Garrison looked uncomfortable for a moment. "Well, that's the thing. I'm not going anywhere in particular. Just wherever the trail takes me," Garrison admitted.

"Tully was right, wasn't he? You are on the run, ain't you?" Beans accused.

"Yeah, he was right," Garrison said with a sigh. "I guess it's best if you knew the truth before you decide whether or not you want to come along."

"Well, let's hear it then," Beans encouraged him.

"I'm a wanted man. Hell, I might be the most wanted man in the country right now. My name's Matthew Lloyd Garrison, but some people call me the Butcher of Bent Pines. Others call me the Pale Rider," Garrison admitted. He paused to see what effect his words had upon his companion.

Beans was staring at Garrison wide-eyed. He wondered for a moment if the younger man might be trying to pull one over on him. But the look on Garrison's face was so serious that Beans soon dismissed that notion.

"Go on," he said, unable to hide the sudden trembling in his voice.

"I didn't butcher anyone at Bent Pines," Garrison insisted. "I was set up to take the fall for that one. But I am the Pale Rider," Garrison continued.

He went on to explain what happened to the Watkins's family and how he had thought up the idea of the Pale Rider to discourage others from preying on the weak. He talked Beans through his attempt to clear his name and how it ended in a disaster. He shared how he had saved the Swansons but then taken the life of the sheriff to avoid capture. He laid his soul bare, leaving out nothing, neither good nor bad.

"I'm not quite the monster some make me out to be, but I'm a long way from being a good man," Garrison concluded, surprised at how good it felt to get all of this out.

Beans had listened in rapt attention as Garrison told his story. At times, he thought maybe he should run in the other direction just as fast as his short little legs would take him. And sometimes he was nearly moved to tears as he thought of all this man had lost in his short life. In the end, it wasn't anything that he heard that made up his mind.

Beans was thinking about that morning, how he had been struggling to mount his horse as the stampeding buffalo were descending upon them. Garrison had already been mounted. He could have ridden off to save himself and left Beans to his fate. But he hadn't. The man had risked his own life to make sure Beans made it out alive.

"Whatever else you've done, good or bad, don't matter much to me. I've known you to be nothing but a good man. A good man who saved my life. I'd be honored to ride with you," Beans responded once Garrison had finished his story.

Garrison was more than a little bit surprised. He thought for sure the man would want nothing to do with him once he knew the truth.

"It could be dangerous," Garrison warned him. He didn't want him going into this blind to the risk he was taking.

"Any more dangerous that what we survived today?" Beans asked. His tone made it clear he didn't think anything could be more dangerous.

"Well, at least the buffalo weren't shooting at us," Garrison pointed out. "Sooner or later, someone always shoots at me. And if you're with me, they'll be shooting at you too," he added.

"That don't scare me," Beans replied.

"Alright, there's one more thing that you need to consider," Garrison told him.

"If I didn't know better, I'd swear you're trying to talk me out of this!" Beans exclaimed.

"No, I just want you to know what you're getting yourself into," Garrison assured him.

"Okay, let's have it then. What's that one more thing?" Beans asked.

"To most folks, I'm an outlaw. If you ride with me, you'll be branded one too. Your good name will be a thing of the past," Garrison warned.

For the first time since the stampede, the older man smiled. Then he broke out into riotous laughter. When he finally got himself under control, he looked at Garrison and, with a twinkle in his eye, said, "You're talking about having a good name to a man that's been called Beans most of his adult life! Can you imagine a wanted poster with my ugly mug on it? And it says something like:

'Wanted dead or alive – the notorious outlaw – Beans.'" The man had barely finished speaking before he once again burst out in uncontrolled laughter.

Garrison just looked at the man for a moment, and then he, too, began laughing hysterically.

Chapter Sixty-One

Rising early the next morning, the two men ate a Spartan breakfast of salted beef and washed it down with coffee, all from Garrison's personal provisions. They had spent much of the previous evening discussing what their next step should be. Beans broached the subject shortly after making up his mind to ride with Garrison.

"We need a plan, Matt. I know you said you just go where the trail leads, but in case you hadn't noticed, there ain't no trails out here. We can't just wander around aimlessly," Beans had insisted.

Before answering, Garrison took a moment to consider their current situation. "The first priority is getting a saddle for your horse," he finally answered. "I'm not lifting and pushing you up on his back all the way to Texas," he added with a smile.

Turning serious again, Garrison said, "We're also going to have to bolster our provisions. We'll burn through what I have twice as fast as I had planned now that there's two of us. You know this territory better than me, so you tell me where we should go."

Beans thought about it for a few minutes and then replied, "I know a feller by the name of Chisholm, a half-breed Cherokee, that's set up a trading post at the mouth of the Little Arkansas River. There's a Wichita Village there that he trades with. We should be able to get what we need from him."

"Okay, that sounds like a good place to start," Garrison agreed.

Beans smiled. "You ain't even heard the best part yet," he said.

Garrison remained silent, waiting expectantly for Beans to continue.

"Chisholm's got another trading post clear down in Indian Territory. Last fall, he was talking about marking a trail between the two posts. If he's managed to do it, we can follow it and get at least halfway to Texas," Beans explained.

"Sounds like we have a plan," Garrison observed with genuine excitement.

"Mind if I ask you a question?" Beans asked.

"Go on," Garrison replied.

"Why Texas anyway?" Beans asked. The tone of his voice made it clear that he did not share Garrison's enthusiasm for the destination.

Garrison thought about it for a minute. "You know, I don't really know. I guess maybe because it's so big. Maybe I'll be harder to find in all that open territory. What have you got against Texas anyway?" Garrison concluded with a question.

With a smile on his face and a twinkle in his eyes, Beans said, "Well, for starters, it's full of Texans!"

Chapter Sixty-Two

Wichita Village, Kansas – August 1865

"There's the village I was telling you about," Beans said, pointing toward a cluster of dome-shaped buildings. He and Garrison were still a long way off but had stopped to reconnoiter their destination from a distance. It was a habit that Garrison refused to break.

Sitting atop Diablo, Garrison turned his spy scope toward the village. Zooming in, he could see that the dome-shaped huts were grass-covered. Some of them were quite large, at least thirty feet in diameter, Garrison estimated. Looking past the huts, he could see crop fields being tended by members of the tribe.

"They're farmers?" Garrison asked Beans.

"This time of the year, they are," Beans answered. "They plant in the spring and harvest in the summer. Come wintertime, they'll abandon the village to hunt buffalo. They'll come back in the spring in time to plant the next season of crops," Beans explained.

Focusing again on the cluster of huts, Garrison zoomed in on one of its residents. The woman wore a dress that appeared to be made of buffalo hide. It was decorated with what looked like teeth. Her most striking feature was the pattern of solid and dotted lines tattooed upon her face.

"I suppose they're friendly given the fact that your friend felt it safe to establish his trading post right next door?" Garrison asked, turning to look at Beans.

"As far as I know, they're friendly," Beans replied. "At least they're friendly with Chisholm. But then again, he is half Indian," he added with a weak smile.

Garrison gave Beans a withering glance. "Just out of curiosity, what's the other half?" he asked.

Beans smiled. "Scotsman," he answered.

"You're joking," Garrison responded, the disbelief written all over his face.

"Come on, you think I could make up something like that? Hell, if my imagination was that good, I'd go back east and try my hand at writing some of them dime novels everyone is so crazy about," Beans exclaimed. Then with a mischievous grin, he added, "But you know what? Maybe I should take a shot at it. I could write all about my adventures with the Pale Rider," he teased.

Garrison shot another withering look in Beans' direction before changing the subject. "You didn't tell me Chisholm was in the cattle business," he said, pointing to their west.

Beans craned his neck to look in the direction that Garrison pointed. He could see a large herd of cattle grazing out on the western plains.

"I didn't know he was," Beans answered honestly. "I've never known him to deal in cattle before, but Chisholm is a shrewd businessman. He's not going to waste his time unless he's sure there's money to be made; you can be sure of that," he added.

"That's a pretty good-sized herd down there, wouldn't you say? Maybe two thousand head?" Garrison asked.

"Probably closer to three," Beans answered. "Why the sudden interest?" he asked.

"I've just been thinking that wrangling might be a good line of work to get into," Garrison responded. "A chance to make a little honest money and keep away from the law at the same time," he explained.

"Alright, we can ask Chisholm about it when we see him. The trading post is down there on the mouth of the river opposite the village. See it?" Beans asked, pointing toward a large wooden structure.

"You think your friend will be there?" Garrison asked.

"Only one way to find out," Beans answered as he spurred his horse forward.

Chapter Sixty-Three

"Let me do the talking," Beans whispered to Garrison as they entered the trading post. Garrison nodded his head in acknowledgment. He realized as he entered that this was the first trading post he'd been to. He had assumed that the interior would be similar to a general store, but he was only half right. It looked more like someone had taken a general store and a saloon and smashed them together. The result was rather chaotic.

To say that it was cluttered would have been exceedingly kind. Shelves lined all the walls. Crates of goods were stacked haphazardly around the room, barely leaving room for the few tables that occupied the remaining space. Furs and tanned hides were stacked in a far corner. A bar occupied the front of the building. According to Beans, Chisholm had just built the place a year ago, but Garrison could already detect a strong musty odor that threatened to overwhelm his senses.

As they approached the bar, a friendly voice called out in greeting, "Beans, my old friend, what are you doing here?"

"Howdy, Jesse. How you been?" Beans asked.

"Doing alright now that the war is over and trade is starting to pick back up," the man said with a smile. "It was hard times there for a while though. Nearly starved to death along with a band of refugees out in the western part of the territory last winter," Chisholm went on to explain.

As the two men exchanged pleasantries, Garrison took the opportunity to observe the businessman. Chisholm was older than he had expected. *Right around sixty,* Garrison estimated. His skin was a dark brown, reflecting his Native American heritage. He had a full head of wavy hair that was mostly gray but with a few streaks of black still hanging around. The ends of his mustache were white, while the hair directly under his nose was a bit darker. He had small bags under each eye. To Garrison, his eyes had a haunted quality about them, as if the man had seen more than his fair share of hard times. Garrison could relate to that.

Garrison tuned back into the conversation just in time to hear Chisholm ask about Tully and the rest of the outfit. Beans was silent for a moment. Chisholm looked expectantly from Beans to Garrison and back as he awaited an answer.

"I'm afraid we run into some real bad luck up on the range a few weeks back," Beans said. "They're all gone. Dead, I mean," Beans added. Beans then told Chisholm about the stampede that only he and Garrison had survived.

"If it wasn't for my friend, Matt, here, I'd be dead too," Beans concluded.

No one spoke for a moment. It was Chisholm who finally broke the silence. "I am truly saddened to hear of their deaths. Tully was a good man. I didn't know the others well but I'm sure they were decent folks too," he said.

Chapter Sixty-Four

Chisholm had insisted on feeding the two men before he would allow any talk of business. Garrison, for one, was grateful. They had nearly depleted his supplies during the journey, eating nothing but hardtack and beans for the past several days.

Chisholm had sat them down at one of the tables and placed a large bowl of steaming beef stew in front of each man. Garrison had attacked his with gusto, emptying his bowl seemingly before Beans had even gotten started on his.

"It's almost as good as yours," Garrison said playfully.

"Bite your tongue," Beans replied in mock annoyance.

Garrison had just opened his mouth to respond when he was cut off by a voice shouting from outside.

"Chisholm! Chisholm, you cheap bastard! You better get your ass out here right now!" the angry voice boomed.

With an annoyed sigh, Chisholm came out from behind the bar and moved toward the front of the building. Garrison began to stand but Chisholm waved for him to stay seated. Garrison and Beans exchanged uneasy glances as Chisholm walked out the front door, neither man certain what to do.

As he stepped outside, Chisholm immediately recognized the two men waiting there for him, one on horseback and the other on foot. He had sold them a pair of horses and some other supplies a couple of days ago. Both men wore the traditional buckskin clothes common among hunters and trappers in the area. The mounted man was small in stature, while his companion was a mountain of a man, standing well over six feet tall with broad shoulders. Both men wore long grizzled beards and apparently neither of them was fond of bathing. Chisholm could smell their stench from several feet away.

It was the larger of the two men who had yelled for Chisholm to come outside. His face was red with rage. He pointed at Chisholm as he spoke, his tone harsh and angry. "That horse you sold me came up lame," he accused. "Bastard threw me in the process. Bent my damn rifle and broke some of my traps," he continued, spit flying from his mouth as he spoke.

Chisholm remained silent and this only seemed to further anger the man. "Didn't you hear me, you half-bred? You owe me!" he screamed.

Chisholm's face remained emotionless, but his voice was like steel when he spoke. "I don't owe you anything."

"Bullshit!" the man yelled at him. "Way I figure it, you owe me a new horse, a new rifle, and let's say two hundred dollars for my trouble," he insisted.

"There was nothing wrong with that horse," Chisholm said firmly.

"You calling me a liar?" the man asked, his tone menacing as his fingers began to tap the grip of the pistol he wore on his left hip.

Before Chisholm could respond, another voice joined the conversation.

"If he's not, I am," Garrison said as he stepped outside. He had shed his jacket, putting his whole arsenal on display.

The two antagonists turned toward the new voice. The smaller of the two men immediately felt a sense of uneasiness wash over him. It took only a single glance to tell that this man was a killer. The larger of the two men seemed oblivious, however.

"This ain't none of your concern, mister. Now, if you know what's good for you, you'll mind your own business," the big man snarled.

Garrison's voice was calm but cold as ice when he replied, "Mr. Chisholm is a friend of a friend, which makes him my friend. I look out for my friends, so if you want to see another sunset, you best be moving on."

This only enraged the big man further. "Who do you think you are threatening me like that!? Do you know who I am?" he asked.

"Don't know and don't care," Garrison said. "To me, you're just another dead man with more guts than sense," he added.

"Them's the last words that'll ever come out your mouth," the man cried as his fingers closed around the grip of his pistol.

Compared to Garrison's lightning quickness, the man's hand moved as if it were stuck in molasses. Garrison drew the Colt from his right thigh and fired just as the man cleared leather. At this range, the round carved a canyon through the center of the man's head.

The other man began to reach for his own pistol but in the blink of an eye, he found himself staring down the barrel of the Colt in Garrison's left hand. The man slowly raised his hands.

"You want to die today, too?" Garrison asked the man.

The man shook his head violently back and forth. Fear had left him unable to speak.

"Good," Garrison said as he holstered both pistols. "Then pick up that trash," he said, pointing to the dead man, "and ride out of here right now. If you ever come back this way again, I will kill you. You understand?" Garrison asked.

The man nodded vigorously as he dismounted and struggled to lift his partner's deadweight up on to the back of his horse. After several attempts, he finally succeeded and then mounted the horse himself. He took off at a gallop and never looked back.

Chisholm and Garrison watched the man until he disappeared from view.

Chisholm turned to Garrison. "There was no need for violence. I deal with men like that every day. They put on a show and act threatening, but they're harmless. Unless you provoke them, that is."

He turned around and went inside before Garrison could respond.

Chapter Sixty-Five

"Why'd you have to go and do that?" Beans asked. "Chisholm is pissed. I thought he was going to ask us to leave there for a minute," he complained. He and Garrison were in the bunkhouse Chisholm used to house overnight visitors.

"Damn it, I was just trying to help," Garrison replied. "He didn't have to go for his gun. He made a choice and he paid the price for it," Garrison insisted.

"Oh, come on, Matt. I'm your friend and even I have to admit that it sounded like you were goading the man into it. It was almost like you wanted him to go for his gun," Beans argued.

"So what if I did? Aren't you the one who's been telling me every day for the past two weeks that I need to embrace who and what I am? That I can't keep running or hiding from the truth?" Garrison challenged.

Beans hesitated. There was some truth in what Garrison said, although Beans now realized that the man may not have grasped the message in quite the way Beans had intended. Before fate and a stampeding herd of Buffalo had brought the two together, Garrison had lived a solitary life, staying away from people as much as possible, fearful that they would recognize him and he would have to resort to violence.

It wasn't fear of his own death or the desire to live that drove him to such a solitary existence. Garrison had admitted to Beans on more than one occasion that he had no great desire to live and nothing to live for. He was simply on the run because he refused to be taken alive and subsequently hanged as a traitor. Garrison was simply going as far as he could until someone finally got the drop on him and ended his miserable existence.

Garrison had also told Beans that in many cases, killing didn't really bother him. He sincerely believed that the majority of the people he'd gunned down had needed to die. No, what ate away at Garrison's soul was when he found himself forced to kill lawmen or soldiers who were pursuing him because they had been ordered to and had been told that Garrison was a traitor and murderer.

That was why he tried so desperately to avoid towns and settlements where he would be more likely to encounter such men.

Beans had simply pointed out that perhaps Garrison thought of his existence as miserable because he wasn't really living. Wouldn't it be better to live, really live, even if just for ten days than to simply exist for ten more years? Beans had readily acknowledged that Garrison would never be able to settle down with a woman and raise a family. But that didn't mean he couldn't enjoy the pleasure of a woman's company every now and then, or a nice soft bed, the occasional bath, a hot cooked meal, or a game of poker.

When Garrison raised concerns about encounters with the authorities, Beans had insisted that Garrison shouldn't feel guilty in the aftermath of such encounters. Garrison wasn't guilty of the crimes he was being pursued for and he had no control over what other people believed about him. "If a man's trying to take your life, you should never feel guilty about doing whatever it takes to stay alive," Beans had argued.

Lastly, Beans had encouraged Garrison to embrace the persona of the Pale Rider when he needed to. Garrison could regret ever leaving that first message all he wanted to, but what was done was done. Besides, there could be times when revealing himself to be the Pale Rider might be enough to intimidate a would-be foe into standing down, ultimately preventing violence.

"Well?" Garrison finally asked, exasperated with Beans' sudden silence.

"Yeah, I did encourage you to embrace who and what you are. But I'm pretty sure I didn't say a word about picking fights and goading men into going for their gun just so you'd have an excuse to kill them!" Beans exclaimed.

Garrison felt like he had just been smacked. "Damn it, Beans! Are you blind? I didn't pick that fight. That big bastard was picking a fight with your unarmed friend. I have no doubt he would have gunned Chisholm down in cold blood if I hadn't stepped in when I did. He was exactly the kind of man the Pale Rider has a reputation for putting down. Aren't you the one who said the Pale Rider is part of who I am and that I shouldn't try to hide from it?"

"I think what I said was don't be afraid to say something like, 'My name is Matthew Lloyd Garrison and I am the Pale Rider,' because it might be enough to make some people back down. But I didn't hear you say anything like that today," Beans said.

"I didn't think that would go over well with Chisholm," Garrison explained. "You think he's pissed now? How do think he would feel if he thought you brought a notorious outlaw to see him?" Garrison challenged.

"You might have a point there," Beans admitted. "Look, why don't we give it a rest and try to get a good night's sleep? Chisholm did let us stay, so he couldn't be but so pissed. I'll get up early in the morning and talk with him about the supplies and tools we need," Beans suggested.

Garrison agreed and soon the bunkhouse was filled with sounds of their snoring.

Chapter Sixty-Six

"Your friend is a dangerous man," Chisholm said to Beans. The two men were seated in matching rockers on the trading post's front porch. Each man held a cup of steaming hot coffee in his hands. It was early morning, the sun just beginning its daily ascent.

"He's a good man, Jesse," Beans insisted.

Chisholm looked at Beans and frowned. "How well do you really know the man?" he asked.

"Jesse, I know him better than I know you," Beans answered. Seeing the scowl on Chisholm's face, he said, "Oh, I may have known you a lot longer, but I've spent more time with him in the last three weeks than I have with you in all the years I've known you."

"If," Chisholm said, putting special emphasis on the word, "he is indeed a good man, that doesn't make him any less dangerous," Chisholm warned.

Beans decided it was time to change the subject. "Thanks for putting us up last night. That bunk sure beat the hell out of sleeping on the ground."

"It was the least I could do for an old friend," Chisholm replied.

"We were hoping we could resupply here before we head into Indian Territory," Beans said.

"Sure. What do you need?" Chisholm asked.

"We're basically starting from scratch. Nothing survived the stampede other than Matt's personal supplies and we've about used them up. I didn't even have time to saddle my horse, so I'll be needing a new saddle. Some salted meat, canned vegetables, coffee, tobacco, whiskey," Beans began rattling off items as they came to mind.

Chisholm held up his hand. "I tell you what. Let's finish our coffee and then we'll go inside and make a proper list," he instructed.

Chapter Sixty-Seven

"That's some list," Chisholm commented as he tore the page from his journal. "You got the money to pay for all this?" he asked, his eyes narrowing in suspicion.

For a moment, Beans seemed embarrassed. "Matt does," he finally answered.

A look of understanding dawned across Chisholm's face. "So, he's footing the bill for this little expedition, isn't he? That explains a lot," he commented.

"Hell, Jesse, everything I owned was destroyed in the stampede. And you know how Tully operated. Nobody got paid until the hunt was over and the hides sold," Beans explained.

"So, is that the real reason you're riding with him?" Chisholm asked.

"What the hell is the matter with you?" Beans asked, clearly offended. "The man saved my life. He's my friend. It's just that simple. I tell you what, you just get our order ready and let us know how much it's going to be," he added curtly and then turned to leave.

"Now hold on just a minute," Chisholm urged. "Don't go getting all riled up over nothin'. I meant no offense. I just thought I might be able to help you out if you were looking to make some money. That's all, honestly," Chisholm explained.

Beans turned back around to face Chisholm. "I'm listening," he said.

"I'm sure you noticed the cattle grazing out on the western plains when you came in," Chisholm said. When Beans nodded, he continued, "I got three thousand head out there. Next month, I plan to drive them up into Osage County to the Sac and Fox Agency. There's only a handful of us going. Nothing compared to the size of Tully's operation, but we could still use a good cook. You know I'll give you fair pay. What do you say?" Chisholm asked.

"What about Matt?" Beans asked.

Chisholm frowned. "What about him?" he asked.

"You got a place for him on this cattle drive?" Beans asked.

When Chisholm failed to respond, Beans spoke again. "Just get our order ready. We want to be on our way by midday." With that said, he stormed off in the direction of the bunkhouse.

Chapter Sixty-Eight

It was just past midday and Beans and Garrison were still making their preparations to leave. Garrison had gone to the stable to prep the horses while Beans paid the bill and collected their other purchases. Chisholm had told Garrison to go ahead and grab a saddle and bridle from the tack room.

Once he had both horses saddled and ready to go, Garrison led them back toward the trading post. Garrison slowed as he approached the building. There was a horse already tethered in front of the building. Garrison hadn't seen it before, so he figured the trading post had a new visitor. He quickly tethered their two horses out of sight and made his way to the door.

Garrison slipped inside as quietly as possible and stood stock-still for a moment, taking in the scene before him. Chisholm was standing behind the bar as usual. Beans stood on the other side of the bar on Chisholm's left. Standing in front of the bar on Chisholm's right was a third man. He looked to be of average height. He wore typical trail clothes, complete with a healthy coating of trail dust.

The man stood at an angle to the bar so that he could face both Chisholm and Beans. From his position, Garrison couldn't see the man's face at all, but he was quick to spot the pistol tied down on the man's right thigh. As Garrison watched, the man removed a tattered yellow piece of paper from his jacket and began unfolding it.

Garrison hoped it was just a list of supplies the man needed, but he was almost certain that the man was unfolding a wanted poster, most likely one with Garrison's own face featured prominently.

"Either of you two gents seen this feller recently?" the stranger asked. He spoke with the drawl of a Texan.

As Chisholm and Beans examined the paper closely, Garrison's right hand wrapped around the handle of his Le Mat. Just then, Beans made eye contact and gave an almost imperceptible shake of his head. Garrison's hand moved away from the pistol.

"I'll be damned," Chisholm muttered after examining the poster.

"You've seen him?" the stranger asked, the excitement evident in his voice.

"Son of a bitch! I don't believe it!" Beans exclaimed. "The bastard was worth $500 dead or alive," he added.

"He was here late yesterday afternoon," Chisholm told the stranger.

"What direction did he head off in and about what time?" the stranger asked breathlessly.

"Whoa now! Don't get too excited," Beans chimed in. When the stranger gave him a puzzled look, Beans smiled and said, "He may have left here but he didn't leave alive."

"He was causing problems, threatening violence if I didn't give him what he wanted," Chisholm explained. "One of my customers came to my aid and when the man went for his gun, the customer killed him."

"You're damn lucky," the stranger told Chisholm. "The bastard was a stone-cold killer. He was wanted for ten counts of murder down in Texas. I don't suppose that customer is still here by any chance?" the stranger asked.

Chisholm glanced at Beans before answering. Garrison tensed, his hands drifting again toward his pistols. "No, he rode out early this morning, headed south toward Indian Territory," Chisholm finally answered.

The stranger frowned. "I'm assuming he took the body with him?" he asked.

Beans and Chisholm exchanged amused glances and then both men broke out in laughter. "The guy you're looking for had a partner with him yesterday. A little runt of a man. We made him carry the body off. Son of a bitch probably went straight to the nearest town and claimed the reward for himself," Beans explained to the bewildered stranger.

"That's a damn shame," the stranger commented. "I guess I'll be on my way then," he said as he turned and headed for the door.

Garrison darted behind a stack of crates just as the man turned around. If the stranger was a bounty hunter or lawman, there was a good chance he'd seen a poster with Garrison's face on it. Garrison didn't want to risk another violent confrontation.

Once he was certain the stranger had left, Garrison stepped out from behind the crates and approached Chisholm and Beans. Seeing him approach,

Chisholm spoke up and said, "Well, Matthew, it would seem that I owe you an apology. Perhaps your instincts are better than I gave you credit for." Beans was silent but he could not hide the triumphant smirk that crossed his face.

Chapter Sixty-Nine

Garrison and Diablo plodded along slowly at the rear of the procession as it made its way slowly toward the Osage River where the Sac and Fox agency was located. Both horse and rider were covered in the dust kicked up by the three thousand head of cattle that moved along ahead of them. Garrison knew that he had been assigned to this position at the rear of the herd, known as drag, because of his relative inexperience with cattle drives.

This knowledge didn't make the chore any more desirable or less miserable. Garrison thought it telling that the man riding drag to his left had been assigned the duty as a punishment. He was a young man, barely eighteen, with an apparent fondness for a strong drink. Last night, the young man, whom everyone called Kip, had let that fondness get the better of him and ended up fall-down drunk. Now he was relegated to the rear of the herd, eating dust alongside Garrison as his penance.

There were a total of six wranglers tasked with keeping the herd moving. Chisholm's trail boss, a man by the name of Tom Dickens, along with another man, rode point at the head of the herd. Two more men rode in the flank position at either side of the herd. Chisholm was somewhere near the front of the procession with the supply wagons. Beans was up there as well, driving the chuck wagon.

Garrison smiled as he thought about the cook. This was the happiest Garrison had seen him since the tragic day of the buffalo stampede. Beans still mourned the loss of his friends, as was to be expected, but Garrison could tell that the man was finally beginning to heal.

Garrison was glad that he had allowed Beans to talk him into joining Chisholm on the cattle drive. He had been hesitant at first. For starters, the cattle drive was going in the wrong direction. He and Beans had traveled to

Chisholm's trading post to pick up a trail into Indian Territory. The cattle drive was heading back up toward the Osage River to the north east. Beans had argued that it shouldn't matter. Garrison had told Beans on more than one occasion that he didn't have a plan or a particular destination in mind. So what difference did it make if they backtracked a little bit? The cattle drive would allow them to make a little money after which they could resume their journey toward Texas.

The other reason for Garrison's hesitation was Chisholm himself. The man had welcomed him when he and Beans had first arrived. But that changed the instant Garrison gunned down a man right in front of the trading post. After that, Chisholm wanted nothing to do with Garrison and had gone so far as to offer Beans a job on the cattle drive. It was not until after the bounty hunter arrived and Chisholm learned that the man Garrison gunned down was a notorious killer wanted for murder down in Texas that the invitation had been extended to Garrison.

Garrison didn't blame Chisholm for this. The man was merely trying to look out for a friend. Riding with Garrison put Beans in danger. Garrison had warned Beans of this from the start. Chisholm obviously recognized this and had offered a safer alternative. Even after he had been invited to join along, Garrison had suggested that perhaps it was time for him and Beans to part ways. This had only set Beans off and Garrison never brought it up again.

Ironically, it was Chisholm who had done the most to try to sway Garrison. The older man had approached Garrison one evening, inviting him to sit down to discuss the matter over a drink and fine cigar. Chisholm had personally asked Garrison to join the cattle drive. There was no telling what dangers they may encounter along the way and he had come to realize that it would be good to have a gun hand along.

Chisholm then increased the incentive by offering both Beans and Garrison a ten percent stake in the endeavor. At five dollars a head, each man stood to make fifteen hundred dollars. If they pooled their money together, they would make more than either man could earn in a year's time.

Garrison had promised to consider the offer and thanked Chisholm for the drink and cigar. He had then returned to the bunkhouse where Beans was waiting anxiously. Beans had nearly lost his mind when Garrison told him about the ten percent cut that Chisholm had offered. He insisted that that type of deal was usually reserved only for the trail boss. Beans had pleaded with Garrison, insisting that it was too good an offer to pass up.

And so, Garrison had finally relented. In the end, it wasn't the money or the personal invitation from Chisholm that had swayed him. He had agreed simply because it was important to Beans. Beans was the only friend he had and, in truth, was one more than Garrison had ever expected to have since going on the run. If this would make him happy, then so be it. A few days of eating trail dust was a small price to pay for a friend's happiness.

Chapter Seventy

With the herd settled for the night, Garrison and Kip were the last two to arrive in the camp. The smell of meat cooking over an open flame wafted through the air and tickled their nostrils as they approached. Garrison's stomach rumbled in response, reminding him that he hadn't eaten in nearly twelve hours.

Cattle-trailing was not what Garrison had expected. The days were both long and tedious. There was little actual work involved. Yet, Garrison found himself exhausted by the time the procession stopped to make camp each day. Thus far, he had done little more than ride along at the rear of the herd as they slowly made their way across the prairie. The pace was leisurely to allow the cattle to graze as they moved along, traveling anywhere from ten to fifteen miles per day. Even so, Garrison soon discovered that ten to twelve straight hours in the saddle took their toll on a man.

Upon reaching camp, Garrison removed his saddle from Diablo's back and took his time rubbing down and brushing the animal. As tired as he felt, he knew Diablo must be even more so. He gave the horse a sugar cube as his reward for another long day of work.

With Diablo taken care of, Garrison joined the others by the fire, doing his best to shake off the trail dust before he got there. He plopped down next to Beans, grabbed a bowl, and helped himself to the stew that the man had prepared.

The trail boss, Dickens, watched with amusement as Garrison shoveled spoonful after spoonful into his mouth. "Work up an appetite today, did you, Greenhorn?" he asked with a smile on his face.

Garrison paused long enough to give Dickens a wan smile. The trail boss' insistence upon calling him Greenhorn annoyed Garrison to no end. Equally annoying was the amusement the other men seemed to get from it. Glancing around the fire, Garrison noticed that even Chisholm and Beans wore amused expressions on their faces.

Garrison shrugged off his annoyance and gave the men a genuine smile. The truth was that he had not felt a sense of comradery like this since his days in the army. All of the men had welcomed him and done their best to make him feel at home. Dickens had begun working with him before the drive had begun, teaching him how to rope and what to expect on the drive.

Garrison was the only man among them who went heels. Beans had wasted little time letting the others know that his friend was a bona fide gunfighter. This had made Garrison somewhat of a celebrity in their eyes. Kip, being the youngest, was particularly enamored.

All of the wranglers, with the exception of Dickens, had clamored to hear stories but Garrison had refused to humor them. Beans, on the other hand, had no problem spinning a yarn or two for their entertainment. Garrison could only shake his head in amazement as he listened to the cook's completely fabricated tales. The man was quite a storyteller, with a far better imagination than he gave himself credit for. Maybe he should try his hand at writing those dime novels after all.

Before the group had left the trading post, Beans had persuaded Garrison to put on a shooting demonstration to entertain the wranglers. The men had hooted and hollered as they watched him shoot cans, first from fence posts and then out of the air. Kip had been transfixed and later begged Garrison to teach him how to shoot. Garrison had refused at first, but the young man had kept at him until he had finally relented.

Out here on the range, the sound of gunfire would spook the cattle and cause a stampede, so the men had to look elsewhere for their entertainment. All but Kip quickly grew tired of Beans' stories. Poker soon became the favored pastime for most of the men.

Tonight, would be no exception. After eating, the men lounged around the fire. Several of them rolled cigarettes, while others pulled cigars from their saddlebags. Chisholm puffed on a pipe as he watched the men unwind. Dickens pulled a harmonica from his pocket and began to play. Garrison didn't recognize the tune.

As soon as Beans finished with the crockery, he joined the group, producing a deck of cards as he sat down. A flask was passed around as the cards were dealt. Garrison, along with Dickens and Chisholm, declined both the cards and drink. Dickens was content playing the sad melody upon his harmonica. Chisholm preferred to read as he puffed on his pipe.

Garrison just preferred a little solitude. Beans had been teaching him how to play poker over the last several weeks, but in truth, Garrison just didn't find much pleasure in it. He moved away from the fire and spread out his bedroll. He leaned back against his saddle as he puffed on a cigar and took occasional sips from his own flask.

Garrison watched the others for a while before turning his eyes heavenward. As far back as he could remember, he had always loved to gaze upon the stars. He smiled as he remembered foolishly thinking that he could count them all as a child. Now as an adult, he knew better and merely contented himself to gaze upon them with childlike wonder.

The card game was still going strong when Garrison finished his cigar. He took a final sip of whiskey before tucking the flask away in his saddlebag. He then rolled over, facing away from the campfire, closed his eyes, and drifted off to sleep.

Chapter Seventy-One

Abilene, Kansas – October 1865

Zeke recognized Garrison and Beans the moment they stepped inside Old Man Jones Saloon. He waved them toward the bar with a big smile upon his face. Unlike the first time Garrison visited, the place was packed. He and Beans carefully threaded their way through the crowded tables until they finally reached the bar.

"I was starting to wonder if you guys were ever gonna come back through this way. Where's Tully and the rest of the boys?" Zeke asked. The smile slowly faded from his face when he saw the looks Garrison and Beans gave each other.

"How about you pour us each a glass of whiskey and then we'll tell you what happened out there?" Beans suggested as he and Garrison each settled down on a barstool. Zeke quickly set a pair of glasses on the counter in front of the men and filled each to the top with strong-smelling amber liquid. He watched in eager anticipation as each man took a small sip.

"Well, what happened?" Zeke asked as his impatience got the better of him.

Beans took a deep breath and then proceeded to tell the bartender about the buffalo stampede that had wiped out Tully's outfit. His voice cracked with emotion and he had to stop to gather himself several times. By the time he finished, his glass was empty and his cheeks were tear-stained.

Zeke quickly refilled the glass. "This one's on the house," he said. "You know, Ike Johnson told me his crew came across a bunch of bodies, men and horses, but there weren't much left but bones by then. Thought it might have been some kind of Indian massacre. It never crossed my mind that it could have been Tully and the boys," Zeke said, shaking his head in disbelief.

"It's a damn shame," he said as he continued to shake his head. "Tully was a good man; he didn't deserve to go out like that," he added.

"Nobody deserves to go like that," Garrison said quietly as images of broken men and horses filled his mind.

"Good point," Zeke conceded.

"Who are all these folks you got in here tonight?" Beans asked, ready to change the subject.

"Hell, Beans, you probably know at least half these folks if you take a minute and really look around," Zeke replied with a smile. "We got old Ike Johnson's crew coming in off the range and Baker's crew just getting ready to head out."

Beans took a moment to look around the room, nodding his head at those he recognized. To say he really knew half of them would be a bit of an overstatement, but he had crossed paths with at least that many over the years. He spotted Baker and gave the man a quick wave.

Turning back to Zeke, he said, "Typical Baker, going out for the big money. I always thought I'd talk Tully into going after winter coats one of these years. I guess it just wasn't meant to be."

"You know, I bet Baker would be willing to take you on," Zeke suggested.

"Nah, I've moved on," Beans told him.

"Yeah?" Zeke asked. "So, what are you up to these days, then?" he asked.

Garrison tuned out as Beans began to weave a yarn about the recent cattle drive. If the stories the man told about Garrison's gunfights were any indicator, Garrison had no doubt that the events would be embellished to such an extent that little of the facts would remain. The man was a natural-born storyteller and he never let the facts get in the way of a good story.

In all honesty, the past several weeks had been the most uneventful that Garrison had experienced in the last year or so. They'd managed to deliver all three thousand head of cattle to the Indian agency on the Osage and Chisholm had collected the promised price of five dollars a head. Chisholm had given his men their cut and then dismissed them.

Before everyone went his own way, Chisholm told them that he was planning a trade expedition down through Indian Territory and into Texas come the first of the year. He said that any of them that wanted in should be back at the trading post by mid-December. Since they were planning to head into Indian Territory themselves, Garrison and Beans had decided to accompany the old man back to the trading post.

But before they headed back, Chisholm had insisted on making a side trip to Abilene. He was hoping to do a little business with the owner of the Frontier Store. Garrison and Beans had agreed to come along. Beans wanted to let Zeke know what had happened to Tully and his crew, while Garrison was looking forward to a meal that consisted of something other than stew.

Much to his chagrin, Kip had insisted on riding with them. Garrison was more than a little uncomfortable to be the recipient of the young man's admiration. It didn't help to have Beans filling the kid's head with fabricated stories that made Garrison sound like some kind of hero.

But that was only half of the problem. The other half was the fact that the kid reminded him so much of young Johnny Watkins. Garrison couldn't think about that young man without reliving his violent death or feeling betrayed. He didn't know if Benjamin had been telling the truth when he named Watkins as his inside man, but the seeds of doubt had been planted in Garrison's mind. But even worse than that, when Garrison thought of Johnny Watkins, his thoughts inevitably turned to Olivia Watkins. When that happened, the pain would wash over him just as fresh and raw as the day he had discovered her lifeless body.

Garrison's thoughts were interrupted when Zeke pointed toward the entrance and asked, "Is he with you guys?"

Garrison half turned on his stool to see who the barkeeper was talking about. *Well, speak of the devil...*Garrison thought to himself. Standing just inside the swinging doors was young Kip. His head moved as if it was on a swivel as he searched for a familiar face. Garrison knew that he had been spotted when he saw the kid's eyes widen as a goofy grin spread across his face.

Chapter Seventy-Two

Beans waved enthusiastically, motioning for Kip to join them. The kid's eyes lit up when he saw them. He waved back with equal enthusiasm as he began to move toward them. Garrison was about to turn around when he caught sight of the holster just barely peeking out from beneath the kid's jacket.

Garrison stood and strode with purpose toward Kip, intercepting him halfway between the entrance and the bar. Without slowing, Garrison wrapped his hand around the kid's arm with a vice-like grip and practically dragged him toward the door.

"Hey! What the hell!" Kip shouted in protest.

"We need to talk. Outside," Garrison said sternly.

Once outside, Garrison guided Kip to the side, away from the entrance. Kip jerked his arm away the moment he felt Garrison's grip loosen.

"What the hell is your problem?!" Kip shouted.

"That's my problem," Garrison answered, pointing toward the gun belt the kid was wearing. "What the hell are you doing wearing a damn gun?" he added.

Kip beamed with pride as he pulled his jacket back to better reveal the pistol that hung from his right hip. "I just bought it over at the Frontier Store," he answered. "Isn't it a beauty?" he asked as he pulled the pistol from the holster and held it out for Garrison to inspect. "It looks like yours, but it's a Remington. The old man at the shop said there was a fire or something at the Colt plant, so they're hard to get now. He said this one is just as good though."

Kip had felt so proud when he had strapped on his new gun belt and tied the holster down on his right thigh. He couldn't wait to show Matt. He had expected his friend to be as excited as he was. He couldn't understand why Matt was acting this way and couldn't help but feel hurt by his friend's unexpected reaction.

"I'm sure it's a fine weapon. But you've got no business toting it around," Garrison insisted, clearly still angry.

Kip slipped the pistol into its holster when it became obvious that Garrison wasn't going to handle the weapon. "I don't see why you're so angry. I just want to be like you…a famous gunfighter," Kip said.

Garrison sighed. "That's the problem. I don't want you, or anyone else, trying to be like me. I know Beans has filled your head full of stories, but barely a word of what he's said is true. Sure, it all sounds glorious, but the truth is it's a terrible way to live. Always looking over your shoulder…"

"I thought you'd be happy that I wanted to follow in your footsteps. I just wanted to make you proud," Kip explained, now sounding dejected.

Garrison's voice and expression softened. "I like you, kid. I just don't want to see you get hurt. If you go around wearing a gun, sooner or later you're going to be put in a situation where you have to use it."

"But you taught me how to shoot," Kip protested. "Didn't I do good?" he asked.

Garrison sighed. "Shooting tin cans and shooting people ain't the same thing, kid. For starters, people shoot back. If you manage to avoid getting yourself killed, you still have to deal with the fact that you killed another person. That ain't always easy to do."

Kip was about to respond when the saloon doors burst open. Beans came barreling through. "What the Sam hell you two doin' out here?!" he exclaimed as he wrapped an arm around each of their shoulders. "It ain't right to leave a feller to drink all alone," he added as he guided Garrison and Kip back in the saloon.

Chapter Seventy-Three

"That's one hell of a story, Beans!" exclaimed the man sitting across the table from Garrison. Beans had introduced him only as 'Baker' and Garrison had remembered Zeke mentioning that the man ran a hunting outfit that was preparing to head out on the range. The man was a head shorter than Garrison and probably ten to fifteen years older. His silver hair was cut short and his beard matched it in both length and color. His clothes looked new and far too expensive to wear on the range. Garrison noted several rings of gold and silver on the fingers of both hands. A platinum pocket watch hung on the front of his vest.

Baker had been sitting alone, nursing a glass of whiskey, when Beans had introduced his friends. Baker had quickly invited them to join him and then motioned for Zeke to bring a bottle and additional glasses. That had been hours ago, or at least it felt like that to Garrison. He and Kip had sat listening in rapt attention as Baker and Beans took turns telling stories of their days hunting buffalo out on the plains.

Each man seemed intent upon outdoing the other and the stories grew more and more preposterous as the night dragged on. Eventually, Baker had produced a deck of cards and suggested they play a little poker. The two men continued to trade stories as cards were dealt and hands were won and lost. Eventually, Beans had begun to tell tall tales starring Garrison. The last of these had drawn the exclamation from Baker.

"And the sad part of it is that not a damn word of it's true!" Garrison said, nearly yelling to be heard over the noise of the packed saloon. This drew a fresh round of laughter from his companions. The whiskey had been flowing freely but Garrison was careful about how much he drank. He wasn't sure the same could be said of the other three.

If appearance was any indicator, Baker had wealth to spare and Garrison, Beans, and Kip were flush from the recent cattle drive. As a result, some of the pots grew rather large and the games more serious. Garrison wasn't fairing any better than the last time Beans had talked him into playing, but he had to admit that he was managing to enjoy himself. But that was all about to change.

Chapter Seventy-Four

Kip had won the last three pots. He radiated confidence as he raised the ante. Baker studied the young man's face closely, trying to determine if he might be bluffing. Baker looked again at the cards in his hand. A straight flush stared back at him. Only a royal flush could beat him and the odds of the kid having that were infinitesimal. His voice ringing with confidence, he called.

Silence descended as Kip slowly laid his cards out on the table, one at a time. The first card was the ten of hearts. This was followed by the Jack, Queen, and King. With a triumphant smile, Kip laid down the ace of hearts, a royal flush.

Kip was all smiles as he began raking the pot toward him. All of a sudden, Baker's hand shot out, catching hold of Kip's wrist. The kid tried to pull away, but the man's grip was too strong.

"What the hell is this?" Baker asked as he reached with his other hand and pulled several cards from Kip's sleeve. "You're a goddamned cheat!" he roared as he held the cards up for all to see.

Beans and Garrison looked at their friend in bewilderment. Kip's cheeks flushed red. He pulled his hand back when Baker released his grip. Every pair of eyes in the saloon was turned toward their table.

"That's bullshit!" Kip protested. "You put those cards there. You're just a sore loser!" Kip accused.

Looking around the room, it was clear to see that no one was buying it. Fueled by anger and humiliation, Kip lurched to his feet. "I'll teach you to accuse me of cheating!" he hissed as his hand hovered above his brand-new Remington revolver.

Baker matched his movement. For a tense moment, the two just stared at each other. Everyone in the room was holding their breath, waiting to see how this was going to play out.

Before either man could make a move, Garrison jumped to his feet and placed himself between the two men. He wasn't thinking, merely reacting, hoping to avoid bloodshed. He stood facing Kip, just a few feet from him. Garrison's left hand flashed toward Kip's waist, and before the younger man realized what was happening, his Remington was safely in Garrison's possession.

Using his right hand, Garrison backhanded Kip with such force that the kid was sent sprawling to the floor. Blood tricked from his lower lip as he looked up at Garrison in shock and anger. Garrison stared back, his features contorted by anger.

"Take that damn gun belt off!" Garrison finally demanded. "You aren't man enough to wear it. You're gonna get yourself killed, you fucking idiot!" Garrison was beyond angry.

Beans stared in wide-eyed wonder. He'd rarely heard Garrison utter such words. He'd seen him gun a man down with far less emotion than this. Beans began to feel a little tickle of fear.

Kip got to his feet and stood face-to-face with Garrison. He was near mad with rage. "I don't gotta do nothing you say!" he snarled, spit flying from his lips. "That's my pistol. You give it here!" he demanded.

Garrison handed him the weapon, grip first. There was a collective gasp from everyone in the room when the kid pointed it in Garrison's face and pulled the hammer back, everyone, that is, except for Garrison.

"You're not such a big shot now, are you? You think you can treat me like that? You're supposed to be my friend!" Kip shouted as his hand began to tremble.

Garrison didn't hesitate. His right hand shot out, his fist connecting squarely with Kip's nose. His left hand shot out to grab the pistol, his first and second finger splitting around the hammer, effectively preventing it from striking home if the kid pulled the trigger. For the second time in as many minutes, Kip found himself sprawled out on the floor. This time, blood gushed from a nose that was almost certainly broken.

The kid scrambled to his feet again. This time, he was met by the cold steel of Garrison's Le Mat pressed against his forehead. Garrison's voice was cold as ice when he spoke. "Kid, I told you before that I liked you. But if you ever point a pistol in my direction again, I won't hesitate to put you down like a rabid dog."

Everyone in the saloon breathed a sigh of relief when Garrison slipped the pistol back in its holster. Two of Baker's men approached and grabbed Kip from behind. They dragged him as he was kicking and screaming toward the entrance and tossed him unceremoniously through the swinging doors.

Garrison tucked Kip's Remington into his waistband at the small of his back. "I'll hold on to this. He's got no business with it in his current state of mind," he said in explanation.

Beans gave Garrison a reproachful look. "Don't you think you were a might hard on the kid?" he asked.

Garrison looked at his friend in exasperation. "He pulled a fucking gun on me. He's lucky I didn't kill him," Garrison replied.

"I mean before that. It might not have come to that if you hadn't humiliated him like you did," Beans said in reply.

"He was about to get himself killed! What the hell was he thinking, cheating at cards anyway?!" Garrison exclaimed.

Beans refused to relent. "I still say you were too hard on him. Made a bad situation worse."

Garrison just shook his head. "You must have lost your damn mind," he muttered as he stormed off.

Chapter Seventy-Five

Chisholm's Trading Post, Kansas – December 1865

The journey south to Chisholm's trading post from Abilene had quickly become tense and uncomfortable for all three men involved. The incident in Old Man Jones Saloon had put a serious strain on Garrison's and Beans' friendship. They hadn't seen hide nor hare of Kip since that night. A stable boy told them that he had come for his horse, riding off without paying. Garrison had settled the bill on behalf of the wayward youth.

Beans had insisted that they wait in town for a couple of days, certain that the kid would come back after he cooled off. When the second day had come and gone, Chisholm refused to wait any longer. Garrison felt bad about the whole thing. He had never intended to run the boy off. He had just wanted to teach him a lesson, one that would hopefully save his life.

Beans had grown fond of Kip and he blamed Garrison for causing the kid to run off. Garrison may have felt bad about the outcome, but as far as he was concerned, he had saved the kid's life that night. He wasn't about to apologize, and Beans doggedly refused to let the subject drop until he did. They had reached an impasse and neither man was willing to give an inch.

The tension between the two men had begun to weigh on Chisholm's nerves. Whenever an argument erupted between the two, Beans had the infuriating habit of looking to him for support. Garrison, on the other hand, was a man of action and once an action was taken, he stood behind it, whether right or wrong. He neither sought, nor needed, validation from anyone else. Chisholm respected that about the man, but it too could be infuriating.

Chisholm had come to consider both men friends and felt like he was trapped in the middle. He had known Beans for nearly a decade. While he had originally had his doubts about Garrison, he had come to both like and respect the man. Chisholm still stood by his assertion that Garrison was a dangerous man, but he had come to realize that the man possessed the restraint necessary to reserve violence as a last resort.

Garrison had demonstrated this the night in question. Chisholm had questioned Zeke about the incident, hoping for a more objective account than either Beans or Garrison were capable of giving. Garrison had acted quickly to prevent bloodshed, even placing himself in the line of fire in the process. He had showed great restraint when Kip had pointed the cocked Remington directly in his face. At the same time, Beans may have been right in thinking that the last part may not have happened had Garrison not struck the boy and questioned his manhood there in front of the entire saloon.

And so, Chisholm could see that both men had valid points. Because of this, he refused to take sides. Instead, he had simply listened in growing irritation as the two bickered back and forth, mile after tedious mile.

Needless to say, all three men breathed a sigh of relief when the now-abandoned Wichita Village came into view, nestled at the mouth of the Little Arkansas River. Its occupants were, no doubt, on the seasonal buffalo hunt, as was their custom. Unlike their white counterparts who hunted the buffalo only for their hides, the Wichita would make use of the entire animal for clothing, food, cooking fat, winter shelter, leather supplies, and medicine.

Opposite the village stood Chisholm's trading post. It was a welcome sight, as was the smoke that poured from its chimney. So too was the smile upon Tom Dickens's face as he watched the trio roll to a stop before the trading post. He stood upon the porch, flanked on either side by men that Garrison didn't recognize.

"Well, ain't you three quite a sight?" Dickens greeted them.

"It's good to see you too," Chisholm responded as he climbed down from the lead wagon. Beans, at the reins of the second wagon, followed suite, giving Dickens a wave and a smile. Garrison dismounted and stretched, relieved to finally be out of the saddle.

"Where's Kip?" Dickens asked with a concerned look on his face. Chisholm groaned inwardly, certain that he was about to be subjected to yet another argument. His concern soon proved warranted.

"Matt ran the poor kid off," Beans replied sourly as the three new arrivals approached the porch.

"Damn it, Beans!" Garrison nearly exploded. "That's horseshit and you know it! I saved that boy's life," he insisted.

"Yeah, maybe," Beans allowed. "But you didn't have to do it by knocking him on his ass and telling him he wasn't man enough to be toting a gun," he retorted.

"He didn't have any business carrying that gun! And he wouldn't have been if you hadn't been filling his head with your bullshit stories," Garrison accused.

"Well…well…well…" Beans stammered as his face grew red.

"Enough!" Chisholm said with enough force to shock both men into silence. "I've listened to this every single day since we left Abilene, and I've had enough," he scolded. Turning to Dickens, he said in a softer voice, "Tom, who are these young men?"

Dickens wore an amused expression on his face as he looked back and forth between the two. "Sure, we might as well get the introductions over with, but I gotta hear this story," he remarked.

"There'll be plenty of time for that later," Chisholm assured him.

"Well then, this here's Pete," Dickens said, indicating the man on his right. He was tall and skinny with sandy hair and a pockmarked face. He had dark purple bags beneath his green eyes, giving them a sunken appearance.

"And this big fella here we call Jumbo," Dickens said of the man on his left. The name fit him well. He was taller than Garrison but every bit as wide as Beans. Garrison guessed he had to weigh close to three hundred pounds. He had a round face that was covered with thick, dark hair.

"I figured we could use a couple more hired hands for this little trip down into Indian Territory that you've got planned," Dickens explained to Chisholm. "They both come highly recommended," he added.

Chisholm shook each man's hand. "Glad to have you," he assured both men. "Sorry you had to hear the bickering, but if you're going with us, you best get used to it," he added with a smile.

"Why don't you two take care of the wagons and horses for Mr. Chisholm?" Dickens suggested. "It seems the rest of us have some catching up to do," he explained.

The two men quickly moved to obey. Chisholm, Beans, Garrison, and Dickens watched silently for a moment or two before turning to head into the trading post.

Chapter Seventy-Six

Garrison stood on Chisholm's porch, a tin cup of hot coffee cradled in his hands, gazing up at the night sky. It was a cloudless night and the air was cold and crisp. He held the cup up close to his face, allowing the steam to momentarily warm his nearly numb nose. After one last lingering look, Garrison turned his back to the stars, gazing instead through a window at his companions who were enjoying the warmth of the fire inside.

While the men all slept in the bunkhouse, they spent a great deal of time visiting with Chisholm in his cottage. It was nothing fancy, but it was cozy and served as his home away from home. Chisholm had originally planned to be back home in the Creek Nation in time for Christmas, but it was not meant to be. While Chisholm, Garrison, and Beans had arrived at the trading post the first week in December, the wagon loads of goods Chisholm had secured from his business partner didn't arrive until late the week before Christmas. At that point, Chisholm had decided they would stay put through the holidays and then head out on the trail the first week of the coming year.

It was Christmas Eve and Chisholm had insisted that they all join him in celebration. The man treated them all as if they were his family, even the two new comers, Pete and Jumbo. Garrison watched through the window as the men inside clinked glasses of eggnog before breaking out in song. Unfortunately, the windowpane wasn't thick enough to spare Garrison from the out-of-key rendition of 'Silent Night' they belted out with drunken enthusiasm.

Garrison had quietly slipped outside when no one was looking. Judging by the look of things, his absence had yet to be noticed. It was just as well. Deep down, Garrison knew he didn't belong.

There was a time when he had looked forward to the holidays and the frivolity that so often accompanied them. But that seemed like such a long time ago now, although in actuality, only a couple of years had passed. Garrison had changed a great deal in that short amount of time. He could feel the difference within himself, even if he could never explain it.

Garrison sometimes thought that it was like a part of him had died, but that wasn't really an adequate explanation. He hadn't lost the ability to feel and to care about others. No, it was more like that part of him had been sealed behind an unbreakable wall. While the wall might occasionally crack, letting a little of the old Garrison slip through, it would never fail completely. Garrison wouldn't let it. He couldn't afford to.

While he had made friends and enjoyed the company of others despite being on the run, most of these relationships were only surface deep. Garrison seldom really let anyone in. It was better this way, for he knew that sooner or later, he would have to go his own way.

There had been exceptions, of course. He'd allowed himself to grow close to both Beans and Kip. And in both cases, the end result was disastrous. Garrison had unintentionally driven Kip away, and Beans seemed determined to hold it against him. No, from this point forward, it would be far better to be friendly but remain emotionally aloof.

Perhaps that was why he was standing in the cold watching Chisholm and the others instead of joining in their merry celebration. He had been riding with Chisholm for nearly six months and had genuinely grown to like the man. But Garrison knew their association would soon come to an end.

Once they reached Texas, Garrison would strike out on his own, while Chisholm would continue to travel up and down the trail between his trading posts. Garrison would be alone on the trail once more, unless Beans decided to continue riding with him. That seemed highly unlikely, given the current state of their friendship. Tired of the constant arguing, the two barely spoke anymore.

Not for the first time, Garrison considered whether it might be better for him to strike out on his own now instead of waiting until they reached Texas. But Chisholm knew his way through Indian Territory and Garrison did not. Plus, Chisholm knew the languages of all the tribes whose territory they would be passing through. But most importantly, Garrison had given Chisholm his word. Since that was about all he had left, Garrison would not break it unless he had no other choice.

Garrison glanced down into his empty cup and gave a sigh. He realized that he could barely feel his fingers now that they were no longer warmed by the hot coffee that he had brought out with him. It was probably best that he rejoined the others anyway.

Chapter Seventy-Seven

It was Christmas day, but there was still work to be done. The horses still needed tending. The cows still needed milking and the chickens and hogs still needed to be fed. Their basic needs couldn't take a break to celebrate the holiday, so neither could the men charged with caring for them.

Because of his natural affinity for horses, their care had fallen to Garrison. He had risen with the sun to get an early start on his chores. He had turned the horses loose in the corral so that he could muck their stalls. He had brought them all in, one by one, wiping them down and brushing them as he put them back in their stalls. He'd given each a feedbag while he tended to the next one.

Now he was finished despite the fact that it was still early morning. He'd leave tending the rest of the animals to Dickens and the others. They were probably all still in the bunkhouse, passed out where he'd left them.

Based upon the smoke he'd seen coming from the cottage's chimney while on his way to the barn, Garrison had assumed that Chisholm had risen early as well. But he couldn't be certain since he had not yet seen the man moving about. Garrison decided that he would refrain from visiting the cottage just in case. If Chisholm wasn't up yet, Garrison didn't want to wake him. He'd just head back to the bunkhouse, maybe catch a couple of more hours of sleep himself.

But as he left the barn, Garrison noted that there was now smoke coming from the chimney of the trading post. Chisholm must have had work that couldn't be put off just because of a holiday, too. *He's probably busy sorting through all his goods, deciding what to take on the upcoming trade run,* Garrison thought to himself.

Garrison had decided to stick to his original plan and head back to the bunkhouse. If Chisholm was busy working, Garrison didn't want to disturb the man. But as Garrison passed by the building, the door suddenly opened, and Chisholm's gravelly voice rang out.

"Good morning, Matthew," he called out. "And Merry Christmas!" he added.

"Merry Christmas, Mr. Chisholm," Garrison replied.

"Please, it's just Jesse. Especially today," Chisholm told him.

Garrison smiled. "Okay. Merry Christmas, Jesse," he said.

Now Chisholm smiled. "Come in and get some breakfast. Plus, I have something to give you, and I'd rather do it when the others aren't around."

Garrison's stomach growled as if to warn him that he had better not pass up the proffered meal. As Garrison made his way toward the door, he couldn't help but wonder what Chisholm wanted to give him. And on top of that, why didn't Chisholm want the others to know about it?

Chapter Seventy-Eight

Garrison scarfed down the last bite of flapjack and washed it down with a swig of hot coffee. "You know, I once teased Beans that you were a better cook, but I'll be damned if it might not just be the truth," Garrison said with a smile.

"I'm glad you enjoyed it," Chisholm replied with a smile of his own. "It saddens me to see you and him at odds like you have been," he added.

"Yeah, me too," Garrison admitted. "But I don't really know what to do about it. We can't even seem to talk about what happened without it turning into another blow up that just makes things worse," Garrison admitted.

"Well, I'm sure it will work itself out in good time," Chisholm tried to reassure him.

"I don't know," Garrison replied doubtfully.

Chisholm rose from the table and cleared the dirty crockery. He disappeared into another room only to reappear moments later with a long narrow package in his arms. It was wrapped in brown butcher's paper.

"This is for you, Matthew, for Christmas," Chisholm said as he handed the package to Garrison.

Garrison couldn't hide his surprise. "Mr. Chi…um…Jesse, you didn't have to do that," he stammered.

"Well, of course I didn't," Chisholm said with a chuckle. "It wouldn't really be a gift, if that were the case, would it? Well, go on now…open it," he encouraged.

Garrison tore away the butcher's paper to reveal a rifle, but one not like any other that he had seen. It was a lever-action repeater, like his Spencer rifles. But unlike the Spencer, which had to be reloaded from the magazine's muzzle end, the loading gate on this rifle was located on the receiver's right side. Also unique were the fully enclosed magazine and the wooden forearm.

"That's a Winchester 1866," Chisholm informed him. "Technically, it hasn't even gone into production yet. That one was part of an early production run, one of several hundred produced as samples. Now that Winchester's got an army contract, they'll start producing them in mass quantities early next year," he further explained.

"I'm not sure how Mead, my business partner, managed to get his hands on a few of them, but when he told me about them, I immediately thought of you," Chisholm continued. "I insisted he include at least one in the loads he was sending down here," he added.

Garrison was speechless. Despite his best intentions, he felt sincere affection for this man. They may have gotten off to a rocky start, but Chisholm had been nothing but kind since then. And now there was this. *So much for remaining aloof,* Garrison thought to himself.

To Chisholm, Garrison merely said, "Thank you." He simply didn't know what else to say.

"You are most welcome, Matthew," Chisholm responded. "I know you already have two rifles, but this one is supposed to be a marked improvement over earlier models."

"Why didn't you want the others around?" Garrison asked purely out of curiosity.

Chisholm smiled. "I make it a point to give my associates a small gift for Christmas, usually something I know they can use. I have gifts for the others, but I fear some may think yours to be a bit more extravagant than theirs," he explained.

"I wouldn't want anyone to think I was playing favorites," he added with a wink.

Garrison rose from the table and thanked Chisholm again for the rifle. "Is there anything I can help you with in here?" he asked.

"No, I'm afraid this is something that I have to do on my own. But there is something you could do for me," Chisholm told him.

"Name it," Garrison replied with sincerity.

"I left the ammunition for that rifle on the wagon with the other rifles. When you go out there to grab a box of ammunition for yourself, will you go ahead and remove the other weapons for me? A condition of doing business with the outposts in Indian Territory is that I not bring any weapons to trade with the native tribes," Chisholm explained.

His words stopped Garrison cold. He hadn't considered the possibility that traveling with Chisholm would bring him into close contact with federal troops. That was a recipe for disaster.

"Is there something wrong?" Chisholm asked with concern upon seeing the look on Garrison's face. "The rifles can wait if..." he began, before Garrison interrupted him.

"No, it's not that," Garrison assured him.

"Well, what is it then?" Chisholm asked.

"I guess it hadn't occurred to me that you do business with the army down there in Indian Territory too, not just the Nations," Garrison answered.

"And that's a problem?" Chisholm asked.

"It sure could be. I don't think they'll be happy to see me. Or they might be really happy to see me but not in a good way," Garrison replied.

"I was under the impression that you served in the Union Army during the war. I take it your service did not end well? You're not a deserter, are you?" Chisholm asked, a hint of alarm in his voice.

Garrison hesitated. "That's what the official record says, but it's not really that simple," he finally admitted.

"It never is. Look, Matthew, I realized the day we met that you were a man trying to outrun his past. The way I see it, a man's history is just that…history. It needn't define who he is, and you've proven yourself to me," Chisholm said.

Garrison was silent. Chisholm just continued to surprise him.

"But I know all too well that sometimes a man's past can come back to haunt him when least expected. Fortunately, there's a simple solution. We'll just have to split up when we come to the forts. We'll separate about ten miles out. Tom, Pete, Jumbo, and I will travel on to the fort, conduct our business, and pull out early the next day. You and Beans can swing wide around the fort and meet us about ten miles from the fort the next day."

Garrison breathed a sigh of relief. Chisholm had obviously already given some thought to this. The only aspect that concerned Garrison was the prospect of being stuck alone with Beans.

A mischievous grin spread across Chisholm's face. "Perhaps the two of you can put the time to good use and work out your differences," he suggested.

"Yeah, if we don't kill each other first," Garrison mumbled under his breath.

"Either way, at least I won't have to listen to the two of you bicker anymore," Chisholm replied, barely able to keep a straight face.

Chapter Seventy-Nine

Beans and Garrison were camped out a mile or so off the trail about ten miles south of Fort Arbuckle. While they huddled close to the campfire to ward of the freezing cold, Chisholm, Dickens, Pete, and Jumbo would be enjoying the warm confines of Fort Arbuckle. This was the third time the group had split up in order to keep Garrison away from the military outposts. They were following the plan that Chisholm had devised back on Christmas morning sitting in the kitchen with Garrison, and thus far, it was working out brilliantly.

Garrison was mildly surprised when not one of the men questioned Chisholm's decision to split up as they had approached that first outpost. Beans, of course, knew nearly every detail of Garrison's recent past. Unless Beans had shared those details with him, Chisholm knew only that Garrison had a past that he was trying to leave behind him. Garrison doubted that either man would have shared those details with Dickens or the two new hired hands, Pete and Jumbo.

Nonetheless, not one of them balked when Chisholm left Beans and Garrison behind, while he and the others traveled on to the outpost. And no one seemed surprised when they rendezvoused with the two men the following day, roughly ten miles south of the fort they'd just left. Beans had turned out to be the only one with complaints about the situation. He was more than a little put out by the fact that he was the one who had to stay behind with Garrison each time.

"I don't see why it's gotta be me every time. Why can't the others take a turn? It just ain't fair!" Beans grumbled as he pulled his blanket tighter around his shoulders. He was talking to himself but loud enough to make sure that Garrison, sitting on the other side of the fire, was able to hear him.

Garrison sighed and shook his head in frustration. This night was starting to play out just like the two previous occasions that he and Beans had been left alone. Garrison had sat and listened to Beans' grumbling until he just couldn't stand it anymore. Not surprisingly, an argument ensued, and it didn't take long for Beans to make it all about what had happened back in Abilene.

"Are we really going to do this again?" Garrison asked with a resigned sigh.

"Do what?" Beans asked innocently.

Garrison gave Beans a withering look. "You know damn well what I mean," he accused.

Beans just stared at him through the flames.

"And if you'd stop to think about it, you'd know why Chisholm insisted you stay behind too," Garrison told Beans.

"Yeah, he's hoping we'll settle our differences, I guess," Beans grudgingly admitted.

"So why don't we?" Garrison asked.

Beans remained silent.

"Come on, Beans," Garrison implored. "Look, I know you miss the kid and you blame me for him leaving. We've been down this road over and over again. What's done is done and there's not a damn thing either one of us can do to change that now."

Beans maintained his silence, but Garrison was good at reading people's faces. For the first time since that night, he thought he might actually be getting through to Beans. He decided to press his advantage.

"We both lost a friend that night, but it could have been worse. At least there's a chance that your paths will cross again. If I hadn't done what I did, Baker would have killed Kip. Then that loss would be permanent. Would you be any less angry with me then?" Garrison asked.

"Naw, I reckon not," Beans answered. "I just miss the kid, and I wonder what's become of him," he added.

"I do too," Garrison admitted. "Maybe I could have handled it differently, but in the heat of the moment, I did what I felt like I had to. It wasn't enough just to stop that fight from happening. I kept thinking of what would happen if the kid did that again sometime when I wasn't around to step in. I wasn't trying to save his life just that one night," Garrison explained.

"I guess I can see where you're coming from," Beans said.

"Like I said before, we both lost a friend that night. I don't want to lose another one, but it's all up to you. Either you can forgive me or you can't. But if you can't, I need you to tell me that now. I'll understand if you can't. But if that's the case, it'll be time for us to go our separate ways. I'll say my goodbyes to Chisholm in the morning and then be on my way. We just can't keep going like this." Garrison fell silent. He'd said all he had to say. It was all up to Beans now.

"Aw hell, Matt! I don't want to lose another friend either. Truth is I don't even know why I've been holding such a grudge. Sure, I liked having the kid around, but it ain't like he and I been through it together like you and I have. I mean we've seen some shit together, haven't we? Hell, you saved my life."

Garrison smiled. "Does that mean we can finally put this behind us?" Garrison asked hopefully.

"I reckon so," Beans agreed.

Beans cast a furtive glance around as if he could see in the darkness that surrounded the camp and then reached into his jacket and produced a small flask. He gave Garrison a sly grin. "I know Chisholm said we wasn't supposed to bring any alcohol down into the territory, but this calls for a celebratory drink, don't ya think?" he asked as held the flask out to Garrison.

Chapter Eighty

"You boys are just in time for breakfast," Beans called out as Chisholm, Pete, and Jumbo climbed down from the wagons that had just rolled to a stop at the campsite. Dickens, who was on horseback, dismounted and hitched his horse before joining the others around the campfire.

"Glad to see you two managed to get through another night without killing each other," Dickens said. "Or freezing to death," he added with a chuckle.

"Go on. Rub it in. Why don't ya?" Beans shot back. "Next, you're gonna tell us all about how you slept in a nice, warm bed, I reckon?" he retorted.

Dickens smiled as he sipped on his cup of hot coffee. "Well, I had to settle for a cot, but I was nice and cozy," he replied.

"Yeah well, if they knew you like I do, they would've made you sleep in the hay with the horses," Beans shot back.

Chisholm smiled as he listened to the good-natured banter. He sensed a change in Beans' demeanor this morning and hoped it meant that he and Garrison had finally settled their differences. His hopes began to diminish, however, when he glanced over at Garrison. The young man wore a troubled expression upon his face.

"Are you alright, Matthew?" Chisholm asked.

"Yeah, Greenhorn, you okay? You're awful quiet this morning," Dickens chimed in.

Garrison had noticed something disturbing when he had watched the men approach the fire. Dickens, Pete, and Jumbo each now wore a six-gun tied down low on his right thigh. Dickens had led the cattle drive from the Wichita Village to Abilene without going heels. And they had traveled almost all the way through Indian Territory without the man feeling the need to arm himself. Why the sudden change? As he pondered the possibilities, Garrison felt a sense of uneasiness wash over him.

Garrison ignored Chisholm and spoke directly to Dickens, "I'm just wondering why you and the boys are all going heels all of a sudden. Do you three even know how to use those things?"

Before Dickens could answer, Pete spoke up. "Well enough," he assured Garrison, sounding defensive. There was a hard look in the man's eyes that Garrison hadn't seen before.

"We picked them up at the fort last night. The post commander warned me that there's a vicious gang of outlaws that's been causing trouble down here lately. He suggested we arm ourselves," Dickens explained.

Garrison considered Dickens's answer as he tried to read the man's face. It was a reasonable explanation, but there was something about the way Dickens spoke that failed to ease Garrison's concerns. It was almost as if the answer was rehearsed.

"We just thought that if we did run into that gang, you might appreciate having some help fighting them off," Dickens offered as further explanation.

Garrison forced a smile. He didn't want to alert Dickens to his suspicions. "Just try not to shoot yourself in the foot," he finally said.

Garrison wasn't the only one harboring suspicions. Sitting next to Dickens, Chisholm found himself questioning the man's explanation. Chisholm had known the post commander for years and found it more than a little strange that the man had not seen fit to share the warning directly with him. He cast a meaningful glance at Garrison as he decided to change the topic.

"I get a sense that our two warring factions might have finally reached a peace accord last night," Chisholm said. "Might that be the case or is it simply an old man's wishful thinking?" he asked.

The smile on Garrison's face now was genuine. "Yeah, I think we did," he answered. His answer was met with a round of cheers from his companions.

"Well, hallelujah!" exclaimed Dickens. "It's about damn time," he added with a smile.

Chapter Eighty-One

Breakfast had been finished and the camp was broken down. Beans had already gone to ready the chuck wagon. Garrison stamped out the last dying embers of the fire. Dickens sent Pete and Jumbo to mount their respective wagons and then headed off to retrieve his horse. That left Chisholm and Garrison standing alone for a moment.

"I am very pleased that you and Beans could come to an agreement," Chisholm said.

"Me too," Garrison admitted. "Did the post commander say anything to you about this gang of outlaws?" he asked.

Chisholm's expression grew troubled. "No. No, he did not. What are you thinking?" Chisholm asked.

"I don't know for sure," Garrison admitted, "but something just doesn't feel right."

"I've known Tom Dickens for many years now and he has never given me a reason to distrust anything he's said," Chisholm told Garrison.

"Let's just hope you'll still be able to say that tomorrow," Garrison replied.

"Indeed," was all Chisholm could think to say in reply.

The two men turned and walked toward the lead wagon, which would be driven by Chisholm. They were met there by an unexpected and unwelcome sight.

"Not so fast," Dickens said. He was flanked on either side by Pete and Jumbo. All three men had their pistols drawn and aimed at Garrison and Chisholm.

"What's the meaning of this, Tom?" Chisholm angrily demanded.

"Come on, Jesse. Are you really gonna sit there and tell me you didn't see the poster in the commander's office last night?" Dickens snarled.

"What poster?" Chisholm asked, genuinely unsure of what the man was talking about.

"The one with his face on it. The one offering a five-thousand-dollar reward for his capture," Dickens answered.

"I don't know what you're talking about. I didn't see any such poster," Chisholm responded truthfully.

"It ain't no matter. Me and the boys have talked it over and we aim to collect that reward. We're taking you back to Fort Arbuckle with us, Garrison. We'd prefer to deliver you alive 'cause it pays more, but we'll settle for dead if you force us to," Dickens said, looking directly at Garrison now.

Garrison and Chisholm stood side by side, both men with their hands raised. For a moment, Garrison thought about going for his guns, just like he did back in Independence. But he had no doubt that these men would not hesitate to open fire, and if that happened, there was a good chance Chisholm would get hit too. Garrison couldn't risk that, not after all the man had done for him.

"Don't do this, Tom," Chisholm implored. Then, without warning, he stepped forward and to his right, placing himself between Garrison and the three gunmen.

"Get out of the way, Jesse," Dickens ordered.

Chisholm simply shook his head, his eyes gleaming defiantly.

"Don't think I won't shoot you if I have to," Dickens warned.

"Move, Jesse," Garrison said softly. "I don't want you dying for me," he added.

Still, Chisholm refused to step aside.

"I mean it, Jesse. Don't make me kill you!" Dickens shouted.

"Your greed is the only thing making you do anything right now," Chisholm replied angrily.

Garrison's eyes widened in surprise as Beans came out from behind the wagon, a large cast-iron skillet held high above his head. With an enraged roar, he charged toward Dickens, Pete, and Jumbo. All three men turned their heads toward the sound. Pete, who stood on Dickens, left, whirled completely around and aimed his pistol at the crazed cook.

Garrison didn't hesitate to take advantage of the distraction. He shoved Chisholm out of the line of fire with his left hand while he simultaneously drew the Le Mat with his right. He started with Pete, on his right, and worked his way to the left, fanning the hammer with his left hand to fire off shot after shot.

All three men went down in a hail of hot lead as gun smoke swirled through the air.

Chapter Eighty-Two

Beans stood stock-still, staring wide eyed at the carnage lying at his feet, the skillet still held high over his head. Chisholm rose slowly to his feet, brushing the dirt from his clothes. Garrison glanced quickly toward him before turning back to Beans.

"You can put the pan down now, you crazy fool," he said as he holstered his pistol.

Beans slowly lowered the pan, holding it at his side. "Who are you calling a fool?" he asked defensively. "I'm pretty sure I just saved your life," he said proudly.

Garrison began laughing. He couldn't help himself.

"What's so damn funny?" Beans asked, sounding defensive once more.

"Three men just lost their lives. I fail to see anything humorous about that," Chisholm said sternly.

Garrison struggled to control his laughter. "I know. I just can't get the sight of Beans charging out from behind that wagon with a damn frying pan out of my head. I don't know anybody else who could bring a frying pan to a gunfight and live to tell about it. I can only imagine what was going through their minds when they turned around and saw him charging at them with that crazy look in his eyes."

Now Beans began laughing as well. Even Chisholm allowed a brief smile to cross his face. "It was quite a sight," he admitted.

The sense of levity soon passed as the enormity of what had just happened began to sink in. For a moment, the three men stood in silence, looking down at the bodies of their former trail mates. Each of them felt betrayed, but none more so than Chisholm. He had known and trusted Dickens for many years. And that trust had been betrayed when Dickens threatened to kill him when Chisholm had dared to stand between the man and his reward.

"Greedy son of a bitch," Beans spat, effectively summing up what each man was thinking.

Garrison was watching Chisholm's face. He thought back on the day they met. Garrison had killed a man in front of Chisholm that day. Chisholm had voiced strong disapproval despite the fact that the man had been threatening his own life. And that man had been a complete stranger. Garrison could only imagine what was going through Chisholm's mind as he stared down at the corpse of an old friend.

"Jesse, I had to do that," Garrison said quietly. "Pete would have killed Beans if I hadn't," he explained. When Chisholm failed to respond, Garrison sighed and said, "But I know it's my fault. If I hadn't been with you, if there weren't a price on my head, none of this would have happened. I think maybe it's time for me to strike out on my own," he suggested.

"Matthew, I told you once before that a man's past is just that. What matters to me is who you are and what you do today, not what you've done in your past," Chisholm said, looking Garrison in the eye as he spoke.

"I killed three men today, one of whom was a friend of yours," Garrison said.

"Yes, you did," Chisholm agreed. "But just as important is what you didn't do," he added.

"I'm not sure I know what you mean," Garrison replied in confusion.

"You didn't go for your gun until Beans' life was in danger. And even then, your first action was to make sure I was out of the line of fire. You could have gone for your gun before that. I know you wanted to. And I know that the reason you didn't was because I was standing right next to you. You made up your mind to give yourself up rather than risk any harm to me. That's what real friends do, Matthew."

"And what's all this talk about taking off on your own anyway?" Beans chimed in. "This is the second time you've brought that up. It had best be the last."

"I just don't want to see either one of you get hurt because of me. Five thousand dollars is a lot of money. Men like these, and a whole lot worse, are going to keep coming. If we're together when they do, you'll be in danger," Garrison explained.

"Be that as it may. That's our choice," Chisholm replied. "I've already told you how I feel about it and I think Beans has made his feelings on the matter rather clear as well."

"Damn right," Beans agreed.

"Jesse, aren't you the least bit curious to know why there's such a big bounty on my head?" Garrison asked.

"No, I'm not. I meant what I said. Your actions since I've known you tell me all I need to know," Chisholm assured him.

"Well, I guess that's settled then," Garrison responded.

"Indeed. Now, what should we do with these three?" Chisholm asked, looking again toward the three corpses on the ground.

"I say we leave them for the buzzards and coyotes," Garrison answered coldly.

"That seems a bit harsh. I almost feel like we have to give them a proper burial," Chisholm said.

"Harsh or not, they earned it," Garrison insisted.

"What do you think we should do, Beans?" Chisholm asked the cook.

Beans hesitated. He looked at Garrison and then at Chisholm before responding. "Fuck it," he said at last. "Let the bastards rot," he answered vehemently.

"Very well then," Chisholm conceded. "Let's mount up and get moving then," he instructed.

Chapter Eighty-Three

Spanish Fort, Texas – March 1866

It had taken over a year and a half, but Garrison had finally arrived in Texas. They had taken their time traversing the latter half of the trail through Indian Territory after the shootout with Dickens, Jumbo, and Pete. They had only come across one additional military outpost along the way and Chisholm had gone there alone, leaving Garrison and Beans to work their way around the outpost. While at the outpost, Chisholm had managed to recruit two new hired hands from among the civilian population there.

Garrison hadn't bothered to learn the names of the two new men. It would be easier to avoid becoming attached to them that way. The incident with Dickens, Jumbo, and Pete had rattled him far more than he let on. While he hadn't been as close to any of them as he was to Beans and Chisholm, Garrison had considered all three men to be friends. Their betrayal had awakened him to the realization that he would never be able to fully trust anyone again. He found himself wondering if there might come a point at which even Beans or Chisholm might be tempted to turn on him.

Garrison tried his best to cast such thoughts from his mind and concentrate instead on the journey that had brought them at long last to Texas. They had forded the Red River a few miles upstream at a place called Red River Station. The river flowed from the panhandle of Texas eastward, forming a natural border between Texas and Indian Territory before running through Arkansas and into Louisiana.

After crossing, they had followed the river along its bank eastward toward Spanish Fort. This would be the last stop before beginning the long trek back to Chisholm's trading post in Kansas. Neither Garrison nor Beans would be making the return trip. Reaching Texas had been Garrison's primary objective since the night he rode out of Atlanta all those months ago. Now that he was finally here, he planned on staying awhile. He hoped that in a state as big as Texas, he would find plenty of open spaces perfect for eluding his pursuers.

With their fractured friendship finally repaired, Beans insisted that he would continue to ride by his side. Garrison had mixed feelings about this. As much as he had enjoyed the company, a part of him had hoped that Beans would choose to return with Chisholm. That would be the safest choice, and Garrison cared a great deal about his friend's wellbeing, even if it meant a return to the solitary existence Garrison had known before meeting Beans. A sudden shout of joy drew Garrison's attention from his thoughts and back to the here and now.

"There it is! Spanish Fort!" Beans exclaimed as the town came into view. Located about a mile south of the Red River, the town derived its name from the nearby remains of an Indian village. The first Anglo settlers in the area had mistaken the ruins for an abandoned Spanish outpost. The name had stuck even after the mistake had been realized.

As they drew closer, Garrison sized up the town. The buildings all appeared relatively new and in good shape. The trail leading into town split just before the town. The left fork led up a hill where a large saloon sat all alone.

The right fork led through the center of town. It was lined with several businesses. Garrison noted with interest that the first building they passed was the sheriff's office. It probably wasn't a coincidence that it was located on this end of town, closest to the saloon. Garrison also spotted a hotel, restaurant, and laundry as they made their way down the dusty street. The livery stable was located on the opposite end of the town. This was where they were headed. There'd be plenty of time to tour the town once the horses had been tended to.

Chapter Eighty-Four

Beans, Chisolm, and Garrison looked up as the man approached them. The three were sitting at a small table in the restaurant, enjoying a hot meal. The stranger walked right up to the table and stood, looking down at them.

"Please pardon the interruption," the man said with a smile. He was tall and lanky. Sandy brown hair hung down to his shoulders from beneath a wide brimmed hat. He had dark eyes and wore a bushy handlebar mustache. He was dressed in town clothes. He wore a pistol across his mid-section, positioned for a right-handed crossover draw. A gold star gleamed from his vest.

"My name is Sam Smith, and I'm the sheriff here," the man explained.

Chisholm smiled up at the man as he wiped his face. "What can we do for you, sheriff?" he asked.

"Oh, nothing. I just saw you fellers ride in a bit ago. I make it a point to introduce myself to any newcomers who pass through our little town," the sheriff answered.

"Pleased to meet you, sheriff," Chisholm said. "I'm Jesse Chisholm and these are my friends Beans and Matthew," he added.

The sheriff nodded at each man. "Beans, huh? That's an interesting name," the man said.

Beans smiled and said, "They call me that 'cause I make the best beans on the plains."

"I see," commented Smith. "Anyway, lots of folks pass through here, and some like to cause trouble. That's why I like to let new folks know right off the bat what's expected. We won't tolerate any drunkenness, tomfoolery, and," he paused to give Garrison an intense look, "absolutely no gunplay," he finished.

Chisholm gave the sheriff a sincere look. "Sheriff, I assure you that you'll get no trouble from us. I've got some business to tend to tomorrow, but I expect we'll be moving on the day after that."

Sheriff Smith smiled. "Well, if that's the case, I hope you enjoy your stay. I'll leave you to finish your meal." With that, he turned and left.

After the sheriff's departure, the three friends looked at one another. "Well, that was a bit strange, don't you think?" asked Beans.

"I suppose," agreed Chisholm.

"Felt more like a warning than a welcome to me," commented Garrison.

"Well, either way, I meant what I said when I told the man that he'll get no trouble from us," Chisholm said. He fixed each man with a stern stare. "Please don't make a liar of me," he implored his companions.

"You've got nothing to worry about," Beans assured Chisholm. Garrison didn't respond. He'd already gone back to eating. Beans and Chisholm quickly followed suit.

"Well, what's next, gentlemen?" Beans asked as the three finished their meal and sat contentedly. Chisholm puffed on his pipe, while Garrison lit a cigar. Beans didn't smoke, so he settled for a slice of peach cobbler and hot coffee.

"A good night's sleep," Chisholm answered.

"That sounds good to me," Garrison agreed.

"Aw, you guys are no fun," Beans complained. "How about we head up to that saloon? Have us some whiskey? Maybe play a little poker? What do you say?" he asked hopefully.

Chisholm frowned. "Beans, you've known me long enough to know that I'm not one to throw my money away."

"How about you, Matt?" Beans asked.

Garrison hesitated. He knew how much Beans enjoyed a lively saloon and he wanted to spend time with his friend, especially now that they had managed to mend their fractured relationship.

At the same time, he couldn't forget how their last visit to a saloon had ended. And that altercation had occurred with one of their own companions. They didn't know anyone here. Garrison could only imagine how much worse things could go.

"I don't think it's a good idea," Garrison finally responded.

"Oh, come on!" Beans exclaimed. "What's gotten into you? You used to enjoy going to the saloon with me. What happened?" he asked.

"Two things," Garrison answered. "First is what happened the last time we stepped foot in a saloon. You know, in Abilene? Second is what happened out on the trail. There's a good chance that posters like the one Dickens saw have made their way down here," he went on to explain further.

"What's either one of those things got to do with whether or not you go to the saloon tonight?" Beans asked.

"That sheriff already warned us about staying out of trouble and Jesse's promised the man that we'll steer clear of any. The saloon is the one place in town where we'd be most likely to run into trouble, especially if someone in there recognizes me. It would be best if I didn't show my face around town any more than I have to," Garrison told him.

"I think that is a wise choice, Matthew," Chisholm chimed in.

"I just think it would be smart to steer clear," Garrison explained. "For all of us," he added emphatically.

Beans gave him a cross look. "You can do what you want, but don't you dare go about assuming you know what's best for me." He stood and thanked Chisholm for dinner. "I'm gonna have me a whiskey or two and play some poker. I'll see you two bores in the morning."

Garrison decided to try lightening the mood. "Well, if you insist on going up there alone, at least do me a favor?"

Beans paused a moment. "What's that?" he asked.

"At least take a frying pan with you," Garrison said, struggling to maintain a straight face.

Beans stood and stared for a moment. Despite his best effort, the anger just drained from his face. Soon, all three men were laughing hysterically, while the restaurant's other patrons stared at them in bewildered silence.

Chapter Eighty-Five

Garrison had gone straight to the hotel after dinner. Chisholm had done the same. Beans had stubbornly insisted on going to the saloon. Garrison had disapproved, but as Beans himself had pointed out, he wasn't the man's keeper.

Now alone in his room, Garrison removed his gun belts and hung them over the bedpost as was his custom. He sat down on the bed and wearily tugged his boots off. He stood and walked to the nightstand sitting by the head of the bed. He snuffed out the flame of the oil lamp sitting there, plunging the small room into darkness. He then stretched out on the bed and closed his eyes. As usual, he slept fully clothed atop the bed sheets.

Garrison was worn down from countless days on the trail, so sleep came quickly. With sleep came the nightmares that continued to haunt him. He was back in Old Man Jones Saloon with Beans and Kip. They were playing cards, trading stories, and laughing with Baker. Then everything went to hell. Baker accused Kip of cheating and the humiliated young man stood and challenged the older man, his hand hovering above his new Remington.

Garrison wanted to intervene, but he was rooted in place, unable to move. He watched in horror as Baker made his play. Everything seemed to unfold in slow motion. Baker fired, the shot resounding in Garrison's head. But it wasn't Kip that Baker shot. Beans' eyes widened in shock as a crimson stain spread across his shirtfront. Baker kept firing again and again, his pistol's ammunition seemingly limitless. Each shot rang loud in Garrison's ears. *Boom! Boom! Boom!*

Garrison's eyes flew open to see early morning light streaming in through the room's lone window. Inexplicably, the shots continued to ring in his ears even now that he was awake. *Boom! Boom! Boom!* His sleep-addled brain finally recognized that it wasn't gunshots that he was hearing but rather someone pounding on his door.

The pounding grew more frantic. They were soon joined by Chisholm's hoarse voice. "Matthew! Matthew! Are you in there?"

Garrison cautiously opened the door. He held a cocked pistol concealed behind his back, just in case. The look on Chisholm's face sent a spike of fear coursing through Garrison's body. The man quickly made his way into the room, taking a seat in the chair that sat across from the bed.

"I fear something terrible has happened, Matthew. Beans was supposed to meet me for breakfast this morning, but he never showed up," Chisholm told him.

Garrison visibly relaxed, easing the hammer forward on his pistol. "He's probably just sleeping off a hangover," he suggested.

Chisholm gave him a withering look. "Do you really think I didn't consider that? I checked with the clerk downstairs. Beans never checked in last night. There's something else too. The townsfolk are acting awfully strange and tightlipped," Chisholm told him.

"Okay," Garrison said as he began to strap on his gun belts. "You wait here. I'll go to the saloon and see what I can find out," he told the older man.

Chapter Eighty-Six

"It's awful early for a drink," said the man behind the bar jovially. The smile disappeared from his face when he looked up to see the stranger who had just entered. It was one of the newcomers who had arrived in town late the day before. Worse, it was the man everyone in town was whispering about, the man loaded down with pistols, the one with the icy blue eyes of a stone-cold killer.

Garrison approached the bar slowly, registering the man's sudden discomfort. The man's hands began to tremble so badly that he had to set down the glass he was busy drying. The man radiated fear and Garrison wondered why.

"What…what…what can I get you?" the man stammered.

Garrison gave the man a smile as he looked around the empty saloon. "Just a little information," he answered as his eyes settled on a large blood stain on the floor near one of the tables. "Did you have some trouble in here last night?" Garrison asked, pointing toward the stain.

"No…not…nothing that we couldn't handle," the nervous barkeep answered.

"A friend of mine was in here last night. Big guy, always smiling. You remember him?" Garrison asked.

The look of fear on the barkeep's face turned to one of abject terror. "You…you…best talk to the sheriff," he answered.

Garrison was becoming increasingly concerned. "The sheriff? Why? What happened?" he asked with an edge to his voice.

"Plea…plea…please, just go see Sheriff Smith," the man pleaded.

Garrison emerged from the saloon to find Chisholm waiting for him.

"Well?" the man asked anxiously.

Garrison frowned. "Something happened in there last night, but the barkeep won't say what," Garrison reported. "We need to go see the sheriff," he told Chisholm.

Chisholm frowned. "That doesn't sound good," he commented.

"No, it doesn't," Garrison agreed, beginning to fear the worst.

Chapter Eighty-Seven

Sheriff Smith was sitting at his desk when Garrison and Chisholm entered. The man looked up when he heard the door open and greeted the two men with a grim expression. He leaned back in his chair, looking the men over.

"Thought I'd be seeing you this morning. Well, Mr. Chisholm, I guess we know your assurances aren't worth much," Smith said.

Garrison was looking at the two cells set toward the rear of the small office. He had hoped to find Beans occupying one of them, but both were empty. Deep down, he knew what this meant, but he needed to hear the sheriff say it.

"What happened?" Chisholm asked, beating Garrison to the punch.

"As best as I can determine, your friend got into it with one of the locals over a card game," Smith explained.

"Where is he?" Garrison asked.

"You friend? I'm sorry to have to tell you…but your friend is dead," the sheriff told them. He didn't sound all that sorry to Garrison.

"You know who did it?" Garrison asked, his voice hard as steel.

"Well, sure," Smith replied. "Got about ten or twelve men that witnessed the whole thing," he added.

Garrison frowned. "If that's the case, why isn't the bastard in one of these cells?" he asked.

Now it was the sheriff's voice that took on a hard edge. "Around here, we don't lock a man up for defending himself," he answered.

Chisholm and Garrison exchanged puzzled looks. "Wait. Are you saying that someone shot down our friend in self-defense?" Chisholm asked incredulously.

"That's exactly what I'm saying," Smith answered.

"That's absurd!" Chisholm exclaimed. "Beans wasn't even armed. I've known the man for well over ten years and in all that time, he's never carried a gun," Chisholm added.

The sheriff's face contorted in anger. "Are you calling me and a dozen decent citizens of this town liars?" he accused.

Garrison spoke before Chisholm could get a word out. "I doubt this town even has a dozen decent citizens," Garrison stared coldly at Smith as he spoke.

The sheriff leaped to his feet, his face turning red with rage. "I've heard enough out of you two! And you," he said, pointing at Garrison, "I can read your face plain as day and I know what you're thinking. Forget about it. You go looking for revenge and you're just gonna get yourself and your friend here killed," he snarled.

"The best thing for the two of you to do right now is go get your wagons and ride on out of here. We'll take care of burying your friend," Smith instructed.

"No," was Garrison's one-word reply.

"Excuse me?" Smith asked angrily.

"We'll go, but we're taking our friend with us," Garrison clarified.

"That's fine too. You can pick his body up at the undertaker's shop down on the other end of town. Just do it now and get the hell out of here before you find yourselves in more trouble than you can handle."

Garrison turned to Chisholm. "Let's go."

"But..." Chisholm began to object, but Garrison was already moving toward the door. He had already reached the conclusion that further talk would accomplish nothing. He knew what needed to be done, but he had to get Chisholm away from here first.

Chapter Eighty-Eight

Sheriff Sam Smith watched the sad little procession as they rolled past his office on the way out of town. He was relieved to see them go. And yet, he couldn't shake the feeling that things weren't over yet. He knew the one calling himself Matthew was hungry for vengeance. The way he was heeled, Smith had no doubt that he was some kind of a gunslinger.

Smith had felt the hatred radiating from him earlier that day in his office. Smith was certain that the man wouldn't hesitate to kill him if given a chance. He was pretty sure that the man had wanted to then, but he had held himself in check. Smith feared that it wouldn't last. Men like that don't just walk away in situations like this.

Not for the first time, Smith questioned his decision not to make an arrest. By the time he got to the saloon last night, the big man from out of town was already dead. He lay in a pool of his own blood. Every man in the saloon, including the barkeep, had insisted it was a case of self-defense. Smith was friends with every single one of them, including the shooter, and he wanted to believe them.

He could see a gun held loosely in the dead man's hand. But he also noticed that the man wasn't wearing a holster and he wondered if someone may have placed the gun in his hand after the shooting. In the end, he had decided not to question it. Hell, it didn't really matter what had happened. With all these witnesses, there was no way a jury would convict the shooter, so why even bother making an arrest?

Smith looked up to see that the gunslinger had stopped right across from him. He didn't say a word. He just sat atop that massive horse and stared at Smith. The look the man gave him made Smith's blood run cold. Now he was certain; this was far from over. Without a word, the man spurred his horse forward to catch up with the three wagons.

They were about two miles out of town when Garrison brought the procession to a halt. Chisholm, in the lead wagon, looked at him expectantly. The two hired hands brought their respective wagons to a halt behind him. They exchanged a worried look. Neither man went heels and they both wanted to avoid any trouble.

Garrison ignored the two hired hands and spoke directly to Chisholm. "You go on ahead. Find a nice spot out on the prairie somewhere to bury Beans. He spent most of his life out there. I think he'd rather be laid to rest there than some two-bit town he spent less than a day in."

"What are you going to do?" Chisholm asked.

Garrison just looked at him for a moment. "I'm pretty sure you already know," he finally answered.

"I'd like to hear you say it, all the same," Chisholm responded.

Garrison shrugged. "Okay, I'm going back to that town. I'm going to find the man that killed Beans and I'm going to kill him," Garrison said.

The casualness with which the man talked about killing scared Chisholm more than a little. "You know that sheriff is not going to just stand by and let you do that," he protested.

"No, I imagine I'll probably have to kill him too," Garrison replied without emotion. "Probably have to kill their friends too," he finished.

Chisholm just shook his head. "That's a lot of killing for one man, Matthew. And for what? It won't bring him back. Do you really think that this is what Beans would want?"

"I don't know that it's what he'd want. But it is what he'd expect. You see, he knew a secret that I guess he never shared with you. A secret about who and what I really am," Garrison told him.

"And who are you really, Matthew?" Chisholm asked.

"My full name is Matthew Lloyd Garrison. Some call me the Butcher of Bent Pines. I don't own up to that one. They also call me the Pale Rider. Death personified. That's who I am, what I am," Garrison answered.

Chisholm regarded him for a moment. "Don't you think you're being a bit melodramatic?" he asked.

Garrison shook his head. "Beans knew it was true and he accepted it. Hell, he tried to help me come to grips with it. It's a shame it took him dying for me to finally get it. But I get it now. I've got to do this. As surely as a man has got to have air to breath, I've got to do this. My mind's made up."

With a resigned sigh, Chisholm asked, "Assuming you survive, will you be meeting up with us somewhere?"

"No, I'll have to go my own way. I'd only bring you more trouble in the long run. Beans wouldn't want that. It's been a pleasure knowing you, Mr. Chisholm." There was a distinct note of finality in Garrison's voice.

"Well, good luck then, Matthew," Chisholm said.

There was really nothing else left to say. He snapped the reins and urged the horses forward, waving for the men in the other wagons to follow. As the wagons rolled past him, Garrison noticed that both men had turned deathly pale and looked on him with wide-eyed fear. They had obviously overheard enough of the conversation to now know who it was they had been riding with these past few weeks.

Garrison sat silently upon Diablo, watching until the wagons disappeared over the horizon. Once he could see them no longer, he set out to find a place where he could prepare. He wouldn't return to Spanish Fort until dusk approached, which gave him plenty of time to do what was needed.

Chapter Eighty-Nine

Night was just beginning to fall as Garrison rode slowly back into the town of Spanish Fort. He came riding in from the west, the setting sun at his back. He rode slowly, in no hurry.

There weren't many folks out and about. The few that were, stopped and stared. Garrison could see a dozen or so people sitting in the restaurant. They too were staring as he made his way past them.

Garrison was sure he made quite the sight. He was dressed all in black. He had decided against wearing an overcoat. He fully expected to need all of his pistols and he didn't want anything to impede his access to them. Of course, this also meant that everyone could see that he was loaded down and ready for battle. He hoped the sight inspired fear.

Garrison had a satchel slung over his neck and left shoulder. Inside, the satchel was divided into two sections. One was filled with paper cartridges for his Colt revolvers. Each cartridge contained a pre-measured load of black powder and a ball, wrapped in nitrated paper. Using these cartridges significantly reduced the time it took to reload.

Even five pistols might not be enough to do what was needed without reloading, so Garrison had come prepared. With the cartridges, all he had to do was slip the cartridge into the front of the chamber and seat the ball with the loading lever ram, located right under the barrel. The last step was to place a cap on the nipple at the back end of the chamber. The second pocket in the satchel was filled with these caps.

Garrison dismounted and hitched Diablo to the hitching post right outside the saloon. He reached into his saddlebag and removed the Remington that he had taken from Kip. He tucked it into his waistband at the small of his back. He might need a little extra firepower before the night was over.

Garrison was just about to ascend the stairs at the saloon's entrance when a familiar voice called out.

"Something told me I would be seeing you again," Sheriff Smith called out.

Garrison turned to see the sheriff approaching quickly. He was flanked on either side by a deputy. Each deputy held a pistol pointed in Garrison's direction.

"I warned you not to try this," Smith told him. "Now I'm going to need you to hand them guns over. All of them," he demanded.

Garrison smiled. He slowly reached for the Colts that hung from his hips, removing them with just his thumb and forefinger. "Sheriff, if you want my guns, all you have to do is come get them," he said as he held the pistols out at arm's length, grips out toward the sheriff.

Sheriff Smith approached warily. This all seemed too easy. He was mere feet away and reaching for the guns when the smile disappeared from Garrison's face. In that instant, Smith knew he was about to die.

Before the stunned sheriff could react, Garrison performed a maneuver that would come to be known as the road agent's spin. Garrison had his forefinger inserted through the trigger guard of each pistol. As the sheriff reached for them, Garrison flicked his wrists in such a way that each pistol pivoted around the forefinger and was flipped back into the firing position.

Garrison fired both pistols pointblank into the sheriff's chest. At such close range, the impact sent his body flying backwards. Before it hit the ground, Garrison adjusted his aim and shot each of the deputies between the eyes.

He could hear the heavy footsteps of several people approaching him from behind, from within the saloon. He holstered his left-hand Colt and spun to face the new threat. Using his left hand, he fanned the hammer of his right-hand Colt gunning down the four men who emerged from the saloon one right after the other.

He quickly holstered the now-empty Colt in his right hand and drew his Le Mat in its place. He also drew the Colt from his left thigh as he rushed up the stairs and crashed through the saloon's swinging doors.

Chapter Ninety

Garrison stood just inside the saloon, a pistol in each hand. Twelve pairs of hard eyes stared back at him. Every man stood. Most of them had been reaching for their guns when Garrison entered. At the sight of him, all motion had ceased. Now everyone stood stock-still, waiting to see what he would do next.

The twelve heavily armed men weren't the only ones occupying the saloon. The barkeep stood behind the bar with his hands raised high over his head. Four women, the town whores, huddled together in the back corner.

When Garrison spoke, his voice was cold and devoid of emotion. "They call me the Pale Rider," he announced. He could see a spark of recognition in many of the eyes that stared back at him. At least some of them had heard the stories about him.

"Oh Jesus!" the barkeep whispered in fear. The women whimpered but no one else uttered a word.

Garrison addressed the women first. "Ladies, I suggest you leave now. Out the back if you will."

They wasted little time making their exit. When the bartender moved to join them, Garrison pointed the Le Mat in his direction. "Not you. You stay right where you are," he warned.

When the women were safely out of the building, Garrison again addressed the room. "Now, which one of you murdered my friend here last night?" he asked.

Garrison's question was met with silence. The men all looked toward one another. Finally, a man standing toward the front of the room, to Garrison's left, spoke up.

"Mister, there weren't nobody murdered here. Your friend was drunk. He accused another of cheating and went for his gun. It was self-defense," the man claimed.

In reply, Garrison simply shot the man in the face. "Don't lie to me," he warned the remaining men. "He didn't even own a gun. One of you murdered him in cold blood and the rest of you lied to the sheriff about what happened," he accused.

Garrison looked toward the barkeep. "Which one of them was it?" he asked.

The barkeep stared back at him, his eyes wide with fear. His lips trembled but he kept his silence. Tears began to stream down his checks when Garrison swung the Le Mat back in his direction.

"You can answer my question or you can die. Those are your two-options," Garrison warned.

Garrison was about to make good on his threat when a voice from behind arrested his attention. "I did. I killed that fat fuck."

Garrison turned to regard the man. He was of average height and weight. He was clean-shaven with medium-length brown hair. There was no fear in his hazel eyes. His clothes were clean and appeared new. A pearl-handled pistol hung from his left hip.

Garrison quickly moved toward the man, positioning his Le Mat directly in the man's face. The man merely smiled.

"What are you going to do about it? Every man here is a friend of mine. They're not about to let you get away with shooting me," he said with confidence.

"Oh, I intend to kill all of them too," Garrison responded icily.

The man smirked. "You're mad! You'll never make it out of here alive, Pale Rider or not."

During the course of this brief conversation, Garrison had subtly flicked the lever on the hammer of his Le Mat into the up position. The Le Mat was a uniquely designed weapon that featured two barrels. The nine-shot cylinder revolved around a separate smooth-bore central barrel that fired twenty-gauge buckshot, effectively functioning as a short-barreled shotgun. With the lever in the raised position, the weapon would discharge the buckshot from the lower barrel.

Now Garrison gave Beans' killer a cold smile. "It doesn't much matter whether I live or die," he told the man, "so long as you die first," he finished as he pulled the Le Mat's trigger.

Chapter Ninety-One

The Le Mat's roar was near deafening inside the saloon. Its impact was devastating. The killer's arrogant smile disappeared along with the rest of his face. The headless corpse stood motionless for a moment and then toppled forward over the table the man had been standing behind. As it did so, the table's oil lamp was knocked to the floor where it shattered upon impact.

Garrison leaped backwards as the burning oil spread across the floor, igniting everything it came into contact with. The remaining men quickly overcame their shock and drew their weapons, preparing to fire on Garrison. Garrison was already turning to open fire on the room when the sight of the spreading flames gave him an idea.

Instead of firing on the men, Garrison aimed for the oil lamps that sat upon the tables. With each shot, one of the lamps exploded, sending burning oil flying in all directions. Tables were quickly engulfed in flame. Some of the men were splashed directly in the face. Others had their clothes set on fire. Agonized screams soon filled the room.

The barkeep's face contorted in rage as he watched his establishment go up in flames. Anger replaced fear and he reached for the shotgun he kept beneath the bar. "You son of a bitch!" he roared as he swung the barrel toward Garrison.

Alerted by the man's shout, Garrison turned and shot the barkeep in the head. The impact spun the man around one hundred and eighty degrees. The shotgun suddenly went off, the blast shattering the liquor bottles behind the bar.

The room was quickly filling with smoke, seriously impairing visibility. The men who had managed to avoid being set aflame were now firing on Garrison, but they were firing blind. Lead flew all around Garrison, but he stood his ground.

On the far side of the room, to Garrison's left, the flames were now climbing the walls. On the near side, the flames crept steadily toward the bar. Garrison watched as the flames reached the spilled alcohol. The bar and the wall behind it were instantly ignited.

Garrison had maintained his position near the entrance. He could easily slip out and trust the fire to finish what he had started. But he wasn't about to do that. Beans' death had put him in a killing mood. He wasn't going to stop until either they killed him or he had killed every last one of them.

Ignoring the lead that continued to fly all around him, Garrison refused to fire blindly into the smoke that now filled the room. Instead, he waited until his enemies fired and then aimed toward the sound of the shots. He was careful to move slightly, first in one direction and then another, lest any of his opponents used the same strategy against him.

When one pistol clicked on an empty cylinder, he holstered it and drew another. He was down to Kip's Remington when the gunshots suddenly ceased. The screams of the men being burned alive had died out long ago. Now the only sound was the roar of the flames that had nearly engulfed the entire building. Still, Garrison hesitated to leave. He waited two full minutes before he became convinced that it was finally over.

Chapter Ninety-Two

Garrison stood in the street in front of the burning saloon, with Diablo by his side. He could hear the cries of alarm ringing throughout the town below. From his vantage point, he could see the throng of people rushing madly toward the scene of destruction.

Garrison ignored it all. He used the light of the burning building behind him to quickly reload his Colts using the paper cartridges from his satchel. He was fairly certain that none of the remaining townsfolk posed a threat, but he wasn't taking chances either.

A noisy throng of people crested the hill and stumbled to a halt. Voices trailed off in mid-cry as each among them laid eyes on the eerie scene before them. The saloon was completely engulfed in flames. The fire had spread to the front porch and even the roof. They watched in horrified silence as the roof caved in on itself with a loud crash.

In the road stood a mounted horse. Silhouetted as they were by the fire behind them, both the horse and rider appeared to the citizens only as shadows, dark and frightening. There was an audible gasp from somewhere within the throng when the massive horse began to move slowly toward them.

As the horse and rider moved into the light, details of their appearance began to emerge. Somehow, the sight proved to be no less frightening. The horse was pale in color, while its rider was dressed all in black. The rider held a cocked pistol in each hand. The pair stopped less than ten feet from the crowd. Not far from them lay the bodies of the sheriff and his deputies.

Garrison silently gazed upon the throng of people, his eyes searching for danger. The crowd seemed to consist mostly of women and the town's shop owners. There didn't appear to be an armed man among them. After what seemed like an eternity to the people, Garrison finally addressed them.

"My name is Matthew Garrison, the Pale Rider," he began. His announcement was met by a chorus of gasps and quiet curses.

"My friend was murdered in that saloon. Your sheriff refused to do anything about it. When I decided to do something myself, he tried to stop me. He died for it. It's true that only one man shot my friend, but everyone in that building was just as guilty. They all lied to help him get away with it. The point is I've done what I came here to do. I'm not looking for any more trouble. But if there's anyone among you that's itching for a fight, I'm happy to give it to you."

Garrison's speech was met with silence. "Well, what's it to be?" he pressed. Without a word, the crowd slowly parted, creating a clear path for Garrison. After a brief hesitation, Garrison urged Diablo forward. He kept his pistols at the ready, but no one dared challenge him.

Garrison holstered his Colts as he left the crowd behind. He rode slowly out of town, heading south. For the first time in years, he felt no inner conflict, and no struggle to understand who he had become or what had happened to the man he used to be. For so long, he had struggled under the impression that he must be either Matthew Garrison or the Pale Rider. In death, Beans had helped him finally accept the truth. Matthew Garrison was the Pale Rider. Perhaps he always had been. A faint smile crossed Garrison's face as he softly uttered the words Beans had once suggested he use to introduce himself.

"My name is Matthew Lloyd Garrison, and I am the Pale Rider."

Epilog

Spanish Fort, Texas – Three Days Later

The stranger came riding in slowly from the east. Given the destruction wrought by the last stranger to visit, the nervous citizens of Spanish Fort watched with trepidation as the man approached. He wore typical trail clothes covered in a fine layer of trail dust. His black duster hung open, allowing all to see the pistol tied low on his right thigh. From a holster on his left hip protruded the handle of a sawed-off double-barrel shotgun. The stock had been removed and the barrels cut down to fit the holster. A Winchester 1866 was stored in his saddle.

A worn and tattered Confederate cavalry hat sat atop the man's head. Dark brown hair fell from beneath its brim at the back of his head and hung down just below his shoulders. A close-cropped beard covered his cheeks and jaw. His eyes were an icy blue.

The horse was a chestnut-colored Morgan. Though compact in size, the animal seemed to exude power. Although no more than fourteen hands high, the animal had well-defined withers and strongly muscled hindquarters. Intelligence radiated from its large eyes. The animal moved with an animated trot as the horse and rider headed for the burned out remains of the building sitting on the hill.

The stranger halted in front of the fire-ravaged building and surveyed the scene. A flatbed wagon had been left in the road directly in front of what was once the town's only saloon. Several men moved through the remains of the building, clearly searching for something. As the stranger watched, the men, working in teams of two, began to remove the charred remains of over a dozen people. The blackened bodies were tossed unceremoniously into the back of the wagon.

Another man stood by the wagon watching the others work. He was significantly older and was most likely there to supervise the others. The man cried in surprise when the stranger seemed to suddenly appear at his side.

"What's happening here?" the stranger asked.

The man regarded the stranger in silence for a moment before he finally answered. The stranger looked familiar, but the man could not say why. "Just trying to get my job done," he answered. "Already put seven bodies in the ground over the last two days. We've got another twelve or thirteen to dig outta here. First, we had to wait for the fire to die out. Then we had to wait for everything to cool down before we could start looking for the bodies. What a mess!" he exclaimed.

Turning again to the stranger, the man introduced himself. "Please excuse my rudeness. My name's Clyde. I'm the town's undertaker."

"It certainly looks like business has been good for you," the stranger observed without even a hint of a smile. "What happened?" he asked.

"It was terrible. Feller got himself killed here a few nights ago and the very next night, his friend rode back into town looking for revenge. He killed everyone in there except for the whores. Burned the damn place down to the ground too, as you can see."

The stranger reached into his coat and pulled out a yellowing piece of parchment. "You seen this man here recently?" he asked as he handed a 'wanted' poster to the undertaker.

The undertaker looked first down at the paper in his hands and back up into the eyes of the stranger. He suddenly realized why the stranger looked so familiar. He audibly gulped as he tried to hide the fear he suddenly felt.

"To be honest with you, if I didn't know better, I'd think I was talking to him now," the undertaker answered. "He was here, alright. Who do you think done this? But you missed him by about three days," he continued.

This answer brought a scowl to the stranger's face. He'd heard the same thing countless times before. He'd been tracking this man for over a year and it was always the same. In every town, someone told him that he looked like the man on the poster. He'd grown tired of it rather quickly. Even more infuriating, he always seemed to be just days behind his elusive prey.

The stranger slowly reached across his body with his right hand, dipping into an inside pocket of his duster. When he pulled his hand free, it was no longer empty, and he tossed the object down to the undertaker. The undertaker caught the object and held it up for inspection. There in his hand was a shiny silver star.

"Lawman?" he asked.

"United States Marshal," the stranger lied. While he had once been a marshal, he had discovered that he could make far more money as a bounty hunter. He kept the star because he had also learned that folks tended to be more willing to share information with the law than a bounty hunter. "My name is Joshua Wayne Garrison. The man I'm after, the man on the poster, is my brother."

To be continued...